FISTFUL OF BENJAMINS

Also by Kiki Swinson

Wifey
I'm Still Wifey
Life After Wifey
The Candy Shop
A Sticky Situation
Still Wifey Material
Playing Dirty
Notorious
Sleeping with the Enemy (with Wahida Clark)
Heist (with De'nesha Diamond)
Lifestyles of the Rich and Shameless (with Noire)
A Gangster and a Gentleman (with De'nesha Diamond)
Most Wanted (with Nikki Turner)
Still Candy Shopping (with Amaleka McCall)

Also by De'nesha Diamond

Hustlin' Divas
Street Divas
Gangsta Divas
Boss Divas
Heartbreaker (with Eric S. Gray and Nichelle Walker)
Heist (with Kiki Swinson)
A Gangster and a Gentleman (with Kiki Swinson)

Published by Kensington Publishing Corp.

FISTFUL OF BENJAMINS

Kiki Swinson
De'nesha Diamond

KENSINGTON PUBLISHING CORP.
www.kensingtonbooks.com

DAFINA BOOKS are published by

Kensington Publishing Corp.
119 West 40th Street
New York, NY 10018

All Kensington titles, imprints, and distributed lines are available at special
quantity discounts for bulk purchases for sales promotion, premiums, fund-
raising, and educational or institutional use.

Special book excerpts or customized printings can also be created to fit spe-
cific needs. For details, write or phone the office of the Kensington Special
Sales Manager: Kensington Publishing Corp., 119 West 40th Street, New
York, NY 10018. Attn. Special Sales Department. Phone: 1-800-221-2647.

Dafina and the Dafina logo Reg. U.S. Pat. & TM Off.

ISBN-13: 978-0-7582-8028-2
ISBN-10: 0-7582-8028-9
First Kensington Trade Paperback Printing: October 2014

eISBN-13: 978-0-7582-8030-5
eISBN-10: 0-7582-8030-0
First Kensington Electronic Edition: October 2014

10 9 8 7 6 5 4 3 2 1

Printed in the United States of America

SPECIAL DELIVERY

Kiki Swinson

PROLOGUE

"**O**h my God, Eduardo. What do you think they will do to us? I don't want to die . . . I can't leave my son," I cried, barely able to get my words out between sobbing and the fact that my teeth were chattering together so badly.

The warehouse-type of room we were being held captive in was freezing. I mean, *freezing*—like we were sitting inside of a meat locker type of freezing. I could even see puffs of frosty air with each breath that I took. I knew it was summertime outside, so the conditions inside where we were being held told me we were purposely being made to freeze. The smell of sawdust and industrial chemicals were also so strong that the combination was making my stomach churn. Eduardo flexed his back against mine and turned his head as much as the ropes that bound us together allowed. He was trembling from the subzero conditions as well.

"Gabby, just keep your mouth shut. If we gon' die right now, at least we are together. I know I ain't say it a lot, but I love you. I love you for everything you did and put up with from me. I am sorry I ever let you get into this bullshit from the jump. It wasn't no place for you from day one, baby girl,"

Eduardo whispered calmly through his battered lips. With everything that had happened, I didn't know how he was staying so calm. It was like he had no emotion behind what was happening or like he had already resigned himself to the fact that we were dead. In my opinion, his ass should've been crying, fighting, and yelling for the scary men to let me go. Something. Eduardo was the drug dealer, not me, so maybe he had prepared himself to die many times. I hadn't ever prepared myself to die, or to be tied up like an animal, beaten, and waiting to possibly get my head blown off. This was not how I saw my life ending up. All I had ever wanted was a good man, a happy family, a nice place to live, and just a good life.

"I don't care about being together when we die, Eduardo! You forget I have a son. Who is going to take care of him if I'm dead over something I didn't do?" I replied sharply. A pain shot through my skull like someone had shot me in the head. I was ready to lose it. My shoulders began quaking as I broke down in another round of sobs. I couldn't even feel the pain that had previously permeated my body from the beating I had taken. I was numb in comparison to the pain I was feeling in my heart behind leaving my son. I kept thinking about my son and my mother, who were probably both sitting in a strange place wondering how I had let this happen to them. That was the hard part, knowing that they were going to be innocent casualties of my stupid fucking actions. I should've stuck to carrying mail instead of stepping into the shit that had me in this predicament. I was the dummy in this situation. I was so busy looking for love in all the wrong places. I had done all of this to myself.

"Shhh. Don't cry. We just have to pray that Luca will have mercy on us. I will try to make him believe that it wasn't us. I'll tell him we didn't do it. We weren't responsible for everything that happened," Eduardo whispered to me.

"But he's the one who got us out so fast. I keep thinking that he only did that because he thought we might start talking. He got us out just so he could kill us, don't you see that? We are finished. Done. Dead," I said harshly. The tears were still coming. It was like Eduardo couldn't get what I was saying. We were both facing death and I wasn't ready to die!

"You don't know everything. Maybe it was something else. Let me handle—" Eduardo started to tell me, but his words were clipped short when we both heard the sound of footsteps moving toward us. The footsteps sounded off like gunshots against the icy-cold concrete floors. My heart felt like it would explode through the bones in my chest and suddenly it felt like my bladder was filled to capacity. The footsteps stopped. I think I stopped breathing too. Suddenly, I wasn't cold anymore. Maybe it was the adrenaline coursing fiercely through my veins, but suddenly I was burning up hot.

"Eduardo Santos," a man's voice boomed. "Look at you now. All caught up in your own web." The man had a thick accent, the kind my older uncles from Puerto Rico had when they tried really hard to speak English.

"Luca—I—I—can—" Eduardo stuttered, his body trembling so hard it was making mine move. Now I could sense fear and anguish in Eduardo's voice. That was the first time Eduardo had sounded like he understood the seriousness of our situation.

"Shut up!" the man screamed. "You are a rat and in Mexico rats are killed and burned so that the dirty spirit does not corrupt anything around it," the man called Luca screamed. I squeezed my eyes shut, but I couldn't keep the tears from bursting from the sides.

I was too afraid to even look at him. I kept my head down, but I had seen there were at least four more pairs of feet standing around. Eduardo and I had been working for this man and had never met him. I knew he was some big drug kingpin inside the Calixte Mexican drug cartel that operated out of Miami, but when I was making the money, I never thought of meeting him, especially not under these circumstances. I was helping this bastard get rich and couldn't even pick him out of a police lineup if my life depended on it.

"Please, Luca. I'm telling you I wasn't the rat. Maybe it was Lance . . . I mean, I just worked for him. He was the one responsible to you. He was the one that kept increasing everything. I did everything I could to keep this from happening," Eduardo pleaded his case, his words rushing out of his mouth.

"Oh, now you blame another man? Another cowardly move. Eduardo, I have people inside of the DEA who work for me. I know everything. If I didn't pay off the judge to set bail so I could get you and your little girlfriend out of there, you were prepared to sign a deal. You were prepared to tell everything. Like the fucking cock-sucking rat that you are. You know nothing about death before dishonor. You would've sold out your own mother to get out of there. You failed the fucking test, you piece of shit," Luca spat, sucking his teeth. "Get him up," Luca said calmly, apparently unmoved by Eduardo's pleas.

"Luca! Luca! Give me another chance, please!" Eduardo begged, his voice coming out as a shrill scream. His words exploded like bombs in my ears. Another chance? Did that mean that Eduardo had snitched? Did that mean he put me in danger when I was only doing everything he ever told me to do? Did Eduardo sign my death sentence without even telling me what the fuck he was going to do? I immediately thought about my family again. These people obviously knew where I lived and where they could find my mother and my son, even after they went back home. A wave of cramps trampled through my guts. Before I could control it, vomit spewed from my lips like lava from a volcano.

"What did you do to me, Eduardo?" I coughed and screamed through tears and vomit. I couldn't help it. I didn't care anymore. They were going to kill me anyway, right? "You fucking snitch!

What did you do?" I gurgled. I had exercised more loyalty than Eduardo had. The men who were there to kill us said nothing and neither did Eduardo. I felt like someone had kicked me in the chest and the head right then. My heart was broken.

Two of Luca's goons cut the ropes that had kept Eduardo and me bound together. It was like they had cut the strings to my heart too. Eduardo didn't even look at me as they dragged him away screaming. I fell over onto my side, too weak to sit up on my own. Eduardo had betrayed me in the worse way. I was just a pawn in a much, much bigger game. And, all for what? A few extra dollars a week that I didn't have anything to show for now, except maybe some expensive pocketbooks, a few watches, some shoes, and an apartment I was surely going to never see again. Yes, I had been living ghetto fabulous, shopping for expensive things that I could've never imagined in my wildest dreams, but I had lost every dollar that I had ever stashed away for my son as "just-in-case" money. I had done all of this for him and in the end I had left him nothing.

"Please. Please don't kill me," I begged through a waterfall of tears as I curled my body into a fetal position. With renewed spirit to see my son, I begged and pleaded for my life. I told them I wasn't a snitch and that I had no idea what Eduardo had done. I got nothing in response. There was a lot of Spanish being spoken, but I could only understand a fraction of it; so much for listening to my mother when she tried speaking Spanish to me all of my life.

"I promise I didn't speak to any DEA agents or the police. Please tell Luca that it wasn't me," I cried some more, pleading with the men that were left there to guard me. None of the remaining men acted like they could hear me. In my assessment, this was it. I was staring down a true death sentence. I immediately began praying. If my mother, a devout Catholic, had taught me nothing else, she had definitely taught me how to pray.

"Hail Mary, full of grace . . ." I mumbled, closing my eyes and preparing for my impending death. As soon as I closed my eyes, I was thrust backwards in my mind, reviewing how I'd ever let the gorgeous, smooth-talking Eduardo Santos get my gullible ass into this mess.

CHAPTER 1

MAIL CALL

Virginia Beach, Virginia, one year earlier

"Excuse me, mister, can you get the dog, so I can bring the mail in?" I called up to the tall, bald, fat Deebo look-alike standing in the doorway of an old, decrepit house on my mail route. The man just grunted like I hadn't even spoken to him. The dog was standing on high alert, tail stiff as shit, eyes focused in on me, like he knew he was going to eat my damn heart right out of my chest. That huge beast of a dog was just waiting for me to open the chain-link gate. I wasn't that stupid. I had been a mail carrier for two years and I already had been bitten by two dogs. I wasn't trying for a third time. I squinted my eyes at the ugly-ass man and tapped my foot impatiently.

"Mister, I am going to ask you again to get the dog or else I'll be forced to return the mail and tell them it was undeliverable," I said as calm and as nice as I could. I really wanted to curse his black ass out.

"He ain't gonna bother you," the man grumbled. "Don't be such a pussy, drama queen. If you take my mail back I'll report you to your supervisor."

It was like someone had splashed me with cold water. I couldn't believe he had just said that shit to me. I was gearing up to curse him out and throw his mail into his yard, when someone approached from across the street. I turned my head because I could see the guy coming toward me from my peripheral vision.

"Yo, Brock. Why your miserable ass giving this beautiful mail lady a hard fucking time? Just take that stupid-ass mutt, that fake-ass Rottweiler, inside that dirty-ass shack you call a house and let her deliver the mail. You ain't getting shit important in the mail, no way. It ain't the first of the month," a gorgeous guy called out as he walked up to where I was standing. I had to turn all the way around to face the guy and he was surely a sight to see. I couldn't stop staring at him. He had the most beautiful face I had ever seen on a man and forget about his swag—it was on one thousand. He was about six feet tall with the smoothest, most perfect cinnamon complexion I'd ever seen. He had a headful of tight, dark curls hugging his scalp that were cut neatly with a fresh line-up making him look clean-cut and sharp. His goatee was also perfectly trimmed and it accented his full, smooth lips. It was his eyes that were the most striking. They were a cross between hazel and green and the shape was hard to describe, but piercing nonetheless. I was stuck on stupid looking at this dude. He was definitely movie-star quality. I suddenly felt a bit shy and awkward. I knew that my U.S. Postal Service uniform didn't do much for my shape and I didn't have on one ounce of makeup that day. I guess that's what I got for rushing out of the house that morning.

"Thank you," I said, blushing like crazy. The guy grabbed the mail from me as the big, ugly dummy inside the gate took his dog inside.

"Don't worry about Brock . . . he's all bark and no ass bite. Give me the stuff, I ain't scared of that big-for-nothing nigga. I'll take the mail up there for you today," the gorgeous guy said, smiling. Damn! His smile was a woman-killer. I was standing there in shock, gushing like a teenage girl who'd just gotten spoken to by her first crush. I couldn't help my eyes from batting like a damn coquettish cartoon character. The gorgeous guy took the mail and tossed it on the steps inside the gate. He came back out to where I was standing and smiled again. Those eyes, those thick lips and perfect teeth were more than I could stand. I knew right at that moment that I wanted to be with this dude in the worst way.

"I'm Eduardo, but my friends call me Eddie," he said, extending his hand toward me. My heart sped up, but in a good way.

"Gabriella," I said, almost whispering. I gave him my hand and thought he'd shake it. Instead, he took it and kissed the top of it. Oh, he was laying it on thick. I swear I almost wet my damn panties. I couldn't even look him directly in the eye, which was a sign that I was feeling him. I looked across the street, trying to see where he'd come from, but there were nothing but abandoned buildings over there. I looked back at Eduardo, not in his eyes, but at his clothes. He was dressed sharply in a pair of neat, slim-fitting True Religion jeans, a Gucci T-shirt, and a pair of Giuseppe Zanotti sneakers. He was too well dressed to be living in an abandoned house. So where had he come from? Strange. Yet, I wanted to know more. I was definitely intrigued.

"Can I call you sometime, Gabriella?" Eduardo asked me, snapping me out of my little daydream. "I think you're beautiful." I thought he would never ask. I almost fainted when he said that I was beautiful. Don't get me wrong; he was fine as shit, but I wasn't so shabby myself. I was a thick-in-the-right-places type of chick with round hips, plump ass, and medium, but perfect, tits. I stood five feet, five inches, I was the color of melted butter, and my skin was blemish-free. My features were typically Puerto Rican—dark, straight black hair that curled up nicely when wet, dark brown, deep-set round eyes, small heart-shaped lips and nice teeth. That day, I had my hair wet and curly, which usually always had dudes on my mail routes trying to holla at me. Trust me, I usually ignored them all, but this was different. Even though I had no makeup on, Eduardo had told me he thought I was beautiful.

"Oh . . . um . . . sure. Thanks again for helping me out. It's so crazy delivering mail around here. All of the houses looked run-down and all of the people have big dogs that they never want to put on a leash or anything," I said, laughing awkwardly as I scribbled down my number.

"Yeah, all these niggas waiting on is SSI checks and letters from the welfare telling them when their next load of food stamps gonna be on their EBT cards. Lowlife shit around here. I would be scared to even deliver mail around this bitch," Eduardo agreed with me. I was smiling all goofy because I had been taking quick peeks at his lips. He was really gorgeous. I couldn't say that to myself enough.

"Well, I have to go. I hope to hear from you," I said, flirting as hard as I could. Truthfully, I could've spent the rest of my workday standing right there talking to him.

"Oh, you'll hear from me baby girl, don't worry," Eduardo said as he turned to walk back across the street. I had an extra pep in my step the rest of that day.

CHAPTER 2

AIN'T NOTHING LIKE GOOD DICK

"Yes! Yes! Fuck me! Harder! Don't stop! Don't ever stop!" I screamed as I dug my nails deep into the skin on Eduardo's back. The more I screamed, the faster and harder he slid his thickness in and out of my dripping wet pussy.

It had been two weeks since our first meeting on my mail route. I usually didn't fuck dudes this fast, but he was just too fine and too smooth to pass it up. He had taken me to three or four nice dinners, brought me flowers, and fucked me right in that short time. I couldn't front, I was being like one of those chicks I always talked about back in high school—sprung off of good dick and nice clothes. I didn't care, either. After all I had been through my with baby daddy, Eduardo was like a breath of fresh air in my life.

"Whose pussy is this? Tell me before I take the dick away," Eduardo huffed into my ear. I guess thinking back, it was a strange question and threat for a new dude to ask a girl he hardly knew, but at that moment I couldn't even think about that.

"Yours! It's your pussy, Eddie! Yours forever!" I screeched like a bubbleheaded bimbo as he plowed harder into my pelvis. I knew my ass was sprung for sure after that. Eduardo had the

best dick I had ever had and he used it expertly. I was screaming from my third orgasm within minutes. That was unheard of
when most of the time during sex I'd hardly ever had even one.

Eduardo busted his nut and he rolled over next to me.
"Damn, girl, you got that good stuff," he panted. I smiled as I
watched his muscular chest heave up and down. This was
definitely the start of something good.

"Your shit ain't so bad either," I said sweetly, reaching over
and rubbing my hand on his tight muscles. He laughed.

"Oh, now you giving me a half-ass compliment," he joked.
I moved closer to him and laid my head on his chest. I closed
my eyes, but not for long.

Eduardo's phone started ringing on the hotel-room nightstand and interrupted our moment. All of a sudden a bad feeling came over me as he pushed me aside, jumped up, looked at
the phone, and grabbed it like he was in a panic. I screwed my
face up as I eyed him evilly. He shot me a worried look and
then he raced into the bathroom with the phone. I pouted
right away. He obviously didn't want me to know who he was
receiving that call from. It was the same story with these niggas. They always had mad secrets. Maybe I was the dumb one.
I was there fucking him like he was my man, yet I still didn't
know if Eduardo had a girlfriend or anything. I just knew I
wanted him to be mine so badly I would've done anything.

I stayed in the bed, thinking that my mother was going to
kill me for staying out and not calling her. She had already
been complaining that I had been basically neglecting my son
for the two weeks I'd spent with Eduardo. I wasn't ready at that
time for Eduardo to meet my mother and my son, Andrew.
Not until I was sure I was going to really be with him. It was
all too much to think about.

I went to grab my cell to call my mother, but Eduardo's
voice getting louder and louder in the bathroom had gotten
my attention. I listened. I wanted to know who he was talking

to like that. It sounded kind of serious, so I moved to the edge of the bed so I could listen.

"What you mean, that nigga got caught? How the fuck did he do that? With all the shit? Do you know what that's going to cost Lance? Cost me, for that matter?" Eduardo yelled at whomever he was talking to on the phone. I was all ears after I heard that. I was glad it didn't sound like a chick he was talking to, but I was also being nosy, since I didn't know a lot about Eduardo and his dealings. I immediately forgot about calling my mother and my son.

"So how we gon' get the fucking packages now? We can't be without a re-up for more than a few hours or our shit will dry up like an old lady's pussy. Lance will be breathing down my fucking neck if he don't get his returns! If he don't get paid, nigga . . . we don't get paid. It's that simple. We have to come up with another way or this shit ain't gonna end good for nobody. I ain't trying to starve—are you?" Eduardo yelled some more. My eyebrows were furrowed in confusion. I got up from the bed and moved closer to the bathroom door, now more interested than ever. Eduardo had been really evasive about what he did for a living and where he lived. I had already figured out that him being near those abandoned buildings the day we met hadn't been a coincidence. Everyone in the Tidewater area knew those buildings were trap houses, including me. In the few weeks I had been spending time with Eduardo, I had already come to the conclusion he was a hustling dude. After my baby daddy I said I wouldn't fuck with any more hustlers, I guess I lied to myself. There was something so attractive about that little bit of danger these dudes possessed that turned me on. I finally heard Eduardo getting ready to hang up so I raced back over to the bed, jumped under the covers and struck a sexy pose. I was hoping he would lay that good dick on me one more time.

★ ★ ★

"Everything okay?" I asked when Eduardo finally came out of the bathroom. He looked pissed. His jaw was rocking feverishly and his nostrils were flaring open and closed. His face was even a different color, I guess from the blood rushing to it while he was yelling.

"We gotta go. Get dressed," Eduardo snapped, being real short.

I felt my heart sink inside of my chest. I didn't want to leave just yet. I wanted to make things better, make him feel better. I had heard his entire conversation and for some reason, I don't know what came over me, but I blurted out, "I think I can help you out."

Eduardo was in the process of putting his pants on when I said it. He paused and looked at me strangely.

My face was serious. I was dead serious. "I know a way that I can help you," I said again. I didn't care if I was being too pushy, I needed this man to want me around. Period.

"Whatcha' talking about, shorty? You don't even know what's up," Eduardo said dismissively.

"It's not that hard to figure out," I said, a little more sternly than I had spoken to him before. He rolled his eyes and continued getting dressed.

"I can get your packages delivered without the risk of using a human mule. As you can see, using those street dudes never works, because they brag, they talk, and the narcos always find out," I said, laying it all out there. Eduardo looked at me with raised eyebrows.

I smirked. "I'm not stupid, Eduardo. I know what you were talking about in there. All I want to do is help out. I really like you and it wouldn't hurt me to have some extra cash for getting it done. It's easy . . . I'm a mail carrier, remember? I would be the one getting everything delivered," I said, continuing to put all of my shit out there on the table. I had done it once or twice for my baby daddy with a couple of weed packages he had come in from Brooklyn. So, it wasn't really a fresh new idea that I had come up with on my own, but that's how I presented it. I wasn't scared to do it, because all of the people who worked in the sorting and weighing area were my friends. The dude Carlos who did the sort for my bundles was basically in love with me and would do whatever I asked anyway.

"Whatcha' mean, get them delivered?" Eduardo finally said, looking at me seriously.

"Just what I said, easy as that. Have your people send the packages a certain way. Make sure they use other items to cover up the scent . . . I hear coffee beans work good on weed. I'll identify the packages. Have someone I know sort, weigh, and scan the packages and I will be the one dropping them off on my route to your addresses. Simple as that," I explained.

"Why, though? Why would you risk it?" Eduardo asked suspiciously.

"The same reason you do what you do: money. And for real, because I like you a lot too," I said honestly, lowering my eyes bashfully. I hated to admit my feelings to him so soon, but what else was I going to say? It couldn't all be just about money, although in my mind at that time, money was my first priority.

"Damn, baby girl. I guess that's as real as it gets. I'm feeling that," Eduardo said, coming over and grabbing me into a huge bear hug. I melted against him, feeling wanted and accepted. That was the start of our thing and I was all in from day one as long as we kept things simple. But, of course, nothing ever stays simple.

CHAPTER 3

MOVING WEIGHT

"Which one you want?" I beamed, pushing a display of expensive watches toward Eduardo. He laughed like I was joking or like he didn't believe that I was going to buy him one of the gold or diamond timepieces.

"I'm dead-ass. Why are you laughing? Pick one out and it's on me," I said.

"Check you out . . . the tables have all of a sudden turned. I'm not the one taking you shopping anymore, huh? Now you can afford to spring on me?" Eduardo joked.

"Don't look a gift horse in the mouth. Pick something. It's my treat for all of the ways you have changed my life," I said, sincerely. "We're not leaving here until you have something out of this case on your arm . . . or in a damn bag." Eduardo shrugged his shoulders, as if to say, *if you say so.* He looked down into the case and studied the watches. He studied them and I was busy studying his fine ass.

Eight months had passed since Eduardo and I had first met that day on my mail route. Eight months of fun, hot sex, money to spare, and smooth business dealings. I had to say to myself that my life had been great. I actually looked forward to going to work every day. Our little system was working like a charm and so far, there had been no glitches. We were moving the packages daily and there had been not one inkling of drama thus far.

Eduardo had copped us an apartment in the Cosmopolitan apartments in the Town Center area of Virginia Beach and moved me and my son in with him. It was the first sign that we were going to be together for the long haul. I had never lived in a building that had a doorman, indoor pool, full gym, and a damn spa all right on the premises. It was like going from hell to heaven all in a short span of time. I had never seen Andrew so happy to be somewhere as when we moved into our apartment and he was able to see his newly decorated Spider-Man room. My son got along so well with Eduardo. It was like God had answered all of my prayers.

Eduardo had even paid off the taxes on my mother's small, raggedy house for the year. I mean, she couldn't move in with us because we wanted to be like a new little family, but I made sure I visited my mother every day and that she had everything she needed since I had left. My mother liked Eduardo a lot, but she also thought he was a car salesman. I couldn't possibly tell her that he was a damn hustler and that I was the one making his hustle happen by putting myself at risk every day. It was something I chose to keep to myself.

I had no complaints about the arrangement at all. I was living better than I had lived all of my life. I was totally in love with Eduardo. I could only hope that he was feeling me in the same way.

"C'mon, Eddie . . . I'm sure about this. Pick a watch. Matter of fact, pick the best one there," I urged.

"A'ight, if you say so, baby girl. But don't get mad at me one day and take your shit back," Eduardo said jokingly. Then he looked down at the case and pointed to a beauty of a watch. "I'll take this one," Eduardo said, pointing to the Breitling with the chronograph face and diamond bezel. I really thought he would pick a Rolex. I had been stashing away for a while just to buy him something as big as a Rolex, but I liked the watch he chose anyway. It wasn't as expensive, but I guess it was close enough.

"We'll take this one," I said to the snobby white saleslady who had eyed us up and down and thought we weren't buying anything or that we couldn't afford anything, for that matter. I plunked down the eight grand for the watch and smirked at the old bitch. Damn, it felt good to do something I wasn't used to being able to do.

"You know I'm taking you home to fuck the shit out of you now, right?" Eduardo said, kissing me and smacking my ass as we headed out of the mall.

We didn't even make it home. When we got back to his Range Rover, he threw me into the backseat and ripped off my pants.

"Hey! Those jeans cost a lot of money," I yelped, giggling like a schoolgirl. Eduardo always made me feel so giddy and childlike when he did spontaneous fun stuff like that. I gladly followed his lead once my pants were off. I opened my legs as wide as the small space allowed. Eduardo lowered his head and I knew I was in for a special treat. He used his fingers to gently part my delicate labia and then took the tip of his long, lizard-like tongue and teased my clit. Not only did my man have a prized dick, he also had a super tongue and the tongue game to match. I was no longer laughing like a teenager; I had changed to panting and sighing like a sexy siren from a porn movie.

"Lick it. Ohh, lick it good," I panted, moving Eduardo's head to the spot where I wanted him. "Stop playing and lick it!" I was tired of the teasing now. Eduardo took my signal and he went to town on my shit. He licked up and down my entire opening. I could feel a mixture of his saliva and my juices leaking down my ass crack. I was in heaven. The more I moaned and cooed, the harder Eduardo went. The slurping noises were making me crazy. I started grinding my hips toward Eduardo's tongue in response. I was breathing so hard my head was swimming. Eduardo pressed his tongue on my clit again and that was enough. I was creaming all over his face within seconds.

"Damn, you know how to push that button," I panted out. My inner thighs were trembling like crazy.

"My turn now," Eduardo panted, pulling his pants down. My knees were bent because of the limited space we had and my ass was sticking to the leather on his seats, but I was ready to receive that long dick in my dripping-wet hot box. Eduardo didn't care that my cum was getting all over his seats, either. He fell between my legs and just as he was about to put that love muscle up inside of me . . . *Bam! Bam! Bam!* Loud knocking interrupted our flow. The whole damn car shook from the banging.

"Oh shit!" I jumped. My heart kick-started in my chest like it had been shocked with paddles. I bumped my head on the door trying to get up fast, just in case it was a cop about to crack on us for public lewdness.

"What the fuck?" Eduardo barked. Through the heavy tint on the Range Rover windows we could see his boy Antoine, who we all referred to as Ant. I kind of felt relief that it wasn't a cop, but I was equally annoyed that Ant had fucked up our moment.

"Why the fuck he banging like he the cops and shit?" I grumbled. I wanted some of that dick and Ant was cockblocking.

I quickly pulled up my pants and Eduardo did the same. He opened the door with fury.

"Nigga! Why you banging on my shit like the police?" Eduardo growled at Ant.

"I saw your shit parked up here by the mall, so I stopped, nigga. I've been calling you for mad long and you ain't answering your shit as usual. So when I saw the truck I stopped and I could see your shit rocking, so I knew you was inside getting it on instead of fucking answering your calls," Ant said, sounding like a complaining-ass bitch to me.

"What the fuck is the problem?" Eduardo huffed. Ant looked through the door at me and then back at Eduardo. *What now?* I was thinking.

"I'll be right back," Eduardo said to me. They stepped away from the car so they could talk. I got out and climbed into the front passenger seat. I couldn't hear shit they were saying, but I saw Ant looking over at me every few minutes like he was scared of something. After a few minutes Eduardo came back into the truck. We sat in silence as he started up the truck. I wanted to ask what was the problem, but decided to play it cool. It didn't take long to get the info.

"Yo, Gabby, shit is getting deeper for us. We got a request that I need to talk to you about," Eduardo said, then he blew out a long breath. I looked over at him, but I didn't say anything.

"Lance wants us to step up the deliveries from one package a day to three. He moving major weight now and stepping back into the white-girl game," Eduardo said, his voice tentative. By "white girl," he meant heroin. I knew that niggas would eventually get greedy. That was how shit always happened. I was the one on the front lines and they were being greedy motherfuckers behind the scenes, calling shots.

I swallowed hard and turned my face away from Eduardo. He couldn't be serious with what he had just asked me. I stared out of the window, speechless. This was not part of the original deal to keep things simple. One package a day had so far kept me under the radar, but more would be too risky. I also didn't know about moving packages of heroin. I mean, ecstasy and weed was one thing, but straight-up hardcore H—that shit wasn't sitting right with me. I'd heard about chicks riding for their men getting more years than the damn dudes.

"I don't know about all of that, Eduardo. Why you want to try and fuck up a good thing? Adding shit to the game is how things always go south," I said, annoyed. "It's already a risk for the one-a-day package. I've been paying that dude Carlos inside of the station who weighs and sorts out of my share of what you give me, but that's for that one package a day. If it gets out of hand, he might get spooked and start acting up. I mean, the only reason why he does it is because I throw him a little flirt here and there and some cash, but putting more packages out there might not be so cool. He is going to be looking for more in return, I can guarantee that. Plus, it might look suspicious if he is grabbing all the big packages and putting them on my truck. If anybody gets suspicious at all, we could all be fucked," I said nervously. I wasn't trying to go to jail and have my son taken from me for no dumb shit. Yes, I had suggested this whole thing in order to snag Eduardo and make some extra cash, but I never anticipated it growing into something bigger. Eduardo let out a long breath like he was sick of hearing my mouth or some shit.

"Gabby . . . when Lance talks, that shit's the final say. He's the boss and he doesn't take *no* for an answer, especially from me. If he asks for something, I mean, I could try to say no, but you don't know that nigga. He is persistent as hell and he could make all of our lives fucked up. He's a kingpin, not some street-corner thug dude. Lance is second in charge in the cartel dudes that work out of Miami. I'm betting the word is coming from Mexico and Miami and that means it is Luca . . . the big, big boss. I don't think we have a choice in this," Eduardo said, looking over at me. I guess he could see in my face that I wasn't happy or swayed by what he had just said.

"It's going to work out. Trust me. Plus, our take will step up from two stacks a week for one package a day to ten stacks a week for three packages a day. I mean, I'm not going to let you take a big risk if it's not going to be worth it for both of us," Eduardo said, looking at me again to see what kind of reaction I was going to have. I guess he knew talking money was going to get bells and whistles ringing in my head. My eyes popped open wide when he said that. In my hood, money talked and bullshit walked for sure.

"Ten thousand dollars a week for three packages a day?" I asked dreamily for clarification. I was in amazement to even think about having that kind of money in my hands every week. I had quickly forgotten about how crazy Eduardo and Lance's request was with stepping up the packages. All I was thinking about now was having that much cold cash in my hands.

"Yeah, baby girl . . . you'll have ten stacks in your hand every week. You'll be able to have shit you never had and your paycheck will become your play money," Eduardo said confidently. I fell quiet. I was already counting up the shit I could do with all of that money. First thing I thought of was getting my mother completely out of the hood, instead of just paying for her taxes on the little shack of a house she had. Next, I thought about taking my son to Disney World or on a cruise for his birthday. Then, I could go to college if I wanted to and pay for it so I wouldn't have loans. All sorts of shit ran through my head when I thought about having that kind of money— tax-free, cash in my hand every week. The one thing I didn't think of after I heard about the money was the risk and the problems of having all of that new money all of a sudden. That was one of many of our mistakes. The one thing about the game you should know, with every dollar comes a higher price.

CHAPTER 4

SPECIAL DELIVERY

"Gabriella, I need to speak with you before you go out on your route this morning," my supervisor Ben said as I clocked in. I didn't like the sound of his voice when he approached me, nor did I like the look on his face. He looked like he was stressed or upset about something. Not a good sign. Ben was usually a happy-go-lucky person who often smiled and tried to keep everyone motivated to work. Not today. I could see stress lines creasing his forehead and there was not a smile even remotely evident on his face. Seeing Ben look so grave was a red flag for me.

"Um, sure . . . is . . . is everything okay with my work?" I asked, barely able to get the words out. I immediately became cold all over my body and my teeth started to involuntarily chatter. I was already paranoid as shit and it had only been one day since the extra packages had started coming through the post office. Could Ben have picked up on it that fast? Did someone become suspicious?

"We can talk about it in my office," Ben said, then he kind of looked around at everyone else as if to tell me with his eyes that he didn't want anyone else to hear what he wanted to speak to me about. Another red flag for me.

All sorts of shit ran through my mind as I slowly followed down the long hallway that separated the bank of offices from the main public area in the post office. Ben was way ahead of me and had made it to the office before I did. He waited for me at the door. Finally, I made it to the doorway. I cracked a weak smile and Ben and I walked into his office, not knowing what to expect. I was feeling like I was being sent to the gas chamber. Ben walked behind his desk and flopped down in his chair. He folded his hands in front of him and looked at me like a father would look at his child who'd gotten in trouble.

"Sit down, Gabriella," Ben said, pointing at one of the chairs in front of his desk. I clenched my ass cheeks together to keep from shitting myself.

"No it's okay, I'll stand up. I'm hoping this is going to be quick. I—I—gotta go on my route," I stammered, cracking a nervous, halfhearted smirk. The truth was, I was too fucking nervous to sit down. Plus, the cramps that were invading my stomach wouldn't allow me to bend my body into the chair even if I wanted to do it.

"Okay, suit yourself. Well . . ." Ben started and then he reared back in his chair, closed his eyes, steepled his fingers in front of his face, and paused. I swear it was like time had stopped moving all over the world. I could hear my heart thumping in my ears. I just knew Ben was going to tell me that he knew what I had been doing and that he was going to call the cops—or worse, the DEA. I could actually picture the feds running up on Eduardo with their guns drawn and throwing him facedown on the ground. I could also see them grabbing me while my son screamed and me grabbing my baby to keep him safe. I saw those bastards snatching my son out of my arms right before I was carted off to jail. The thoughts threatened to make me cry.

"Gabriella, I wanted to ask you something," Ben said, snapping me out of my nightmarish reverie. Blinking rapidly, I looked across the desk at Ben. I still needed to try and focus on keeping my cool so that Ben couldn't read me.

"I know there's been some things happening in the station," Ben said, his tone even but serious. His words sounded as if they were coming out in movielike slow motion. I kept staring and blinking. All of a sudden, I was so hot all over. I wanted to just bolt out of the chair. My mouth had gone cotton-ball dry.

"So, I wanted to ask if you could cover another route in addition to yours," Ben finally said. I could hear my own relieved breath escaping my mouth after I had finally started to breathe again. I felt a whoosh of relief wash over me. *This is what he wanted that was so important. If he only knew how fucking scared he made me,* I said to myself.

"I mean, you've been doing such a good job getting yours done that I felt with Angie gone on maternity leave that you might be able to cover hers too," he said, like he regretted to have to ask me. I smiled. The biggest, brightest, widest smile I could get across my face. Ben just didn't know that I wanted to jump up and kiss his ass. He would never know how fucking grateful I was that all he wanted was to ask me to pick up another route.

"Oh, yeah. That's no problem at all. I'll cover her route. In fact, I'll do her route first and then I'll do mine afterwards. It's really not a problem. I'd be happy to help out." I was rambling because my nerves had my tongue loose and my brain like mush. I was giddy as fuck at that point. Ben was looking at me strangely, so I finally snapped my lips shut and stopped talking. *Don't overdo it, Gabby.*

"Well, then, I guess that settles it. Great. I guess that was easier than I thought it would be. Most of the workers at this station always gripe and complain when I ask them to do anything outside of their normal duties. I want to say thank you for being such a team player," Ben said, standing up from behind his desk. I was moving on my legs like I had to take a piss real bad.

"No problem, Ben. Anytime," I said, still a little caught up. With that, I turned and damn near ran from Ben's office. I rushed to the sorting room because I needed to tell Carlos about the increase in packages before he found out. I was too late, Carlos was already waiting for me. And he did not look happy.

"Gabriella, what the fuck is going on?" he whispered harshly, grabbing me by the arm.

"Nothing. Ben just wanted to ask if I'd—" I started, but Carlos quickly cut me off. I wrestled my arm out of his grasp.

"No! I mean with the extra packages from Florida? There's more than one today. It's supposed to be one a day . . . not fucking three. What is this all about Gabriella?" Carlos gritted.

"Just calm down," I whispered, urging him to follow me into a corner so we could speak away from nosy ears. "It'll be fine, Carlos. Just keep doing it the way we always have, but now with two extra packages. I will make sure nothing happens."

"This is a higher risk. You know that when it comes to sorting, this many packages each week from the same place is going to raise suspicions. You have to change something up, Gabriella, or else things are going to get blown," Carlos replied, looking around like he was expecting someone to jump out of the walls at us.

"Just do it like we always did," I hissed, annoyed. He was starting to look like a weak-ass complainer. Nothing turned me off more than a weak-ass man.

"I want more money and more of your time," Carlos said, grabbing back onto my arm forcefully. It was like he'd hit me over the head with a hammer. I expected him to ask for more money, but was he actually asking me to spend time with him—as in fucking him? I wrestled my arm away from him once again. This time I didn't care if we made a scene.

"What the fuck are you talking about?" I whispered through clenched teeth.

"I'm talking about some of what I've been asking you for all of these years. You think I'm going to keep helping you for nothing," Carlos said lecherously. He was dead serious too. I couldn't believe he had really gone there. I had considered him a cool work friend. Just thinking about Carlos touching me made me throw up a little in my mouth. Not only was he almost three hundred pounds, he was also hairy like a caveman and he smelled like day-old cheese and hot dogs. I was cool with him at work because he was my sorter and he'd been easy to get on board with Eduardo's deliveries, but now Carlos was taking this shit to a whole other level.

"My time you can't have, but I will double what I've been giving you in cash," I tried to placate without spitting in his fucking face or slapping the shit out of him.

"I want double of that and I want once a week with you . . . my apartment. Me and you, together," Carlos repeated like a fucking pervert.

"You can fucking forget that shit. I can't believe you even went there," I growled, my jaw rocking feverishly. Carlos let out a snort type of laugh, like he thought I was fucking joking with him.

"Either that or none of these packages get delivered and a little note goes out to the postmaster general and maybe even the DEA," he threatened with a smirk.

"You can't be fucking serious, Carlos," I hissed, my eyes squinted into little dashes. If looks could kill Carlos would've instantly dropped dead.

"I am serious. I've been looking out for you, haven't I? Well, I'm not going to fantasize about you anymore, Gabriella. If you don't want to go to jail, then you'll do what I say," Carlos replied snidely. With that, he wobbled away. Leaving me standing there mouth agape and insides burning up with anger.

CHAPTER 5

RISKY BUSINESS

"What's wrong with you?" Eduardo asked, looking at me strangely. "You been acting real funny lately. You starting to make me wonder about you. You got some nigga out there hollering at you? Or you tired of me? What's the deal?"

He was hitting me with the fifty million questions because I had pushed him away from me when he'd tried to initiate sex; something I would've never have done under normal circumstances. As much as I loved Eduardo's dick, he knew just as well as I did that I would've never turned down an opportunity to feel it inside of me. So when I rejected him for the third night in a row, Eduardo knew something was up. I'd usually be the one trying to damn near rape him, but after what I'd been going through to keep the packages coming in for him, I wasn't in the mood to be touched by a man at all.

"You gon' tell me what's up or you gon' leave me to come up with some shit on my own?" Eduardo pressed. I rolled my eyes and ignored him at first.

It had been three weeks since we'd started moving more packages and each week I'd had to go to Carlos's house and fuck his nasty ass. The first time, I literally threw up right after he'd touched me.

Carlos was a nasty motherfucker who wanted to have his small, sweaty, fleshy, soggy, musty dick sucked, although it smelled like he'd never washed it in his life. That was where I had drawn the line. "Fuck you! I'm not sucking your dirty dick for nothing!" I had barked at him. I was really close to stabbing him full of holes that day.

"Remember, I hold the key to your freedom, Gabriella. I know you don't want that little boy of yours to grow up without his mother. And what will Mama Vasquez think of her only daughter . . . the drug courier?" Carlos had said when I had told him I wasn't sucking his dick. He knew the right things to say to hit home with me. My mother and Andrew were the two most important people in the world to me. They were the real reason I had started doing the packages in the first place. After more threats from Carlos and more reluctance from me, I finally gave in to his disgusting request. I swear, when I put that piece of flesh in my mouth, I died a million deaths inside. Something deep down inside of me really died and I knew that I would never be the same again. Ever! As I choked and gagged from the odor of Carlos's dick, I had so many devious thoughts running through my head. The first thing I thought about was biting down on his shit until it was almost cut off and he died from the pain.

After I left there that day, I had rushed straight to the drugstore and purchased at least five different mouthwashes and tried to wash every bit of him out of my mouth. I didn't think the musty taste would ever leave my mouth. I still don't think my sense of taste or smell will ever be the same.

Eduardo was still complaining about me rejecting him. Finally, I glared at him. I wanted so badly to scream at him and say, *You have no fucking idea all I've been doing for you! Don't complain, because I've been making the ultimate sacrifice for your ass.* But I didn't say what I was thinking.

"Nothing is wrong. I'm just not in the mood. I'm not always ready to be at your beck and call, you know," I snapped, then turned my back toward him. Just knowing that I was sacrificing so much to help him and to be with him had already started making me feel annoyed around him.

"Well, you used to be ready for me all the time. You used to want me all the time. So, now that you're acting like this, I know something is wrong. This is not the Gabriella I know. You sure you a'ight?" Eduardo said. I never answered him. I just laid there waiting for it to be my time to leave.

"I'll see you later when you come through with the packages. Remember, the ones with the gold stars go to Ant now and not me. Don't mess that up or else I'll have no way to get all that shit over there carrying it on the streets," Eduardo instructed. I wanted to tell him to shut the fuck up with all of his fucking instructions. I bit my tongue and stayed quiet.

"One last chance for you to tell me what's the matter," Eduardo said with the silly but sexy smile he always used on me. I just grumbled. He shrugged, then he kissed me. I pushed him aside. One minute I would feel like he was concerned about me and down for me; but it never took long for Eduardo to bring the topic back to the packages and his money and Lance and what Lance wanted, blah, blah, blah. Frankly, I was sick of the entire operation.

I got up from the bed and stomped into the bathroom. Once inside, I slammed the door so hard I almost broke the door frame. I plopped down on the toilet and put my face in my hands. I began to sob. I had done all of this just for Eduardo and now, once a week, like fucking clockwork, I was being raped against my fucking will and I couldn't even tell Eduardo what was happening. Just thinking about the task I had at hand that day was driving me crazy. I knew right as I sat there that fucking pervert Carlos would be waiting for me to get to his house so he could come up with one more freakish thing for me to do. I wondered if I had told Eduardo, would he say *fuck the packages* and go fuck Carlos up for me? There was no telling, so I just sucked it up and continued to do what I had to do to make sure everything continued to run smoothly.

That morning I arrived at Carlos's house just like always before our shift. Like usual, as I walked inside I had to cover my nose until I could get used to the smell of rotting garbage, dirty clothes, and stinking ass. Carlos was a fucking slob in every sense of the word. His house was dirty as shit, with food containers strewn all over the floor and tables, and dishes piled high in the sink that looked like they hadn't been cleaned in years. Flies buzzed around everywhere and dirty clothes were piled up in several different corners of the place.

I wasn't in the mood for any small talk or bullshit. I wasn't in the mood for much that morning and I was feeling like it was time to put an end to the madness. I had put a butcher's knife that I had taken from my kitchen in my bag. I told myself that I was sick of his fucking abuse and I was going to end it once and for all.

"You ready, sweet girl?" Carlos asked, rubbing his crotch lasciviously. I eyed him evilly and I could actually see myself pulling out that knife and gutting that fat bastard like a slaughtered pig. The way I was feeling, I could've probably stabbed him a thousand times and would not have felt any remorse about it.

"Don't talk to me. Seriously. I'm not your fucking girl and I'm not here because I want to be here, so do not fucking speak to me at all," I said through clenched teeth. Carlos laughed like I had just told him the funniest joke in the world. My eyebrows shot up in disbelief. He watched me as he continued to rub himself.

"I love it when you get upset. It turns me on even more," he replied. I bit down into my lip until I could taste the tinny taste of my own blood. My chest was moving up and down like someone was pumping it with a machine.

"I don't know when you'll get used to this, Gabriella. I thought by now you would be enjoying it. I enjoy it. You're doing this for your man, right? To protect that little punk who could give a damn less about you. Or wait—maybe a guy who would let his girlfriend deliver drugs in the most dangerous neighborhoods in Virginia Beach really does love you. I don't fucking think so," Carlos said rudely.

"I'm warning you, Carlos, shut the fuck up today. Don't talk to me at all because I might just lose it on your ass. Don't speak about my boyfriend, about me, about nothing—or else," I replied. I was not joking with him, either.

"Okay, baby. I'm sorry if I made you mad," Carlos said tauntingly. Something about the way he spoke incensed me. It was like he was enjoying this torture he was putting me through a little too much. As if I was some dumb, love-struck girl who was just an asshole for putting myself out there for Eduardo.

"Come over here and sit by me," Carlos said, patting a spot on his bed. I rolled my eyes and reluctantly walked over. I sat down and Carlos immediately reached out and grabbed a handful of my breasts. His touch felt like a million needles stabbing me on every inch of my body. I closed my eyes and pretended I was someplace else, which was hard to do given the fact that this nigga stunk like shit.

"Gabriella, you feel so good. You're so beautiful," Carlos panted, sounding like he'd run ten miles. I had to swallow hard to choke back the vomit that had crept up my esophagus. My stomach churned as wave after wave of nausea passed through my gut. I was saying a silent prayer that I wouldn't lose it. If I had murdered him, I'd go to jail for life. That's what I had to tell myself to stay calm.

"Today I want it from the back. I want to feel every part of you before this is all over. I know you are going to stop coming to see me one day and then you'll be in jail and I won't ever get to feel you again," Carlos said, breathing hard like he was excited just thinking about it. I set my jaw and my hands involuntarily curled into fists. This motherfucker must've been losing his fucking mind if he thought I was going to let him fuck me in my ass. I loved Eduardo and I didn't even let *him* fuck me in the ass.

"You're not fucking me in my ass, Carlos!" I growled, jumping up from the bed. I wanted nothing more than to get away from him.

"Don't make this harder than it has to be, Gabriella. I thought you might resist, so I want to show you something," he said. He stood up too.

I clutched my bag and I could feel the handle of the knife. My blood was boiling inside. I was looking at this slob in disbelief as he went to retrieve his laptop. For the two years I had been with postal, I'd thought of him as a cool coworker. Yes, he used to flirt, but so did most men in the workplace. I would've never thought he would have blackmailed me into sleeping with him like this. I wanted to torture and murder him for this shit.

"Here you go," Carlos said, putting the laptop down on his nightstand and clicking a few buttons. My mouth dropped open when I saw the videotape footage of the inside of the packages. Carlos had actually opened up a few of Lance's packages and taken video of the drugs inside. Then he had video of me instructing him to make sure those packages got into my mail truck. *How could I be so stupid? I knew better than to put myself out there like that!* I was screaming inside of my head.

"Now, if I were you I would hurry up and get this over with. We both have to be at work soon and you wouldn't want Ben to catch your packages before I did, now would you?" Carlos said flatly. I could feel tears burning at the backs of my eyes.

"Take off that uniform and show me that beautiful ass of yours," Carlos wheezed. I stood there, contemplating taking that knife out and doing this bastard in.

"Don't just stand there. We both have to be at work before

those packages get picked up by someone else, right?" Carlos reiterated, his words giving me the motivation I needed to move. I used one hand to slowly slide out of my pants. But I was still clutching my bag with the knife inside.

"Mmm, yeah, that's what I'm talking about. I don't think anybody expected you to be so fine under that uniform. Now come over here and let me see that ass that I'm about to get," Carlos huffed. I stood up in front of him and turned around, barely able to get my legs to cooperate. I flipped up the flap on my pocketbook and slid my hand inside. I was about to dead this nigga.

"You know, if anything happens to me, I have a way of letting everyone know you were here. That is not the only video I have," Carlos said. I guess he was smarter than I'd ever given him credit for. I froze, my hand no longer going to my knife. I guess it was final. I was going to be his fucking sex slave until something else changed.

"Yeah, there's a camera around here somewhere. Too bad I can't tell you where. And if you ever think about telling on me or not coming back here anymore, I have something for that too. You see, Gabriella, my brother-in-law is with the DEA. It would just make his day to have you and your little boyfriend served up on a platter for trafficking heroin, weed, and ecstasy over state lines and through the mail, which constitutes its own federal crimes. I would act like I never knew you had drugs in those packages when I sorted them. I would act like I just got suspicious one day because there was so many coming in, not from the same address, but with the same postal coding, from the same area and going to the same houses on your route day after day after day. I would say I was just giving the DEA a tip because I was too scared to confront you for fear that your big, bad boyfriend and his goons would come after me. Then, you know what would happen? The DEA would come on down and get you and your handsome hunk within the blink of an eye. I think you would get ten-to-twenty in federal prison for the type of stuff you're riding dirty with every day," Carlos said cruelly. It was his only way of getting me to submit. He pulled me closer to him. He probed my ass with his fat, sausage fingers at first. Each touch felt like sharp-bladed razors tearing into my skin. Tears ran a race down my face and I was sick to my stomach. I couldn't believe that I was standing there letting this happen to me. All because I was protecting Eduardo and thinking about my mother and my son. I kept telling myself that I was doing this for a good reason. I was protecting everyone that I loved.

"Bend over, baby," Carlos panted like the animal he was. He pushed me over and attempted to stick his shriveled-ass dick into my ass. It felt like someone was slapping a wet noodle over my ass. His dick was cold, limp, and clammy. Carlos was getting frustrated because he couldn't get that little flat dick to go where he wanted it to go. I was breathing hard because the anger inside of me was boiling over now.

"Aghh," Carlos moaned as he finally found his way inside of my tight anal opening. His dick was so small that it didn't hurt; it was more annoying and humiliating than painful. I gripped two handfuls of his dirty bedsheets and closed my eyes. The shame was trampling over my mood like a herd of wild animals. The tears were falling fast and furious now. They were more tears of pure, white-hot anger than tears of sorrow. Carlos was grunting and wheezing like he would just fall over and croak at any moment. That was exactly what I was praying would happen too.

"Yeah. Your ass feels so good," he wheezed as he plowed his fat body into me from the back. Feeling his overhang gut touch me made my skin crawl.

"I wonder if your boyfriend knows what a good piece of ass he has," Carlos said. It was like he had plucked the last string of sanity that I had left.

"Shut the fuck up! Don't talk to me or I'll fucking kill you," I barked so loud that I even surprised myself. I could tell he was startled. Carlos didn't say another fucking word after that. He did his business and just as fast as it had started, it was over. I climbed off the bed and raced into his bathroom to clean myself up. I swore I felt like I was being attacked by flesh-eating bugs all over my skin. I kept swiping and wiping like there was shit crawling on me. Now I could understand what people meant when they said their skin felt like it was literally crawling. Mine was alive; every pore felt like it was moving. When I got to the sink inside of Carlos's small, cramped, dirty bathroom, I looked at my reflection in the filthy mirror hanging over the sink. More tears dropped from my eyes and I shook my head from left to right, trying to make sense of what I was doing. I clawed at the skin on my own face until I felt welts cropping up on my cheeks. I didn't even recognize myself anymore. I didn't want to be me anymore. I could barely stand to look at myself. That was the moment I decided that I would not endure anymore of this abuse. It was also the moment I would live to regret later, like so many other moments that came after.

CHAPTER 6

TIME TO FACE THE MUSIC

"Gabby! Gabby are you here?" Eduardo called out to me. The sound of his voice seemed so loud, like he was standing next to me screaming in my ear. I wanted to disappear. I didn't want to face Eduardo, so I didn't answer him.

"Gabriella?" he called out again. I could tell he was in the bedroom now, but I still kept my eyes shut and my head tucked between my knees. I had been sitting in the dark, on the floor of our bedroom, naked with my knees pulled up to my chest, just rocking back and forth for hours now. I had a bottle of Vicodin and a razor right next to me on the floor. I had contemplated several times just ending my misery. Finally, Eduardo came all the way into our huge master suite and found me sitting on the floor in the corner. He clicked on the bedside lamp and I buried my face deeper to hide from the light. I didn't want him to see my red-rimmed, swollen eyes or the self-inflicted scratches that painted my face now.

"Gabriella? What are you doing sitting in the dark? Naked?" Eduardo asked, bending down in front of me. The smell of his cologne used to comfort me, but at that moment it made me afraid. I couldn't face him; the shame and guilt were too much to handle.

"Gabriella? What's wrong?" He tugged on my arms, trying to get me to look at him. I just started to sob again for the one-hundredth time since I'd been sitting there. I didn't answer him. I think my deep, guttural sobs were enough to tell Eduardo that something was seriously amiss.

"What the fuck is going on, Gabriella?" he asked, grabbing me up from the floor. He carried me over to the bed and put me down. I kept my eyes tightly squeezed. I could hear the concern in his voice. Then he must've noticed the razor and the pills on the floor.

"Talk to me, Gabby. Did you take something? Did you try to hurt yourself?" Eduardo asked frantically. I don't even think he realized how hard he was shaking me, as if he could shake the answers out of my mouth.

"Did something happen to Andrew? Is something wrong with your moms? Something at work?" Eduardo asked. I whimpered like a wounded puppy, but I couldn't speak. The words were on the tip of my tongue, but they just wouldn't come.

"Please, Gabby, talk to me. I can't help you if you don't tell me what's wrong, baby. It's me; I'm here for you, but you've got to tell me, please," Eduardo pleaded. I could feel my heart melting. I wanted and needed to share my pain with somebody.

"He—he—" I started, but I couldn't bring myself to say it. I was ashamed to say that I had let this happen to me so many times. I also didn't know how Eduardo was going to take it if I told him I had slept with another man behind his back, even though it was to protect him.

"Who? What? He who? Who did something to you?" Eduardo urged, concern lacing his words. I was overcome with more wracking sobs. I pulled my knees up toward my chest and lay there curled like a baby on my side. Eduardo laid next to me and held me.

"Shhh, just tell me, Gabby. I won't be mad. I just want to

make it better," Eduardo said sweetly. He was in my head. He made me feel so safe at that moment.

"He raped me! He fucking raped me! He made me do it over and over again!" I finally blurted out. It felt like I had thrown up the worst dinner I'd ever eaten. My stomach felt lighter. My brain felt relief. My body felt more relaxed than it had in a month. After I got those words to come out, I felt like a thousand-pound weight had been lifted off of me. Eduardo let go of me. He stood up from the bed, but he didn't say anything at first. I opened my eyes to look at him. His face was scowling and his fists were clenched at his sides. I had never seen his face fill up with blood that fast. It looked as if someone had pulled a red veil over his eyes. He was baring his teeth like a vicious dog about to attack.

"Who! Who the fuck touched you?! Tell me right now!" he boomed. I jumped. I was shivering now; a combination of fear and suddenly going cold. He was moving on his legs like he was getting ready to run out of the room at any minute. Eduardo's reaction made me feel even worse about the situation.

"Tell me now! Right now! Who the fuck was it, Gabriella?" Eduardo screamed. I had never seen him like this.

"It—it—wa—was Carlos," I sobbed, barely able to speak. Eduardo stopped moving as if I had hit an imaginary pause button. His eyebrows dipped low on his face and he cocked his head to the side. His eyes went into little dashes.

"Who? Carlos? You mean the nigga you was telling me about at your job that makes sure you get the packages? The fucking sorter that you've been hitting off with cash?" Eduardo asked for clarification. "The fat nigga?"

"Yes," I mumbled, feeling so much shame my cheeks flamed over.

"How? How could his fat ass rough you up? At work? He had a gun? Where was everybody else at when this happened? Did you scream?" Eduardo replied, shooting questions at me rapid-fire. All of his questions made me cry even harder. I mean, that was how rape usually happened, right . . . by force?

"No . . . nothing like that. He didn't hold a gun on me and it didn't happen at work," I cried. Eduardo's face curled into a confused frown. I knew he wouldn't get it.

"Then how the fuck he rape you?"

"He made me come to his house and do things with him. He said he would call the DEA on you and on me if I didn't do it. He said he would make sure CPS took Andrew away and he would tell my mother that I was transporting drugs. He said he had video and he showed me some video of the packages— the heroin inside of the coffee beans," I explained. "I did it for you, Eddie. I did it for us. But this last time, he—he—hurt me," I said, almost whispering. The words felt like huge rocks coming out of my mouth. They fell around the room with the same type of *thud* that an actual rock would've made. Eduardo seemingly lost his legs. He slumped down on the end of the bed and put his head in his hands. I could see him squeezing his head like he was trying to get what I had just told him to settle into his brain. He turned toward me, his face showing confusion.

"So you fucked a nasty nigga like that all to protect me? More than once?" Eduardo asked, his voice low and sympathetic.

"I didn't fuck him! He blackmailed me and then raped me! I went along with it to protect you! All for you! From the beginning, everything I've done was just because I wanted to be with you!" I screamed. Eduardo came over and grabbed me into a big bear hug. I choked on my tears as a wave of nausea rippled through my stomach, making me want to hurl.

"Get dressed, Gabriella. I can't let this go," Eduardo said, stroking my hair. I immediately pushed away from him and broke from his embrace. I looked at him, terrified.

"No! Please, just leave it alone. If he knows that I told you he will go to the feds. He says his brother-in-law works for the

DEA. We will all go to jail. Andrew will have to go to foster care. My mother would probably die if she found out what I've been doing. We can't say anything right now," I cried, shaking my head from left to right. Eduardo grabbed my face and forced me to look him in the eyes.

"There is no fucking way I am letting a nigga get away with what he did to you. I don't give a fuck who he knows or who he threatens to tell! He hurt you and I'm going to see that nigga!" Eduardo gritted.

"Now, get up and get dressed and take me to his house. Now! I'm not asking you, I'm telling you!" Eduardo yelled at me. I knew this wasn't going to end well. It was going to be the first of many things to go wrong with our little business.

Eduardo barely waited for me to get out of the car before he was banging on Carlos's door like the police right before a raid. When Carlos pulled back the door he had no time to react before Eduardo bulldozed his way inside. Carlos didn't stand a chance against the force of Eduardo's strong, muscular frame. Carlos's round, wobbly frame was knocked off balance and he fell back flat onto his back. Seeing him lying there like a fat lump of shit gave me a quick fleeting feeling of satisfaction.

"No, please don't hurt me. I have no money here. Please, I can get some money, but I don't have anything of value in the house," Carlos cried out, begging like the fat-ass punk bitch that he was.

"What nigga—you think I'm here to rob you? You got me fucked up, you sloppy piece of shit. Nah. You should wish I was here to just rob your ass. Fuck that, your fate is going to be much worse, partner," Eduardo said through clenched teeth. That is when I finally stepped from behind Eduardo and looked Carlos in his evil fucking eyes. When Carlos saw me, his eyes almost popped out of his head. Eduardo was standing over him, so there was no place for Carlos to run or to hide.

"You fucking piece of shit," I spat, hawking up the biggest wad of spit I could and spewing it down on Carlos.

"What—what's this—this all about Gabriella?" Carlos stuttered, trying to act like he was so innocent. I just stood there looking at him evilly.

"You blackmailed my girl into fucking you? You raped her by threatening to tell the feds on her—on me? Then you threatened her seed too? You ain't no fucking man. We got a term for niggas like you in the hood: bitch-ass nigga. That's what the fuck you are for preying on a woman and her kid," Eduardo growled. Carlos shot me a look. Terror flashed in his eyes and across his entire face. That was confirmation enough. Eduardo slammed his left fist straight into Carlos's face. I jumped because I had been so busy locking eyes with Carlos I hadn't been paying attention.

"Ahh!" Carlos screamed out in a high-pitched voice like a woman. "Help me! Please, somebody help me!"

"Shut the fuck up!" Eduardo hissed, slamming more fists into Carlos's face. Each time Eduardo let his left or right fist land at will, he would say something else to Carlos about being a bitch-ass nigga. Eduardo was not stopping until he felt satisfied. He was possessed. He slammed another hard blow to Carlos's face and that time a gush of blood spurted from Carlos's nose and lips in a spray. Carlos was crying like a woman and pleading for mercy. He'd even asked me to call Eduardo off. I stood there watching and thinking that he was getting everything he deserved.

Eduardo was saying things, but he was so winded and seemingly possessed as he rained down an onslaught of strikes that I couldn't even understand him. When he was tired of punching, Eduardo lifted his foot and began kicking Carlos all over his body.

"You threaten anybody that works for me and you die, motherfucker. You threaten my business and I fucking kill you," Eduardo huffed. Those words struck me like an open-handed slap to the face. I wondered right then if the real reason Eduardo was fucking Carlos up was because Carlos had threatened to tell and to shut down the business. As much as I wanted to believe that Eduardo was doing this to get revenge on Carlos for raping me, something in my heart said he was doing it to ultimately protect himself.

Carlos was barely conscious, but Eduardo wouldn't stop hitting and kicking him.

"That's enough," I said. "He's not even moving anymore."

"Enough? You think I'm leaving this nigga alive so he can snitch? You think I came here just to beat his ass for recreation? Nah, I wanted him to suffer first, but this nigga gotta go, so go get me a pillow and get a towel," Eduardo replied, winded and sweating. He was dead serious too. I was frozen in place. Murder wasn't what I had bargained for.

"Go! Do what the fuck I said!" Eduardo barked at me, spurring me into motion. My legs were moving, but they didn't even feel like they belonged to me. I knew my way around Carlos's apartment, but I wished that I didn't. I came back and handed Eduardo the pillow.

"Use the towel to wipe your prints from this fucking place. But not before you take the laptop and any disks you find that might have any videos on it," he instructed.

"If—if you kill him—who will we have to get the packages done?" I asked softly, too afraid to upset Eduardo any further. It was a valid concern, although I knew it wasn't a big enough concern to save Carlos's life. I wanted him dead too, I just didn't want the police to suspect us.

"That's for you to figure out. This nigga right here ain't no more good to us. He will never stay loyal after this. Plus, if I know Lance, he wouldn't like to know that he threatened our entire operation," Eduardo said with finality. I scurried away and grabbed up the laptop and whatever else I thought could be holding any incriminating videos. Then I began wiping the hard surfaces clean of my prints. *Pop! Pop!* Two muffled shots rang out. I squeezed my eyes shut tightly and tensed my shoulders in response to the noise. I bent over at the waist and threw up all over the floor.

"Yo! Now you gon' have to use bleach or something to clean that shit up. That shit will have your DNA all over this fucking place," Eduardo yelled at me. I certainly hadn't thought of that when I was hurling up my guts. That scared me about Eduardo. It was like he was an expert on this type of shit. He had just killed a man and his hands weren't even shaking. His face showed no emotion: not fear, not remorse, nothing. He was simply cold, like nothing had just happened. All of the anger he was previously displaying against Carlos had seemed to subside. It was like the murder had brought him some type of calming relief. Me, I was a fucking wreck. Even after everything Carlos had done to me, I was still not really prepared to see him lying there stiff and dead like that. My hands and legs were shaking. I was crying and shivering. I was scared to imagine how I would be all night. Every time I closed my eyes I was sure I would keep replaying the murder over and over again.

"Let's fucking go, Gabriella. I'm hungry and I have shit to do," Eduardo demanded. I could do nothing but look at Eduardo like he was crazy. I had just assisted in committing a cold-blooded murder and this nigga was talking about he was hungry. I couldn't imagine eating one bit a food at that moment. There was blood on my hands. We had committed the ultimate sin. I would never be the same after that and I knew it. I had gotten myself caught up in a truly risky business.

CHAPTER 7

MIXING THINGS UP

I didn't sleep for days after Carlos's murder. Just like I imagined, I couldn't eat, sleep, think, interact with my son, nothing. Each time I tried to do anything—when I closed my eyes or even when they were opened—I would see Carlos's fat, bloodied dead body. I was spooked as shit when I returned to work. Everyone was talking about how Carlos had been gunned down in his own house. It had been on the news and everything. I could barely look anyone at work in the eye. Since Carlos had hardly called out in the ten years he was with the Postal Service, when he didn't show up to work for three days everyone grew suspicious. Ben was the one who'd sent the police to the apartment. They'd broken down the door and found him damn near rotting inside. It was a huge news story, which only served to scare the shit out of me even more. Of course, Eduardo wasn't fazed at all.

People at work started looking at me for answers. They were asking me when was the last time I had spoken to him; if I knew of any other friends and family he might've had and if I knew of anyone who would've wanted to hurt or rob him for any reason. I was annoyed as shit about all of the questions. Why would they assume I knew the answers? What would have made people believe Carlos and I had spoken outside of work? Right away, I wondered if Carlos had been spreading rumors that he and I were somehow romantically or sexually involved. Just the thought of anyone else at the job knowing what had happened between us made me shudder and feel sick to my stomach. It would've been a little more than just regular embarrassment if anyone else even suspected us.

"Gabriella," Ben, my supervisor, said as he touched my shoulder from behind me. I almost jumped out of my skin as if a bolt of lightning had struck me. Ben snatched his hand away quickly and took a few steps backwards, like a snake had bitten him. That is how hard and fiercely I had reacted to his touch.

"Did I startle you?" he asked, his face folded into a confused frown. I swallowed hard and put on a fake smile.

"Um . . . no. I was just daydreaming and didn't hear you coming, so I was a little thrown off when you touched me. I've just been feeling a little stressed with everything going on . . . you know," I said, my voice shaky. My nerves were on a hairpin trigger. I couldn't stop my hands from shaking. I shoved them in my pockets and even that didn't help.

"I know you of all people heard about Carlos. I know you must be taking it hard," Ben said sympathetically. I looked at him strangely as if to say, *What the hell do you mean by that? Carlos wasn't my fucking man!* I guess Ben read my mind and the expression on my face.

"What I mean is, you've worked so closely with him since you've been here and he always spoke so highly of you. He told me that you had been bombarded by a lot of deliveries lately and that you were doing such a great job with it. I think Carlos really cared about you, Gabriella," Ben continued. A pang of guilt flitted through my chest. I had no idea Carlos had been sticking up for me and giving me compliments at work. I had to shake off those thoughts and remember that Carlos also made me sleep with him through fucking blackmail.

"What a senseless tragedy," Ben said, shaking his head. "He

was such a nice guy. I don't know who would do such a terrible thing to an innocent, harmless person like him." I had to really choke back down my words. Obviously, my opinion of that fat pervert was the total opposite.

"Yeah, a tragedy," I repeated, at a loss for better words.

"Well, we are all prepared to do our part to help get to the bottom of this. So, I wanted to let you know that there are a few police detectives who are coming in today to speak with some of us here who worked with Carlos. We all know Carlos didn't have any family, so we were the closest thing he had to one. I guess they want to try and get a better sense of how something like this happens to a guy like that. I told the detectives that you and Carlos had a pretty close relationship," Ben was saying. I was too nervous to even let him finish.

"We weren't close! We worked together and that's it! Why do people keep saying we were close!" I snapped, annoyed that everyone kept insisting that Carlos and me were so damn close. Ben looked at me, clearly taken aback.

"Well, I would see you talking to him all the time—that's all I was saying. I mean, he was your sorter and I could've sworn you guys were like friends. You all seemed to have gotten closer over the past months too. So I just assumed . . ." Ben replied, his eyebrows in high arches on his face.

"Don't assume. Carlos was my sorter and I used to speak to him at work. But, that's it. I can't stand to hear people keep saying we were close, as if we did things together or told each other our closest secrets. We weren't friends outside of work or personal or close or anything like that. It was just a work thing . . . nothing more than that," I rambled, immediately on the defensive. I was coming apart at the seams and I knew it. I had to get away from Ben before he figured it out. This was definitely more than I had bargained for. And where was Eduardo? Nowhere around to deal with the backlash of his fucking actions.

"Well, the detectives will be here when you're done with

your route. So make sure you check back in because they want to speak to as many people as they can, so they can try to make some sense of this horrific incident. I told them we'd all help as much as we could. I told them it was important to speak to you, out of all of us," Ben said, repeating the same thing again as if he was sending me some sort of message. He was still eyeing me suspiciously.

"Okay, I'll be here," I said, as calmly as I could. I knew that I had no intention of coming back that day. I didn't know if I'd ever come back. That was, of course, until I spoke to Eduardo.

After my conversation with Ben, I headed into the sorting room. When Carlos first went missing from work, I had asked Ben if I could sort my own packages. Ben allowed it, but had said he was working on finding me a new sorter. That wasn't good at all, but at least that day I was able to get Eduardo and Ant's packages and get them delivered, so there was no lapse. When I got to my last stop that day and met up with Eduardo I told him what Ben had said about the detectives coming by to speak with everyone.

"So? Just got back down there and talk to them," Eduardo had said nonchalantly, like it was no big damn deal. My eyebrows shot up into arches. I was really starting to think this nigga was straight-up crazy.

"I'm not going back to speak to any cops, Eduardo!" I snapped angrily. "Do you know how nervous I would be? They would be able to tell right away from my body language that I knew more than I was saying. No way," I continued my tirade, on the brink of tears. I was feeling weak and I knew how persistent cops could be. They would've been able to crack me like a fragile egg in the state of mind I had been in since the murder.

"Yes, you are. You are going to speak to them fucking pigs and act like you know nothing about what happened to that nasty nigga that was blackmailing and raping you. You can play dumb or put on a good show. I don't really care how you do it, but dipping out is not an option. Avoiding shit is never an option, as you can tell from that nigga pushing up daisies right now," Eduardo demanded.

"What if they feel like I know something?" I complained, biting down on my bottom lip.

"They won't know shit, because you don't know shit. If you start telling yourself you weren't there, you don't know what happened, you had nothing to do with it, then you will believe it when you speak to them. You're going to play it cool; you have no other option. What we got is too good to fuck up right now, Gabriella. You making more money than you could've ever dreamed up. We got a good thing together. Your kid is happy. That lame-ass baby daddy of yours is finally out of the picture. Your mother is proud of you. What more can you ask for? If you want to risk all of that, then you'll fuck this up. If not, you got this. If you play your hand right, everything will be all right. Don't let some bullshit nerves fuck this up for everybody," Eduardo said convincingly. I closed my eyes for a few minutes to contemplate his words. He was right. My son was so happy. My mother was happier than I'd seen her in years. I was able to buy whatever they wanted and needed with no questions asked.

"C'mon, baby girl. Think about it and then go down there, speak to those fucking cops, and convince them that they are barking up the wrong fucking tree," Eduardo said, grabbing my hand. I opened my eyes and looked at him. Before I could say anything to evoke any more doubt, Eduardo stuck a wad of money—my weekly pay for the deliveries—in my hand. I guess that was his way of helping his little pep talk hit home. I looked down at the money, which usually made me feel happy and excited, then I looked back at Eduardo. Money wasn't enough to calm down the torment I had going on inside of me, but I still didn't let the money go. I stuffed it into my pocketbook and turned back toward the man I had done all of this for.

"What if, Eduardo? I mean, I don't know how good I can hide because I'm so fucking nervous I can't even keep down any food," I whined. Eduardo made a face like he was growing sick of me.

"Gabriella, for the last fucking time! Calm the fuck down and just go talk to them. If you avoid them that's like admitting you're guilty about some shit. You can't fuck this up because if you do, shit will get worse for all of us than just a few homicide cops investigating a murder. It'll be fucking DEA, FBI, and all types of feds breathing down our necks. You think they gonna take lightly to you, working for the federal government and doing the shit you've been doing? Hell no—they're going to come down harder on you than even me or Lance. Forget what Luca might do if you fuck up his entire flow. You better go in there and act like you about to win a fucking Emmy award. No joke, you better act like an innocent angel and be damn convincing about it. I don't care how you do it, just do it. I'm not going to talk about this shit anymore," Eduardo replied, and the tone of his voice was borderline threatening. I looked down at the money sitting in my bag, seemingly glaring back at me. I wondered right then if it was worth it. Was a couple thousand dollars that would've never made me rich anyway worth digging deeper and deeper into the quicksand of my actions? Or signing my life away, for that matter.

CHAPTER 8

CONSPIRACY THEORY

When I got back to the post office after my routes, Ben was there with two white detectives waiting for me. Talk about bag of nerves—my damn teeth were hitting together like it was zero-below outside. I had tried to stall and take as long as I could, but that just caused Ben to call me up on my personal cell phone. I guess that was how badly those detectives wanted to speak to me. Apparently, they had already spoken to all of the other mail carriers, clerks, sorters, and packagers at the station. I walked inside slowly, with my head down, too afraid that if I made eye contact they'd be able to read my guilt right away.

"Ah, there she is," Ben said, rushing over to me. "Whew! Gabriella, I thought you weren't going to show up. They've been waiting a long time for you. What took so long? I had to keep making excuses," Ben whispered through his teeth. I didn't answer him or look at him, either. Ben pushed me in the back, ushering me toward the two detectives as if I needed help walking.

"Gabriella, these are Detectives Sinclair and Boules. Remember I told you that they wanted to talk to you about Carlos?" Ben introduced, his voice jumping and nervous. He was so damn jittery he was making *me* jittery. What the fuck was he nervous for? I barely opened my mouth to greet the two men, who were both dressed in their obligatory sand-colored trench coats, wingtip shoes, and cheap Men's Wearhouse suits and ties. Because the inside of my mouth was so dry, it felt like I'd eaten a jar of paste.

"Hello, Ms. Vasquez," one of the detectives said. He had a friendly enough face, unlike his stony-faced partner. I barely opened my mouth again. I just nodded at the detective, who I could tell was just being nice as a tactic.

"They've been speaking to everyone in the break room," Ben interjected, motioning for me to follow him and them. Apprehensively, I followed Ben and the detectives to the break room. With every step I felt like I was walking into uncertain doom. My legs felt like two lead pipes. I was thinking all sorts of shit now. What if they had found a video in Carlos's house that I had overlooked? What if Carlos left some kind of death manifesto, letting them know everything? What if I had left DNA or fingerprints somewhere in the house, even though Eduardo and I had tried to clean it up? But just as fast as those thoughts came into my head, I started replaying Eduardo's words over in my head as well: *Your kid is happy and your mother is so proud of you.* What he'd said was more important to me than anything else. I decided then that I was going to have to put my big-girl drawers on and ace this fucking interview as if was the last test of my life.

"We can take it from here," the detective with the friendly face said to Ben. Ben gave my shoulder a squeeze as if he could transfer some strength from himself to me. With that, Ben was gone and I was alone with the two detectives. Friendly-face was tall, bald, slightly overweight, and breathing hard like he'd just run for miles. He stuck out his hand and introduced himself as Sinclair. Stone-face was also tall, but he was muscular; I could tell that by his thick neck. He seemed to be the paramilitary, clean-cut, by-the-book-type that kicked ass and took names after. He didn't bother to extend his hand or introduce himself. He just kept eyeing me evilly. I guess their good cop-bad cop routine was starting already and it wasn't hard to tell who was going to play which role.

"Ms. Vasquez, I know your supervisor told you we wanted to speak to you to find out some things about Carlos Ortega and that is partially true. But before I ask any questions and you give any answers, let me start by saying, we know some things already. We've done some digging beforehand and I think we are pretty well prepared to talk to you," Sinclair said, looking over at evil-face Boules for confirmation. Boules nodded and grunted.

"So we want you to know from the very beginning that telling the truth is the only way to go here. It saves you the heartache of lying to us and getting caught up, and it saves us the heartache of painting you as a liar and, in turn, a suspect," Sinclair said, looking at me with a serious—yet still friendly—gaze. My insides immediately started feeling funny, kind of like I was hungry and had to take a shit at the same damn time. I folded my arms over my abdomen, trying to get the feeling to go away. It was as if my organs were grinding against one another. I stayed quiet after Sinclair's little spiel. Listen to the questions and give them answers—that was all they wanted me to do.

"So to start with, without asking a bunch of bullshit, we think you know some things about what might've happened to Carlos and we would like to know just how much you know," Sinclair said, leaning in closer to the table. I moved back a bit from the table, clearly uncomfortable.

"Let's face it, Carlos was a little more than just your coworker . . . maybe even a little more than a casual friend," Sinclair said, raising one of his eyebrows knowingly. *What the fuck does he mean by that? What does he know about me and Carlos? Oh, my God! Does he know I was fucking that nasty pig?* I was screaming in my head and praying that, as terrified as I was, my fear wasn't playing out across my face. Now, my heart was hammering in my chest. The evil-eyed detective, who I assumed was the one Ben had introduced as Boules, stood up and forcefully slammed a case file and a video DVD on the table in front of me. I almost fell out of the chair when I saw the video DVD. I just knew they were about to tell me I was going to jail for the rest of my life for being an accessory to Carlos's murder. I was blinking rapidly. *Maybe Carlos did have more hidden cameras in his apartment. They must have me and Eduardo on tape.*

"Is there anything you want to tell us?" Sinclair asked, as Boules drummed his fingers on top of the video. I kept thinking about what Eduardo had told me. I had to play it cool, even if the detectives seemed like they knew everything. I decided to stick to that plan and see where it took me. If they knew something more, they were going to have to pry that shit out of my lips.

I shook my head left to right, signaling that I didn't have anything to share with the detectives. Boules let out a long, exasperated breath and stopped moving his fingers. There was a few minutes of mind-bending silence. It was so quiet my breath was loud in my own ears.

"You and Carlos Ortega were good friends here at the job, no? This video from the camera shows you having long conversations with him every day—even the day before he was murdered," Sinclair said, moving in closer to the table and eyeing me closely. I swallowed hard, thanking God silently that the videotape wasn't from Carlos's building, apartment or some shit like that. These stupid-ass cops had just told on themselves. I was thinking, *You dumb asses should've bluffed a little longer and you might've scared the truth out of me.*

"We weren't friends. He was my sorter, so I had to spend time talking to him about routes and packages . . . you know, work stuff, but that was it. Everyone thinks that we were closer than we actually were. I guess that was the way Carlos made it seem to everyone. He was a really lonely man, but I guess you already know all about that. I am just a person who is always nice to everyone. I felt sorry for Carlos, because he was always talking about wanting to have a family, a wife, or even just a girlfriend to take on dates, so I was always nicer to him than everyone else here. People can be very mean. You know because he was . . . was . . . different," I said, widening my arms so that they got my drift. Both detectives were hanging on my every word. Evil eye twisted his lips like he wasn't so convinced by my rousing speech.

"The other day he told me he was going to meet a girl on craigslist; you know, so he could have sex or whatever these men do when they pick up strange women from a Web site like that. I was kind of shocked. I knew Carlos was lonely, but I never expected him to really be into like, prostitution—well, digital prostitution. I told him not to do it. I warned him that not only was it illegal, it could be dangerous meeting strange women like that, because they could rob him or worse, set him up, and have their real boyfriends or pimps hurt him. I don't know if Carlos went through with his plans to meet the strange woman and this is the result or not. I sure hope that you guys look into that; because honestly, I don't know anyone else who would've wanted to hurt him," I fabricated on the spot, lowering my voice like I was really sad and concerned. I had surprised even myself with my lying and acting skills. Shit, like Eduardo said, I deserved an Emmy or Oscar for that performance. I was clapping for myself in my head.

Sinclair and Boules looked at each other like they were considering what I'd told them. I'm sure the dumbfounded looks on their faces meant that they were probably thinking this was the first time they were hearing anything about a craigslist date. I even had two seemingly seasoned detectives second-guessing their investigative skills.

"What do you know about the packages Carlos sorted every day? Aside from the fact that he just gave them to you for delivery *every day*," Sinclair asked, stressing the words *every* and *day*.

"Did he ever say anything to you about any strange packages that he'd been receiving? Any packages that were coming from the same place? In another state, maybe?" Sinclair asked. I immediately felt sweat beads running a race down my back. I balled up my toes in my shoes and bit into my bottom lip. *Stay calm, Gabriella. They don't know shit. Stay calm like Eduardo said. Just answer what they ask.*

"I don't know anything, except he sorted the stuff for my routes and I delivered them. I'm just the little ol' mail lady; I never get caught up in where packages came from or really who they were going to. Especially express-mail packages. I just dropped them wherever they needed to go. Carlos certainly never spoke to me about any one package in particular. All of our conversations were just general," I replied, lowering my eyes. My legs involuntarily started to swing in and out under the table. I tried to control them, but they would just start back up again. Boules and Sinclair looked at each other again. This time their exchange was more like a knowing smirk rather than a dumbfounded, confused look. That seemed like a bad omen to me, but I continued to wear my poker face nonetheless.

"Humph," Sinclair said, looking at me through squinty eyes. "So you know nothing about the packages? You just delivered them to the correct addresses as they were listed on the boxes?

"Yes, sir," I said, all official-like. The detectives looked at each other again.

"And you're sure this is all you know?" Sinclair asked, his tone suspicious.

"Like I said, I'm just the mail lady," I replied. Boules stood up first. He still wore a pissed-off scowl, but that wasn't anything new for him. I was more concerned about Sinclair's facial expression. His eyes and face were no longer so friendly. He wore a scowl as well now. He kind of looked like I'd insulted him in some way.

"You have a nice day, Ms. Vasquez," Sinclair said as Boules picked up the stack of stuff from the table. Sinclair stood up next. He started gathering up his pen and pad too.

"That's it? We're done here? Just like that? Seems so—so— abrupt," I said nervously. Neither of the detectives responded.

"Is there any other information about who might've done this? Are you going to check out the craigslist lead? Is there anything else I should worry about?" I asked a bunch of dumb-ass questions. It was my nerves; they'd finally gotten the best of me. I was fucking bugging for that, but I needed to know why they had ended the interview so abruptly. I was nervous as shit about that. What did they know about the packages? Why were they even asking about the packages?

"We have no other information, Ms. Vasquez. We are still investigating. I can tell you this much, something about Carlos Ortega's murder smells very fishy. And for some reason, I just keep thinking it has something to do with his job. Something to do with someone close by. Something to do with those packages we asked you about. I guess you can just say this is not my first time at the ballpark, so I'm a little smarter than the average gumshoe out there," Sinclair said snidely. I didn't know what else to say to that.

Both detectives gave me a knowing glance before they walked out of the break room, leaving me there alone, para-noid and scared shitless. Now I had to decide just how much I was going to share with Eduardo.

CHAPTER 9

GETTING OUT OF THE GAME

"What the fuck you mean, *you want out?*" Eduardo screamed after I told him what the detectives said. Finally this nigga was showing some emotion through all of this.

"You think it just works like that: One minute you're in and the next minute you're out? This ain't the fucking postal service, Gabriella," he barked.

"Eduardo, I don't like the way those cops ended the interview. I'm telling you, it's like they knew something and they were just waiting for the setup," I explained with urgency, underlying my words.

Eduardo waved his hand and exhaled a windstorm of breath. This nigga was not trying to hear me when I told him I wanted to quit our little arrangement. "You don't have to be out there being all scared and shit. I really think they are snooping around, Eduardo. I have too fucking much to lose," I said. It was the truth. Something about the way those detectives just abruptly ended the interview didn't sit right with me. I was scared all day and all night after that.

Eduardo, however, felt like everything was fine; that we had nothing to worry about.

"I'm out, Eduardo. Tell them not to send any more packages, because I'm not going to intercept them. I'll just let them go to whomever. I'm serious. I can't and won't do it anymore," I kept insisting. Eduardo turned toward me, his face painted with an evil snarl. He rushed toward me and bulldozed into me so hard I stumbled backwards and twisted my ankle. I didn't even have time to react before he grabbed my face roughly and got close enough to it that I could damn near taste his lunch.

"Let me tell you one fucking thing. You are in it. There is no going back now, Gabriella. Understand something, these people we work for are not to be fucked with. I can't just call up the fucking deadly Calixte cartel and tell them to stop sending their fucking product. It doesn't work like that. It doesn't stop until *they* say it stops. I will not have Lance breathing down my neck about these packages, so you better continue working it out however you been working it out. These are very dangerous people we are dealing with. You are all in and there is no backing out now or ever—except if your ass ends up dead," he breathed hard in my face. I could've sworn I could see fire flashing in his eyes. For the first time since we'd been together I felt fearful of Eduardo. The kind of fear that makes you lose your breath.

That evening when I got home from work, I decided I was not going to speak to Eduardo at all, after his little tirade that morning. I wanted to get to my safe, count my money that I had been stashing, and start mapping out an exit plan. Fuck what Eduardo was talking about—I was getting the fuck away from it all. I had saved enough money to at least get me started someplace else. I wanted out of this deal before I ended up going to jail or worse, dead from a bullet.

I turned my key in the lock to the apartment and stormed straight past the living room without looking. I knew Eduardo was home because I could hear voices from the TV. I knew my mother had my son, so there was no reason for me to stop, since I wasn't speaking to Eduardo enough to even say hello. I was almost past the doorway to the hallway that led to our bedrooms when I heard it.

"Ahhh, so this is the famous Gabriella," I heard a man's voice say. I had walked right past the living room, assuming it was just Eduardo watching television alone. I hadn't even looked to notice that someone else was in the house. The voice gave me chills although I could not identify the source. Those chills quickly turned into straight- up panic.

"Mommy! Mommy! I want my mommy!" I heard Andrew call out at the top of his little voice. I stopped dead in my tracks. Dread overcame me and my heart raced painfully against my sternum. I turned back and walked into the living room to investigate now. My eyes almost came out of my head when I saw Andrew there looking like he was terrified. He was supposed to be with my mother. I hung my head low with my feet in full view. I had suddenly became lightheaded and my body was beginning to shut down. I felt like my legs would give out at any moment.

"Come join us, Gabriella," the man said with a sinister smile planted on his lips. I furrowed my eyebrows in confusion. Eduardo was sitting up erect on the opposite couch, his face pale as shit, like he had seen a ghost too. I looked at him through squinted eyes, my head tilted slightly.

"Gabby . . . this—this is Lance," Eduardo stammered. I looked back over at the man. I swallowed the tennis ball–sized lump that had formed in my throat.

"Mommy!" my son called out for me again.

"I know, baby," I said, on the brink of tears and hysteria.

"Eduardo, how did Andrew get here?" I asked, my voice coming out raspy and hoarse. I already knew the fucking answer. Eduardo had picked up my son from my mother so that they could use him against me. I know my mother wouldn't have given my baby to anyone other than Eduardo because, just like me, she trusted him. I looked from Eduardo to Lance and back again.

Lance was a broad-shouldered hulk of a man. His hard facial features, beady eyes, charcoal-dark skin, and glistening, bald head made him look like a serial killer from a scary movie. The long scar that ran the length of his left cheek didn't help much, either. He was flanked by two big, bouncer type of dudes and he had my son sitting on his lap. I could barely lift my hand to wave, much less say anything else to this monster.

"Please, this is your home, right? So come join us for a quick minute, Gabby," Lance said, signaling me to sit down and calling me by my nickname like we were old friends.

"Mommy!" Andrew stretched his little arms toward me and tried desperately to run to me. Lance gripped my baby tightly around his waist and he started to scream and cry like he'd been hurt. Hearing his wails ripped me to shreds inside. Tears immediately sprang to my eyes. I had done this to him . . . to us. My fucking greed had done this to my son. I closed my eyes and bit down into my jaw. My fists were curled so tight my knuckles paled. I was a mother watching her child in distress . . . not a pretty picture.

"Not so fast, little man. I need to have a chat with your mommy," Lance said, his words coming out like snake hisses in my ears. Watching him use my son to get to me made me despise Lance and I didn't even know him.

I slowly sat down. My legs were quaking in my work boots. I looked at Lance, trying my best to keep from jumping up and gouging his eyes out.

"So I hear that one of my packages went missing," Lance started. I didn't let him even finish. I immediately jumped up like I had springs on my ass.

"No way! I always deliver everything! I would never take anything from you or let those packages go missing! I've been doing this faithfully for eleven months—almost an entire year, and I never had anything go missing!" I blurted defensively. Lance put his hand up, halting me. My little tirade hadn't swayed him one bit.

"Gabriella, only guilty dogs bark. Now, sit the fuck down and hear me out," he growled, yet he still had an eerie calmness to his tone. "You may speak to your chump-ass man like that, but not to me. I'm a fucking boss and you will respect me as such. Sit the fuck down," Lance said through his teeth. Andrew was screaming, kicking, and crying harder now. Maybe Lance was pinching him or something or maybe he just wanted to be with me. Either way, I felt like my heart was being ripped out and stomped on.

I slumped back down on the chair. I could see Eduardo out of the corner of my eye and for the first time since we had been together I was completely turned off by him. I had always hated weak men all of my life. My father was a weak bitch-ass who had walked out on us. I would've never taken Eduardo for that type, but seeing him sitting there silently, letting me be accused while my son was being kept from me was enough to make me look at him like a weak piece of shit. What a fucking punk bitch I was dealing with! Eduardo was cowering at the end of the couch, not saying a word to help me. He fucking knew I would never have stolen anything from him, much less Lance—and even worse, Luca. My mind was racing in a million directions, trying to figure out what Lance was talking about. I had never messed up the deliveries. Ever.

"Now . . . I came by personally to tell you that my package of H better show up by the end of your route tomorrow or this little precious commodity you have here will really have a reason to cry . . . or maybe you'll have a reason to cry over him," Lance said evilly. "There will be no negotiating. I want my shit or else, Gabriella."

Lance went to set Andrew down on the floor. Before my son's little feet could fully plant on the floor he was running toward me. He jumped into my arms, sobbing. I had never felt my son hold on to me so tight in his entire life.

"Mommy, that man scary," he said. I squeezed him tightly and closed my eyes.

"It's okay, baby. Mommy is here. Mommy is here. I'm never going to let anyone get to you again," I spoke softly in the soft skin of my son's little neck. His little pulse was throbbing fiercely, which made mine pick up speed as well.

"We on the same page?" Lance asked me as he stood up and hovered over me and Andrew. I just shook my head. What else was I going to do? I had no idea what had happened to his package. The only explanation I could come up with was that one of Lance's packages from Miami accidentally got delivered to the wrong address. I was so nervous at work now that it was totally possible that I had started mixing things up. Now, I would have to go back over all of my last stops and find it. I just prayed that whoever received it hadn't already opened it, found the drugs, and called the police.

CHAPTER 10

UNDER SUSPICION

I rang the bell at the address where I thought I might have mistakenly delivered Lance's package. I shifted my weight from one foot to the other as I waited for someone to answer. I prayed that this was the right address and that the person still had the package.

"C'mon. Be home. Open the door," I whispered out loud as I looked around. I was all sorts of paranoid after that visit from Lance. I felt like my bladder would bust, my nerves were on edge so bad. I rang the bell one more time, said another quick prayer, and peeped at the huge bay window on the front of the house. *Fuck! Fuck! Fuck!* I screamed in my head. What was I going to tell Lance now? My shoulders slumped and my stomach cramped up.

Just as I was about to turn to leave, I heard the locks clicking on the door inside. My eyes went wide with excitement. *Please let them have this package. Please let them have this package,* I chanted silently in my head.

"Hello?" a feeble old woman croaked from behind the screen door. She didn't know how happy I was to see her ass.

"Yes. Hello, ma'am. I am your mail carrier and I think I

delivered the wrong package to you yesterday by mistake. I really, really need to fix it and I apologize," I said, rushing my words out.

"Oh, yes. I remember," the woman said. Her voice was wet and shaky, like she was going to cough up phlegm at any minute. *Yes!*

"Good . . . can I get the package back and give you your correct package?" I asked, hopeful that this was going to go as smoothly as I wanted it to. "My boss will be so happy that I was able to fix this problem. I'll give you some free stamps every day for a year," I said, trying to make small talk and ease the situation.

"Well, baby. I'm going to tell you. Me and my Edgar opened that package thinking it was ours," the lady said. My knees immediately went weak.

"You did?" I asked almost frantically.

"Yes . . . we were looking for our delivery of adult diapers and all we found inside of that box was a bunch of coffee beans," the lady said innocently. *Whew!* I breathed a sigh of relief.

"Yes . . . you're right. That was the package I am looking for. I have your package here. I'm sorry about you not getting your diapers. If you go get the other package I'll make this right," I said, trying to usher the lady along. I was already thanking God they didn't find the drugs and report it.

"Okay . . . let me see what we did with it. Hold on right there," the lady said as she disappeared from the door. I had my fingers, toes, eyes, arms, and legs crossed. It seemed like an eternity before the woman returned to the door with the box. I felt so relieved when I saw that package that a few drips of piss escaped my bladder anyway.

"Great!" I cheered. "Let me help you." I snatched that box from her little wrinkled hands so fast I almost caused the old lady to fall over. I pushed her correct package inside, took Lance's shit, and sped down to my mail truck. I felt like singing and dancing, but I kept my cool. For the first time since I had started riding dirty on my mail route, I was excited as shit to be bringing drugs to a trap house.

Although I wasn't speaking to Eduardo, I was happy as shit to see him that day. It was more of an evil satisfaction than happiness to see him.

"Here is Lance's missing package. I was able to get it back," I said flatly, shoving the package into Eduardo's hands. I turned to leave. I wasn't fucking with him and he knew it. I had taken Andrew and started staying with my mother. Eduardo had crossed me in the worst way when he gave my son over to Lance like that.

"Gabriella . . . wait," Eduardo said, grabbing me by the arm. "I want to holla at you about what happened." He looked so pitiful. He was still fine as hell, but this time, that wasn't enough for me. I wanted to spit in his fucking eye. Now he wanted to holla at me about what happened? He wasn't saying that shit when Lance was fucking threatening me with harming my son.

"I have nothing to say, Eduardo. I'll continue to deliver the packages because you bastards won't let me out of this shit. I want to continue getting paid, but other than that, I have nothing more to say to you or Lance or anyone associated with either of you," I retorted. Eduardo let me out of his grasp.

"Lance is asking for more packages to come in every day. He is not taking *no* for an answer," Eduardo blurted as I started to walk away. I felt like Eduardo had kicked me in the back of my head when I heard that. I whirled around so fast I almost did a full pirouette. My face was folded into the fiercest scowl I could muster.

"Tell Lance and Luca and whomever else you need to tell that I'm not fucking doing it. Enough is enough. If you want to go to jail, you find someone else to do it," I gritted, jutting a disapproving finger in Eduardo's face.

"All I'm doing is sending the message. You know the rest. If you want another visit from Lance, suit yourself. As you can see from the other day when I had a gun stuck in my fucking mouth until I gave in, I am not a one-man army," Eduardo said, throwing his hands up. I never said anything to him in response. I had nothing to say. I stomped away and got back in the mail truck. I drove a few blocks away. When I was finally far enough, I pulled over.

"*Agghh!*" I screamed, slamming my fists on the steering wheel over and over. "Why did you get into this shit, Gabriella! Why!" I chastised myself. I was in too deep to even pull myself out. I knew then that nothing about this was going to end well for me or my family, for that matter.

CHAPTER 11

MY WORLD WAS FALLING APART

I hadn't slept in two days. That had become more the norm for me the past few months. My usually long, luscious locks of hair had become dry, brittle, and had started breaking off. I hadn't gotten my nails done in weeks. My usually smooth, clear, blemish-free skin was breaking out with acne and I had lost my curvy shape because my appetite was nonexistent. *Stressed* was an understatement. It showed all over me from head to toe. There was no end in sight to the stress, either. In fact, it just kept getting greater and greater.

By force, Luca and Lance had again upped the package deliveries from three a day to six a day. Their greed and disregard for the risk I was taking didn't even surprise me anymore. Nothing surprised me anymore.

I had a new sorter, which was a challenge in itself. The new bitch who had my packages was going to be crazy. I already had to practically curse at her to get her to put all six packages on my truck, along with the stuff that was legit. That bitch had given me several icy stares and evil looks, but I couldn't care less, until the morning it happened—shit blew up. I came into the post office station ready to go and found Ben standing over my bundles and packages. *What the fuck he want? This is all I fucking need right now. I am not in the mood for him!* I huffed to myself. I put on a fake smile, said good morning to Ben, and proceeded to pick up my stuff as if he wasn't standing there glaring at me.

"Gabriella, it is my understanding that you had Tanya put all of these packages from Florida on your truck?" Ben said, getting right to the point. No *good morning* or anything.

"Yeah . . . most of these are my regular customers, so what's the problem? I deliver to them all of the time," I said, trying to keep calm. Ben never really questioned how we did things in the station, as long as the mail got delivered. He wasn't asking just to be asking.

"I don't see the big deal," I followed up, stopping so I could look at him.

"I'm just concerned that you're getting bogged down with express-mail deliveries and not your regular stuff. We can share these out. There's no reason for you to take everything that comes in. Express mail doesn't really have to go by regular routes," Ben replied, reaching down toward Lance's packages.

"No!" I snapped, stepping in front of the packages to block Ben with my body. I didn't even realize how fiercely I had protested. Ben kind of took a step back at my response. With all of my nervous reactions over the past few weeks, Ben must've thought I was straight-up crazy.

"I mean—I—I—can handle it. Please just let me do it. I'm okay, I promise and everything gets there on time," I said nervously, trying to clean it up. I couldn't afford to have Lance's packages fucked with. Ben just didn't know that my life and my son's life depended on those damn pieces of express mail in that bin. I knew the next time anything went awry, Lance wasn't just going to hold Andrew hostage on his lap in front of me: It would definitely be a worse fate for my son. The thought of that was enough to make me crazy for real.

"Okay. I'm trusting you, Gabriella. I'm trusting that since you are one of my best workers that everything is on the up-

and-up with you. I'm putting my job on the line based on this trust. Please don't make me regret this decision," Ben said tentatively. I felt bad that he had so much faith in me, when I knew damn well if the shit hit the fan he might take a fall for my actions too. I couldn't even look Ben in the eyes after he said that he trusted me. I grabbed my mail bundles and all of Lance's packages and loaded up my stuff. As I slid behind the steering wheel of my mail truck, I looked over to the door real quick. I saw Ben standing there with his arms folded, watching me. A cold chill shot down my spine. Something about the look in Ben's eyes and on his face told me that I was already under suspicion. Even if he said he trusted me, Ben was watching me closely and he wasn't as nice and gullible as he made everyone believe. As I pulled out of the garage, Ben didn't budge. He was letting me know that he had his eye on me. There was no turning back now, I had to deliver those packages. I had people to protect.

Each day that I delivered the extra load of Lance's packages, Eduardo tried to speak to me. I didn't have shit to say to him. Now, with the increase in packages, I was getting $15,000 a week, but the money didn't mean shit. It didn't ease the fact that I was always worried about my son and my mother. All I could do with the money now was start stashing it for them, because I already had a feeling that things weren't going to end well for me.

Four days after my encounter with Ben and the fight over the extra packages being sorted into my route, I reported to work as usual. I was already exhausted from not sleeping, so I was really not in the mood for any bullshit. The first thing that was different was Tanya, the sorter who had taken Carlos's place, was not there. "What the fuck is going on now?" I mumbled when I found some white dude, who looked like he had just gotten out of the army, standing there sorting my stuff.

"Who are you?" I asked with an attitude. This was not good and I was certainly not up for the same fight I had been having with Tanya on an almost daily basis.

"I'm Mark . . . I'm filling in for Tanya today," the man answered. A funny feeling went through my stomach. I squinted my eyes and surveyed him up and down. I immediately didn't trust him.

"All these packages are the same weight . . . humph— that's unusual," Mark said to me as he lifted one of Lance's packages. *Fuck! This is all I need. A nosy motherfucker questioning shit.* My heart immediately started jackhammering against my chest bone. I had already told Lance not to have the fucking packages all the same weight on the same day coming from the same place. It was apparent that these bastards didn't give a fuck about anything except getting their drugs delivered.

"I don't know. Why you asking me like I sent the packages? I guess when people send things to their family or whomever they don't think about the packages being the same weight as someone else's package. Can't it just be a coincidence?" I snarled. He didn't answer.

"Are they ready for me to go?" I asked, tapping my foot impatiently. Mark smiled and nodded. The smug look on his face gave me pause. Something in the back of my mind was telling me to run; to go far away while I still could. This dude was not on the up-and-up. I didn't listen to my instincts. I grabbed up my stuff and began heading out. The next thing that was different were the four strange men in the garage when I began heading to my truck. I had never seen any of their faces before. They weren't mail carriers, mechanics, sorters, nothing. I noticed that Ben was there as well. I got so nervous I had to put my bundles down for a minute.

"Oh, Gabriella. I was waiting for you," Ben said. He didn't

smile. He wasn't upset. He had no emotion at all. Not like Ben at all.

"We have a new truck for you. I remember you complaining about the old one." I looked at him suspiciously. I didn't remember complaining about my mail truck at all.

"Um . . . my truck is fine. I'll just take it. I have my seat adjusted and everything already," I insisted. Then I looked at the guys who were with Ben. They were all dressed like Postal Service mechanics, but something told me otherwise.

"Ma'am, I'm sorry. You'll have to take the new truck. Headquarters is making us retire the old one once we issue a new one," one of the men told me. Ben shook his head yes. I reluctantly took the keys from the guy's hands. I looked around the inside of the new truck. It was much more modern than my old one. It was clean and had that new-car smell. Still, I didn't have a good feeling about it as I slowly loaded my stuff, including Lance's drugs inside.

"You like it?" Ben asked because he was standing there watching me.

"Honestly, not really, Ben, but I didn't have much of a choice," I shot back.

"Well, Gabriella, sometimes we have to do things we don't like in the name of our job. I guess it's all in the name of the game," he said. I looked at him for a long, hard minute trying to read him, but one of the strange mechanics came over to us.

"Everything all right with the new truck, miss?" the guy asked. I climbed up into the truck and turned toward the guy and Ben.

"I guess I'll know after today if everything is all right with it, now won't I?" I replied. I don't know to this day why I didn't listen to my gut, which was telling me to drive a few blocks, ditch that fucking truck and run far, far away, but I didn't.

It was the end of my routes that day and, as usual, I started delivering Lance's packages to his trap houses. I had the routine so down pat I could've done them in my sleep. My brain was definitely on autopilot. I had way too much on my mind. First, I went to Ant, then to a new dude named Brick, then to Pablo, then to Lance's club, and lastly to Eduardo. Before I got out of the truck at my last stop to give Eduardo his package, I had the urge to call my mother and speak to my son.

"Mommy loves you no matter what, okay?" I had said to him. I could feel my heart breaking into a million little pieces as my baby told me that he loved me back. I did the same with my mother. Of course, she kept me on the phone longer because she was asking me over and over again if I was okay. She also had a lot of questions. It broke my heart to lie to her, but had I tried to get near the truth with her it would've just caused me strife and heartbreak. I assured her that I was fine, that I loved her even when I didn't say it, and reluctantly I ended the call.

As I walked up to the steps of the trap house to meet with Eduardo, I felt it. It was like someone was standing so close to me I could feel them breathing. Although there was no one right behind me, the presence was felt. It was an instinct, I guess, because I knew they were there. The heat from what felt like a million sets of eyes on me. I was walking slowly because at that point I was sure. I had told myself that it was the end of the line. I silently asked God to forgive me for what I had done to my son and my mother. I could've turned and ran back to my truck. I could've ran—period, but I didn't. I thought about it and I knew that if they were watching me, I would be severely outnumbered. I kept walking slowly up to the door with what I believed was the last of the drug deliveries gripped tightly in my hands. I knew that there was a difference in the box. I had been delivering them for an entire year; I knew how they should feel, look, and even sound. I felt the weight of all of the packages Ben had set aside for me earlier that morning and I knew none of the packages were the same as I'd always had. Yet, I didn't warn Eduardo or Lance; instead, I went about delivering every single one of them. They wanted more deliveries and that was just what I had given them that day.

An unusual calm had settled over me as I reached the door. I guess it was something like acceptance that I had come to the end of the line. I lifted my right hand and banged on the door with the same force I always used. I did my usual three bangs, paused, and three more. That invisible presence I'd felt when I first got out of my mail truck seemed like it was hovering closer now. The hairs on the back of my neck and on my arms stood up. I let out a long, soul-cleansing breath. *It's finally over, Gabby. You did it and now there is no turning back,* I spoke to myself.

I didn't turn around. I didn't look left or right. I didn't cry. I didn't try to warn Eduardo or anything. Like always, he opened the door in anticipation of his drugs. In his hand was my envelope filled with my weekly pay. Eduardo smiled like usual too. He was still trying to win me back. Even though I hadn't been fucking with him lately, he would always smile and tell me he missed me. He would always try to get me to come back to the apartment to live with him again. But, today, after a few seconds his smile faded off of his face as fast as it had come over his face.

"Gabby . . . what the fuck did you do?" he asked, his face folding into an evil scowl. Eduardo was set to run, but there was nowhere to go.

"It wasn't me," I said calmly as the presence I had been feeling finally revealed themselves. I heard the shouts behind me so loud I felt like they were screaming directly into my ear.

"Federal agents! Let me see your hands! Now! Put your fucking hands up! Now!"

I think I stopped breathing for a few minutes. My ears were ringing and everything around me seemed to stop. I could hear my heartbeat pounding in my ears. I raised my hands slowly over my head and turned around just as slow. The envelope Eduardo had given me fell to the ground and the money lay littered around my feet. Some of it blew in the wind, just like my life at that moment. That's all it had amounted to after all I had been through. The money was dirty and it was now just useless as I was.

"Gabriella Vasquez, you are under arrest. You have the right to remain silent. Anything you say can and will be used against you in a court of law. You have the right to an attorney . . ." one of the agents rattled off at me as he roughly grabbed my arms and forced them behind my back. There was no fighting, no fussing, no resisting, and no words right then. I was numb all over.

"What the fuck did you do, Gabriella? What the fuck did you do?" Eduardo shouted from the prone position they had him lying in on the floor. "You set me up! Why? Why did you do it?"

I didn't say another word to him. I whipped my head around and read the backs of the jackets of all the agents there. I saw DEA, FBI, ATF, and standing there smirking were also the Virginia Beach police detectives who had interviewed me after Carlos was killed.

As a female DEA agent was searching me, Detective Boules walked over, his stony face now wearing a look of satisfaction. I rolled my eyes when I saw him coming.

"Didn't think you would see us again, did you?" Boules said snidely. I squinted my eyes into dashes and flexed my jaw. *Fuck you asshole!* I shouted in my head.

"You've been doing this a whole year, missy, and you almost kept getting away with it. Couldn't quite get you on the murder of Mr. Ortega, but watching you distribute drugs was good enough. And, I must say, using you to bring down such a big operation was lots of fun for us cops," he said smugly. The look on my face must've been one of shock because Boules broke into a full smile, like he was getting a hard-on just watching my pain.

"Oh yes, Ms. Vasquez, those packages you delivered today,

every one of them was equipped with a nice, government-monitored GPS tracker. That's right . . . so you took us right to every hot spot in town. We even got the boss—what's his name, Lance Baxter or Big Lance. What an ugly fucker he is," Boules continued. I just hung my head. What a dummy I was for not listening to my own gut feelings. I had probably single-handedly helped bring down Lance and Luca's entire Virginia Beach operation.

"Yep . . . we followed Lance right to your house immediately after we purposely mixed up your package delivery. We kind of knew that would get him to come out of the wood-work—missing drugs does it every time. You know these ghetto bosses are so predictable. You were a great target to fol-low too—you never burned us because you are so oblivious to your surroundings. How did you not notice four cars follow-ing you for days? Ha! You would think a girl who chose to be a drug-delivery service would be looking around all of the time—nope, not you," Boules laid it all out. I felt so stupid. Then it happened; I couldn't help it. My stomach had begun to swirl so badly that I just bent over and threw up. The vomit went all over Boules's shoes and the bottom of his pants. He jumped so high he looked like he was on a trampoline.

"Oh God! What the fuck!" he screamed. I was too sick to smile, but I felt at least a little vindicated inside. Right after that I was forced inside of a waiting unmarked police car. I looked out of the window and watched all of the feds swarm like flies to shit over Eduardo's spot.

"Get that mail truck. That's one of ours. It has the cameras inside. If that shit goes missing we won't be able to catch any more postal workers riding dirty. I am not trying to have HQ breathing down my neck about their new toy," the female fed-eral agent who had searched me yelled out to the other agents who were busy rushing around the truck and the house. I knew I should have never gotten in that truck that day, but what choice did I have? It was either go through with getting arrested, or get killed by Lance or Luca or whomever. I just hadn't realized that it was going to be a little bit of both. The day of the arrest, I had accepted the fact that I might spend the rest of my life in jail. I just didn't anticipate that the drama wasn't over.

CHAPTER 12

COMING TO AN END

When I was led into the pale-brick federal building in handcuffs, I was purposely taken past a row of doors with small glass windows. Inside, I saw Eduardo in one room surrounded by two DEA agents, Lance in another sitting alone, Ant in one with two more agents, and Brick in one acting the fool, yelling and screaming about his lawyer.

Boules was telling the truth when he'd said everyone had been taken down from the packages I had delivered. That wasn't a good feeling. Not because I cared about those dudes, but because of the implications it had on me and my family. Tears welled up in my eyes because nothing about the situation could be good. I was put inside of one of the same types of rooms. It was really like some shit I had seen on TV. There was nothing in the room but a metal table, three metal chairs, and the usual double-sided glass mirror. It smelled of fresh paint and Pine-Sol. That didn't sit well with my already fragile stomach.

"Have a seat, Ms. Vasquez," the same female agent said, pointing to the lone chair opposite the table. The male federal agent who was with her took off his DEA jacket and hung it on the back of the chair he was about to sit in. She kept hers on, but before she sat down she swept it back at the waist so I was able to see her gun, belt badge, and extra ammunition on her belt.

"I'm Special Agent Christy and this is Special Agent Farmington," she introduced all official, her voice devoid of any emotion. I rolled my eyes and turned my head to the side.

"You have some choices to make today, Ms. Vasquez. You can cooperate with us or you can never see this little guy again," Agent Christy said, sliding a picture of Andrew across the table at me. *How the fuck did they get that? Why are all of these bastards using my son against me?* Tears burst from the sides of my eyes instantly, like she had pressed some button in my brain. I tilted my head back and let out an exasperated breath. I refused to look at Andrew's little chubby face. I couldn't afford to let me son make me weak.

"The situation can end up a little better for you than those guys out there," Agent Farmington chimed in. "The way we see it, Gabriella, you were doing a favor for your boyfriend and it just got out of hand. They probably told you that you couldn't stop because it was going so well and so easy for so long . . . right? We know how this story goes. Nice working girl gets caught up with bad boy. Bad boy asks her for a one time favor, but it turns into many favors and then she just can't get out," Agent Farmington said. I finally made eye contact with him. He was basically telling my story. He seemed to get a little excited that I was looking at him. I guess he thought he was making some progress with getting me to talk.

"Listen, Gabriella. We see this story all too often in our line of work. You're not the big-time drug dealer or distributor. We know that and we are prepared to tell the judge that on your behalf, but first, we need to know some things from you," he continued. That's where he started to fuck up. I broke eye contact with him and hung my head. Just like he had seen cases like mine so many times, I had also seen these scenarios—like the one I was in right now—too many times on TV. I wasn't stupid. I wasn't speaking to those agents without a lawyer. In my assessment, I had enough money stashed away that my mother could get me a lawyer.

"You told me I had the right to remain silent. I am exercising my right and I want a lawyer," I said flatly through dry, cracked lips. I could see the blood rush to Agent Christy's face and her fingers curl into fists. Agent Farmington grabbed her arm, I guess to keep her from reaching across the table and pounding me in the face. She was the bad cop, I guess. I chuckled inside. Through my eyes that bitch was weak without that gun and badge.

"Suit yourself, Gabriella, but this won't end well for you or your son. See, your mother is facing accessory to distribute charges, because when we executed the search warrant at her house—your last known address—we found stacks and stacks of dirty money. House is in her name . . . she is responsible. She goes to jail too. Not a pretty sight when we had to take that adorable little boy of yours to child protective services, kicking and screaming for his grandma and mama. I don't think I've ever heard a baby cry so hard and so loud. That's some set of lungs that kid's got. Guess he's never been away from you or your mom overnight. Now he has to stay in a strange place all night, alone. Better hope his foster parent isn't some registered sex offender that fell through the cracks," Agent Christy said vindictively. I couldn't stop the waterfall of tears from falling, but they were hot, angry tears this time. I was breathing hard and thinking if I could be alone with this bitch for ten minutes what I would've done to her ass.

"Foster care, wow, all because his mother is a fucking drug distributor who made pennies compared to the people she is choosing to protect. What a shame. Wonder what kind of story that little boy will grow up and tell his friends about his loving, wonderful example of a mother. Oh—and Mama Vasquez, she's old with arthritis. Spending her nights in a cold, unforgiving jail cell will wreak havoc on her aching joints. What a shining-star daughter you are too. And all for those lowlives down the hall who are more than likely pinning all of this shit on you right now. Oh yeah, dudes like them will make you out to be the mastermind of this whole drug operation and then guess who gets one hundred years behind bars? You . . . not the so-called kingpins," Agent Christy continued, her words feeling like a knife to my heart. I probably would've actually rather someone stab me a million times in my heart than to hear about what was happening to my mother and my son. It was all my fault. From day one, I put myself in this position. I was so desperate for love and acceptance after that horrible relationship with Andrew's father that I would've done anything. My head immediately began pounding with an instant migraine. The harder I thought about it the worse my head ached. I started imagining my baby daddy picking Andrew up once the foster care system got in touch with him. I knew he would use my son against me.

More tears started falling, but this time I put my head down on the table and hid my face. The feds were driving a hard fucking bargain, but snitching wasn't an option for me. I would just have to take my chances with a court-appointed attorney and one who could get my mother off. They still didn't know about the cash I had in safe deposit boxes at two different banks. It probably wasn't enough for two lawyers, but it would be enough for my mother to have a good one.

There was a long few minutes of silence in the room. I guess the feds were waiting for me to fold to their demands. I contemplated it, but it just wasn't in my nature.

"So . . . what's it going to be, Ms. Vasquez," Agent Farmington asked. I still didn't look at him. "Are you going to let your mother and son suffer?" he asked. I inhaled deeply. My anger was starting to well up like a volcano. The fucking nerve of him to use my family as a pawn in this game! This is what the feds did, though. I heard all about it. They broke up families and put innocent kids in the system just so that they could get stats and bonuses at the end of the year. I wasn't giving them any more satisfaction over me.

"Go fuck yourselves," I gritted. My chest was heaving with anger by then. Sweat was dancing down the sides of my face. Agent Christy jumped up from her chair so fast and furious that the chair slid back and hit the wall behind her. I didn't even flinch. I eyed her, daring her to hit me. I knew that she was going to do her bad-cop, intimidation tactics now. I smirked at her. She knew fucking better.

"You fucking stupid ghetto bitch. I hope you never see your son again. Bitches like you don't deserve to be mothers. You're fucking ghetto trash!" Agent Christy snapped. She was so close to my face I could see that her pupils were dilated. I didn't back down or move back. I had come too far in this game to stop fighting now. I tilted my head at her as if to say, "Go ahead and hit me, bitch, so I can own you."

"C'mon . . . she's not worth it," Agent Farmington said, pulling his female counterpart away before she caught a brutality charge—or worse, a fucking career-ending lawsuit. I laughed as they started to leave the room. It was a crazy, maniacal laugh, but it wasn't because I found anything funny. I laughed because it was all I could do to keep myself from screaming to the top of my lungs.

CHAPTER 13

FEDERAL CUSTODY

I spent two days in a federal holding cell before my first court appearance. I felt sick, dirty, and weak. I hadn't eaten, slept, or drank anything since I'd been locked up. My legs felt like they weren't even connected to my body. My stomach was growling too as I was pulled from the courthouse holding cell.

"Vasquez! It's your time to shine," a court officer called to me.

I barely had the energy to walk. When I was led to the defendant's table inside of the courtroom, I was shocked to see a different lawyer standing there waiting for me, instead of the court-appointed attorney I had seen the day before.

"Ms. Vasquez, I'm Saul Shapiro, your new attorney," the slim, white man said, extending his hand for a shake. My eyebrows dipped low on my face.

"Where's Mr. Baum?" I asked, confused as hell. Mr. Shapiro wore a tailor-cut suit, Rolex watch, and a Gucci tie, so I knew full well he wasn't one of those low-paid court-appointed attorneys.

"He's been replaced and I've been hired to represent you. I'll explain later. Let's just say you have friends in high places," Mr. Shapiro said. *Or enemies,* I thought to myself. I turned slightly and looked around to see who was in the courtroom.

Sure enough, at the back of the room were two rows of very scary-looking Hispanic men, all dressed in their goon-outfit suits and wearing the obligatory dark shades. They looked very similar to the bodyguards who had showed up to the apartment with Lance the day he threatened me. My heart started rocking in my chest. I quickly turned back around, too scared to return all of the glares I had received from the goon squad. The judge came to her bench and she was saying something. I couldn't even concentrate on what she or my new, apparently expensive, attorney were saying. All I could think about were those men glaring at me from the back. I knew all of them had to work for Lance—or worse, for Luca.

"Your Honor, I'd like to enter myself as new representing counsel for Ms. Vasquez," Mr. Shapiro called out, flashing a big smile like he was a celebrity. I couldn't believe he had the balls to smile at the judge. The judge was an evil-looking old lady who wore wire-rimmed glasses that sat so far on the tip of her nose I wanted to rush up to her and push them up.

"And just what fairy godmother came down and paid your ridiculous retainer for this poor little drug-dealing postal worker?" the judge replied sarcastically, looking over the rim of her glasses at my attorney. Mr. Shapiro chuckled and flashed that smile again. I looked at him like he was straight crazy. Didn't people get held in contempt of court for stunts like this?

"Well, hello to you too, Judge Hartwell. It has been a while since we've shared our moments, huh," Mr. Shapiro joked with the judge. I took it from the exchange that he and the judge were very familiar with one another. The judge grunted as she examined some of the paperwork in front of her. Mr. Shapiro said some more legal-speak that I didn't understand and the next thing I heard was . . .

"Bail is set for two hundred thousand dollars. Passport needs to be turned in by four o'clock today. We are on for three weeks from today. Make sure your client shows up, Mr.

Shapiro, or else I'll send the entire United States Army to find her," the judge said, banging her gavel.

"I guess I owe you one," Mr. Shapiro joked.

"Don't push your luck, counsel," the judge grumbled.

My attorney turned toward me, flashing the brightest-veneered smile I'd ever seen on an older white man who wasn't a Hollywood actor.

"Well, sit tight for a few and your bail will be posted. I'll meet you at the doors when you're released. I have a few more people in your crew to represent and everyone will be re-united like one big, happy family," he said with a fake cheeriness that made me want to spit on him. I wasn't smiling or happy about my abrupt release. It smelled of a setup for sure. I shot a quick glance to the back of the courtroom and all of those scary dudes were gone. There was nowhere to run now.

CHAPTER 14

DEATH BEFORE DISHONOR

Waiting around to be released from the courthouse jail cell had to be one of the most nerve-racking things I had gone through during this entire ordeal. My imagination, combined with the paranoia I had been experiencing, were getting the best of me. It was not every day someone came along and paid a high-priced attorney to spring you from facing a long prison sentence. There was certainly more to it than Luca or Lance wanting to thank me for my year of service to their drug operation. I knew for a fact it had not been Eduardo who'd paid Mr. Shapiro to come sweep me out of jail, because Eduardo's ass was in the same boat I was in. When the court officer finally came and called me for release, I sat on the jail-cell bench for a few extra minutes, contemplating whether I should've just voluntarily opted to stay in.

"Vasquez! I said, let's go!" the officer boomed for the third time. Reluctantly, I pulled myself up off the bench. *Well, whatever your fate is going to be . . . it will be,* I told myself. I was processed out, handed the tiny bit of belongings I had been arrested with, and released into the custody of Mr. Shapiro. Just like he promised, when I was released Mr. Shapiro was standing right there, wearing that big-toothed smile, holding onto his Louis Vuitton briefcase and wearing his expensive threads. He was the epitome of the criminal lawyer. I walked toward him tentatively, not knowing what to expect. Was he going to take me home? Was he going to walk me outside and shoot me himself? All sorts of shit ran through my mind as I looked at him, wide-eyed.

"C'mon, put a little pep in your step. I don't bite—except, of course, if you're a federal agent," Mr. Shapiro said jokingly. I didn't laugh. In fact, I thought all of the joking he did was always at the most inopportune fucking times.

"Okay . . . I see you're not in the mood for the small talk. How about we go get you some food? Maybe a shower and a change of clothes. You look terrible," Mr. Shapiro said brightly. Food and a shower sounded like heaven to me. Thinking of those things made it a bit easier for me to follow him. I still didn't trust him, though. I couldn't really be sure who'd hired him and why. As we walked together toward the courthouse doors, I looked around to see if anyone else was there, but there was no one else around who seemed interested in me. I guess that was a good sign. Besides, at that point, following Mr. Shapiro wasn't one of many options I had: It was the only option I really had. What other choice did I have? Could I have refused to go with him? I highly doubted it.

We walked out of the courthouse together. There were people bustling about, but none of them drew any suspicion from me. I had a quick, fleeting thought about the goons I'd seen in the back of the courtroom; however, I quickly shook that off. The less I saw of them, the better for me. I followed Mr. Shapiro down the steps to his waiting Audi A8. He opened the door for me kindly and I got in. He slid into the driver's seat and just began driving. He never asked me where I needed to go. I didn't say a word. He tried to make small talk, but I wasn't in the mood. He stopped at a small diner on the outskirts of town.

"As promised, I am stopping to get you something to eat. I

could hear that belly of yours growling from miles away," he said playfully. His lighthearted, carefree mood was grinding on my nerves. We went into the diner and I ordered breakfast. He just had coffee. Mr. Shapiro was gabbing away about his clientele and his job and blah, blah, blah. I was looking at him in amazement. He might've been taking me for my last meal, yet he expected me to get all chummy with him. We left the diner and just like the showboating asshole he was, Mr. Shapiro threw a one hundred dollar bill on the table for the food, which could not have cost more than twenty dollars. Back in the car, he started talking about some drug family up in New York that he'd got off scot-free from RICO charges they were facing. This man just loved to speak about himself. That was apparent. After driving for what seemed like two years, Mr. Shapiro slowed the car down. We had reached this unknown destination that he hadn't bothered to tell me about. But that I also hadn't asked about.

Finally, we pulled up to a chain-link fence. Outside of it was a small keypad with numbers on it. I looked around at the deserted-looking place beyond the fence. It seemed like some kind of industrial park. Suddenly, my heart started up. This wasn't some place you'd expect your lawyer to bring you. It certainly didn't look like a lawyer's office.

"What's this place?" I finally asked. Mr. Shapiro ignored me as he punched in a few numbers and just like that, the two gates pulled apart and invited us to drive through.

"Mr. Shapiro! What is this place?" I asked more urgently. He didn't answer, but he drove a little faster. I could hear the gravel crunching under the car tires. With each pop and crunch I felt more and more like impending doom. Behind the gate was a nondescript, deep-red brick building with no windows. I was thinking, What type of building didn't have windows? There were rows and rows of black-and-white vans parked out front too. I didn't see any people in the immediate area.

"Mr. Shapiro! Tell me what the fuck is going on!" I screamed. Mr. Shapiro stopped the car and he remained calm as a cucumber. He pulled out his cell phone and hit the speed-dial button. I was still screaming. I went for the door handle, but really, where was I going to run?

"Yeah. It's done," I heard Mr. Shapiro said into the phone receiver. That was the first time I'd felt anything resembling emotions since leaving the courtroom. A ball of panic erupted inside of me like a fireworks display.

"You fucking crook! You set me up!" I barked at him.

"Well, kiddo. This is the end of the line. My job is done. Everything comes with a price," Mr. Shapiro said, and for the first time he wasn't smiling or making jokes. His voice was grave. I looked over at him, my eyes squinted into dashes. If eyes could kill, that Jew bastard would've burst into flames and flew down to hell at that moment. Suddenly, out of my peripheral I saw at least five goons moving toward the car. Mr. Shapiro put back on that silly smile he'd been flashing since I'd met him. I wanted to slap that shit right off of his face. Before I could react, my door swung open. A gush of hot air hit me in the face. Next, I felt huge, monstrous hands on me. They were grabbing me roughly, pulling on me with brute force.

"No! Please! Don't leave me here! Please! I didn't do anything!" I screeched at the top of my lungs as I kicked my feet. I knew I had caught one of the goons in his nuts, because I saw him go down moaning. "Aggh! Somebody help me! Help me!" I hollered. It was all for nothing. Who was I kidding? There was probably no one around for miles and miles out in that deserted industrial area. I kept screaming, though. I was in a fight for my life. I was finally out of the car. My ass hit the gravel with a *thud*. I kept kicking and swinging my arms wildly. It wasn't long before a huge hand covered my mouth and nose, muffling my desperate cries for help. I struggled to breathe and my legs were moving like I was running as I was hoisted up in the air like a little rag doll. I flailed and kicked and tried to scream, but my efforts proved futile. I tried to open my mouth enough to bite down into the hand that was suffocating me, but I couldn't get my teeth close enough to close in on the skin. I was getting exhausted from trying to fight. But, I continued. My fight-or-flight instinct was in full effect right then. I was no match for the hulk that was carrying me into the scary building. And I knew I was finally in over my head.

CHAPTER 15

MY LIFE WAS SLIPPING AWAY

"Mmmm!" I moaned from the depths of my throat, but the sound wasn't enough. I heard what sounded like big steel doors slam shut once they carried me inside. That was it. I just knew I was a dead woman.

I was finally dropped onto a hard concrete floor. My back ached when it hit the floor. I immediately scrambled onto my knees in an attempt to get to my feet so I could run. "Help me!" I cried out again. That's when I noticed Eduardo balled up in a corner of the room. I had never been so happy to see him. I crawled over to him as fast as I could. Whether I was speaking to him or not, he was my only source of comfort now.

"Eduardo! Help me! Don't let them hurt me!" I screamed as I reached him. When I got close enough to see his condition, my heart sank. There was no way he could help me now. He was barely able to sit up himself. His once strikingly handsome face was now a bloodied, bruised, closed-eyed mess. Eduardo inched himself up into a sitting position, wincing in pain with every move he made. He parted a halfhearted smile when he saw me. He reached out and grabbed my hand.

"Oh my God! What did they do to you?" I hollered. Eduardo tried to shush me, but I couldn't stop screaming. "What did they do to you! You didn't do anything! It wasn't us!" I screamed some more. I was fucking losing it. I felt like I was snapping. "Eduardo, we have to get out of here! Let's run! Let's go!" I shouted.

Suddenly, I felt a shooting pain in my scalp that radiated over my entire head. It was like a bolt of lightning had hit in me in the head.

"Aggh!" I shrieked. Instinctively my hands flew up to my head in an attempt to stop the pain. That's when I realized my body was moving across the floor. I was being dragged by my hair like a piece of garbage. I had never felt pain like that in my head. It felt like my entire scalp was being ripped off. Not to mention the friction burns I was getting on my back from the concrete floor.

"No! No! Get the fuck off of me! Let me go!" I screeched, digging my nails into the skin of my attacker's hands in a last-ditch effort to get some relief from the unbearable pain. "Ah! This fucking little bitch scratched the shit out of me," the man who'd been pulling my hair barked. I was finally let go, but with force. My head was thrown down as if were some type of ball. The back of my head crashed to the concrete floor with so much force I thought my brain would shoot through the front and burst out through my forehead. I knew now what people meant when they got hit and said they were seeing stars. My head hit with such force that little squirmy flashes of lights invaded my eyesight for at least twenty seconds. I was dazed and confused and the pain was like nothing I'd ever felt.

I moaned from the pain, trying to keep my head still so that it wouldn't feel so bad. I tried to keep perfectly still, but my minute of peace was short-lived.

"This is the bitch who brought the feds down on us," I heard someone growl from somewhere to my left. Then, I felt the presence of several pairs of feet next to me. I tried to gather up my senses so I could try to roll away, but I wasn't fast enough on the action. My brain wasn't sending the right signals to my body to tell it to move.

Wham! Crack! Bam! Crunch! were the sounds that filled my ears next. More pains erupted on every inch and pore of my body. The bones in the side of my skull felt like they'd come loose. My teeth clicked together so hard I knew that some of them were knocked from my gums. My jaw ached so badly that my ears rang. I felt like both of my eye sockets had been caved in. The bridge of my nose cracked under two or three hits. This pain was the result of the bevy of punches being rained down on my face and body landing at will.

"Eduardo, help me," I croaked, but I couldn't even get enough air into my lungs to scream properly. I tried to curl into a fetal position, but another set of hands forcefully unbent my body. Next, a huge men's boot slammed into my abdomen, then with the force of a wrecking ball the boot slammed into my rib cage. A cough involuntarily escaped my lips as the wind was knocked out of me. My bladder released all over my clothes. I was hurting so badly, even my eyeballs ached.

"Please," I begged through my constantly swelling lips. "Have mercy."

"Luca wants her alive when he gets here, so enough," I heard one of the men say to the ones beating me. He just didn't know how grateful I was to him for stopping them. My body curled in on itself and I sobbed. It even hurt to cry at that point. I could smell and taste my own blood. Death would've been a welcomed thing with the way I was feeling at that moment.

"Get her up. Put her with that bastard man of hers and let them wait for whatever Luca has planned for them," the same voice instructed. I immediately tightened my aching body and tried to fight them off.

"Get off of me! Don't touch me!" I managed, although it hurt like hell to even whisper.

"Shut the fuck up, before I put a bullet in the back of your head, you fucking snitching-ass bitch," one of the men growled as he forcefully pulled me up off the floor. Again I was dragged, this time into another room. I was immediately freezing. I was thrown practically on top of Eduardo, who had been beaten just as badly, if not worse, than me. He reached out an arm and held onto me. He wasn't showing any emotion. I kept shaking him, but he was stoic, cool even. That pissed me off. We were both forced to sit up. Our shoes were removed and so were our shirts.

"What's happening?" I cried. My spine felt like someone had replaced the discs with ice blocks. Eduardo and I were forced together back-to-back. His skin still felt warm against mine. The contact gave me a quick feeling of comfort. It didn't last, though. The men used a thick, scratchy nautical rope to bind Eduardo and me together. The heavy rope was forced around our chests and stomach. Then it was run around our ankles. I felt like my skin would bleed. That is how tight they had that coarse, harsh rope against the delicate skin of my stomach and chest; even my ankles burned from the touch of it.

"Look at the two snitching pigs tied together, ready for the slaughter," one of the men said. The others laughed. Their words and the sound of their laughter stung my ears. I thought about my mother and Andrew. They would never get to lay eyes on me again. The pain from knowing that was even harder to bear than the bruises, broken ribs, fractured nose, and facing death.

"Gabriella," Eduardo mumbled, leaning his head back against mine. I was overcome with sobs.

"Oh my God, Eduardo. What do you think they will do to us? I don't want to die . . . I can't leave my son," I cried, barely able to get my words out between sobbing and the fact that my teeth were chattering together so badly. The warehouse-type of room we were being held captive in was freezing. I mean, *freezing*—like we were sitting inside of a meat locker type of freezing. I could even see puffs of frosty air with each breath that I took. I knew it was summertime outside, so the conditions inside of where we were being held told me we were purposely being made to freeze. The smell of sawdust and industrial chemicals were also so strong that the combination was making my stomach churn. Eduardo flexed his back against mine and turned his head as much as the ropes that bound us together allowed. He was trembling from the subzero conditions as well.

"Gabby, just keep your mouth shut. If we gon' die right now, at least we are together. I know I ain't say it a lot, but I love you. I love you for everything you did and for the shit you put up with me. I am sorry I ever let you get into this bullshit from the jump. It wasn't no place for you from day one, baby girl," Eduardo whispered calmly through his battered lips. With everything that had happened, I didn't know how he was staying so calm. It was like he had no emotion behind what was happening or like he had already resigned himself to the fact that we were dead. In my opinion, his ass should've been crying, fighting, and yelling for the scary men to let me go. Something. Eduardo was the drug dealer, not me, so maybe he had prepared himself to die many times. I hadn't ever prepared myself to die, or to be tied up like an animal, beaten, and waiting to possibly get my head blown off. This was not how I saw my life ending up. All I had ever wanted was a good man, a happy family, a nice place to live, and just a good life.

"I don't care about being together when we die, Eduardo! You forget I have a son? Who is going to take care of him if I'm dead over something I didn't do?" I replied sharply. A pain shot through my skull like someone had shot me in the head. I was ready to lose it. My shoulders began quaking as I broke down in another round of sobs. I couldn't even feel the pain that had previously permeated my body from the beating I had taken. I was numb in comparison to the pain I was feeling in my heart behind leaving my son. I kept thinking about my son and my mother, who were probably both sitting in a strange place wondering how I had let this happen to them. That was the hard part, knowing that they were going to be innocent casualties of my stupid fucking actions. I should've stuck to carrying mail instead of stepping into the shit that had me in this predicament. I was the dummy in this situation. I was so busy looking for love in all the wrong places. I had done all of this to myself.

"Shhh. Don't cry. We just have to pray that Luca will have mercy on us. I will try to make him believe that it wasn't us. I'll tell him we didn't do it. We weren't responsible for everything that happened," Eduardo whispered to me.

"But he's the one who got us out so fast. I keep thinking that he only did that because he thought we might start talking. He got us out just so he could kill us, don't you see that? We are finished. Done. Dead," I said harshly. The tears were still coming. It was like Eduardo couldn't get what I was saying. We were both facing death and I wasn't ready to die!

"You don't know everything. Maybe it was something else. Let me handle—" Eduardo started to tell me, but his words were clipped short when we both heard the sound of footsteps moving toward us. The footsteps sounded off like gunshots against the icy-cold concrete floors. My heart felt like it would explode through the bones in my chest and suddenly it felt like my bladder was filled to capacity. The footsteps stopped. I think I stopped breathing too. Suddenly, I wasn't cold anymore. Maybe it was the adrenaline coursing fiercely through my veins, but suddenly I was burning up hot.

"Eduardo Santos," a man's voice boomed. "Look at you now. All caught up in your own web." The man had a thick accent, the kind my older uncles from Puerto Rico had when they tried really hard to speak English.

"Luca—I—I—can—" Eduardo stuttered, his body trembling so hard it was making mine move. Now I could sense fear and anguish in Eduardo's voice. That was the first time Eduardo had sounded like he understood the seriousness of our situation.

"Shut up!" the man screamed. "You are a rat and in Mexico rats are killed and burned so that the dirty spirit does not corrupt anything around it," the man called Luca screamed. I squeezed my eyes shut, but I couldn't keep the tears from bursting from the sides.

I was too afraid to even look at him. I kept my head down, but I had seen there were at least four more pairs of feet standing around. Eduardo and I had been working for this man and had never met him. I knew he was some big drug kingpin inside the Calixte Mexican drug cartel that operated out of Miami, but when I was making the money, I never thought of meeting him, especially not under these circumstances. I was helping this bastard get rich and couldn't even pick him out of a police lineup if my life depended on it.

"Please, Luca. I'm telling you I wasn't the rat. Maybe it was Lance . . . I mean, I just worked for him. He was the one responsible to you. He was the one that kept increasing everything. I did everything I could to keep this from happening," Eduardo pleaded his case, his words rushing out of his mouth.

"Oh, now you blame another man? Another cowardly move. Eduardo, I have people inside of the DEA who work for me. I know everything. If I didn't pay off the judge to set bail so I could get you and your little girlfriend out of there, you were prepared to sign a deal. You were prepared to tell everything. Like the fucking cock-sucking rat that you are. You know nothing about death before dishonor. You would've sold out your own mother to get out of there. You failed the fucking test, you piece of shit," Luca spat, sucking his teeth. "Get him up," Luca said calmly, apparently unmoved by Eduardo's pleas.

"Luca! Luca! Give me another chance, please!" Eduardo begged, his voice coming out as a shrill scream. His words exploded like bombs in my ears. Another chance? Did that mean that Eduardo had snitched? Did that mean he put me in danger when I was only doing everything he ever told me to do?

Did Eduardo sign my death sentence without even telling me what the fuck he was going to do? I immediately thought about my family again. These people obviously knew where I lived and where they could find my mother and my son, even after they went back home. A wave of cramps trampled through my guts. Before I could control it, vomit spewed from my lips like lava from a volcano.

"What did you do to me, Eduardo?" I coughed and screamed through tears and vomit. I couldn't help it. I didn't care anymore. They were going to kill me anyway, right? "You fucking snitch! What did you do?" I gurgled. I had exercised more loyalty than Eduardo had. The men who were there to kill us said nothing and neither did Eduardo. I felt like someone had kicked me in the chest and the head right then. My heart was broken.

Two of Luca's goons cut the ropes that had kept Eduardo and me bound together. It was like they had cut the strings to my heart too. Eduardo didn't even look at me as they dragged him away screaming. I fell over onto my side, too weak to sit up on my own. Eduardo had betrayed me in the worst way. I was just a pawn in a much, much bigger game. And, all for what? A few extra dollars a week that I didn't have anything to show for now, except maybe some expensive pocketbooks, a few watches, some shoes, and an apartment I was surely going to never see again. Yes, I had been living ghetto fabulous, shopping for expensive things that I could've never imagined in my wildest dreams, but I had lost every dollar that I had ever stashed away for my son as "just-in-case" money. I had done all of this for him and in the end I had left him nothing.

"Please. Please don't kill me," I begged through a waterfall of tears as I curled my body into a fetal position. With renewed spirit to see my son, I begged and pleaded for my life. I told them I wasn't a snitch and that I had no idea what Eduardo had done. I got nothing in response. There was a lot of Spanish being spoken, but I could only understand a fraction of it; so much for listening to my mother when she tried speaking Spanish to me all of my life.

"I promise I didn't speak to any DEA agents or the police. Please tell Luca that it wasn't me," I cried some more, pleading with the men that were left there to guard me. None of the remaining men acted like they could hear me. In my assessment, this was it. I was staring down a true death sentence. I immediately began praying. If my mother, a devout Catholic, had taught me nothing else, she had definitely taught me how to pray.

"Hail Mary, full of grace . . ." I mumbled, closing my eyes and preparing for my impending death. As soon as I closed my eyes, I was thrust backward in my mind, reviewing how I'd ever let the gorgeous, smooth-talking Eduardo Santos get my gullible ass into this mess.

Boom! Boom! Boom! Three shots caused my eyes to pop back open. Suddenly, Eduardo's cries abruptly stopped. My entire body went limp. I closed my eyes back because I knew then that Eduardo was dead. I heard footsteps coming toward me and I continued to pray harder. I was next. Finally, the footsteps stopped. Without opening my eyes, I could tell someone was standing over me. There was more Spanish being exchanged. Next, I felt hands on me. "Hail Mary, full of grace . . . Hail Mary, full of grace . . ." I chanted as I was brought into a sitting position.

"So you're Gabriella," I heard a voice say. I slowly opened my eyes to come face-to-face with Luca. He was not a bad-looking older man. His skin had an orange glow like he'd spent most of his recent days lying out on a yacht, soaking up the sun.

"Yes," I whispered, unable to get my voice to go any louder than that.

"You were doing a great job with my products, but I guess these guys got greedy, eh?" Luca said. I furrowed my eyebrows in confusion. I'd always thought that the demand to increase the packages had come from Luca. I started to breathe hard as he continued.

"I would've never put an honest, working woman like you in that kind of risk with the feds. Lance and Eduardo got greedy. They put all of the risk on you and it backfired on them. I know what you did when those DEA agents tried to force you to talk. I know you refused—I got the word from those on my payroll," Luca said sincerely. I let out a long, gasping sob. My body rocked.

"Lance and Eduardo weren't so loyal. They were both ready to make a deal that would've exposed me and would've put you away for life," he continued. I could not stop crying.

"I never turn my back on those who are loyal to me. About the beating . . . my men didn't know this information I am telling you now until I got here, so I will see to it that you get the proper medical care. Your case . . . it is done. You don't have to show back up to the courts. I have taken care of that. Now, I will need to take care of you and your family. Your son, your mother; they are awaiting your arrival at my house on the beach. You will stay there for three days, but after that, you will use the tickets I have purchased and you will take your family and move to Puerto Rico. I have left more than what you've made . . . a sufficient amount for you to live," he told me. I looked up at him with tears rolling down my face.

"But why? Why are you doing all of this for me? It was my fault that the feds followed me," I replied, thinking that what he was telling me was too good to be true.

"No . . . it was Eduardo's fault. It was Lance's fault. They were the ones who caused it. You were just doing what you were asked to do like a loyal worker would. I recognize that," he said. "Gabriella . . . don't look a gift horse in the mouth. I am usually not this kind," Luca said. With that, he stood up. He spoke to his men in Spanish. I was helped up and practically carried to another room. I was wrapped up in a blanket and carried to a van. Fear still gripped me around the throat, but for some reason, I didn't believe I was going to be killed.

I was left at the emergency room at the hospital. I was admitted and treated for a broken nose, three fractured ribs, and two missing teeth. The injuries to my head were all surface, no skull fractures.

After my second day in the hospital, I was in and out of sleep from the pain meds when I heard a light tapping on the door. I rolled my head toward the sound with my eyes halfway open. When I saw who was at the door, no drug could've kept me asleep and no pain could've kept me from jumping out of the bed. I jumped up, pain and all, and raced toward them. It was my mother and my son. Andrew jumped into my arms and almost knocked me backward. I was still too weak to move another inch. My mother immediately grabbed me into a tight embrace. We all stood there, hugging for what seemed like an eternity. I would not let them go at that moment or ever. I had never been that happy and relieved in all of my life. I can now move forward and go back to living a normal life. Fuck the money, expensive cars, shoes, clothes and the sheisty niggas that come along with it! It's about family. Thank God I got another chance at life.

GUN PLAY

De'nesha Diamond

CHAPTER 1

THE LOVER

Cozumel, Mexico

Cartel Princess Cataleyna Rosales stands smiling like a glittering Spanish rose at the top of her father's spiral staircase while a sea of Mexican drug lords and chieftains applauds her grand entrance to her twenty-first birthday party. She takes a breath and then descends the staircase in a red-beaded Givenchy gown with a grace she'd inherited from her mother. Diamonds and Tahitian pearls adorn the sides of her hair while the back hangs iron-straight past her shoulders.

A pack of gold-digging she-wolves surrounds the young Afro-Latina, beaming jealous smiles. Cataleyna pays them no mind. Everyone knows that there's no *real* love in the cartel. They're latched onto her to gain political and personal favors from her father.

Vicente Rosales steps forward at the base of the staircase, his eyes wet and glowing with love. "Ah. I wish your mother had lived to see this day. She would be so proud." He leans forward and brushes a kiss against her dimpled cheek. "You're so beautiful."

"Gracias, Papa." She plasters on a bright smile and is probably praying that he can't read her traitorous thoughts.

Tonight is the night. She's officially a player in a dangerous game, but can she outmaneuver the master—her father? The stakes have never been higher.

"I have something for you, Bella."

She stiffens at the use of her mother's name—something that has become a habit in the three years since her death—just like him keeping her caged in this gilded Caribbean estate. He claims he's protecting her from his enemies, a job he failed to do for her mother. In truth, he's smothering her and preventing her from finding a life and love on her own.

Vicente turns toward me. I'm caught slipping'.

"Julian," he hisses.

I jump, shame-faced that I've been caught gawking at the boss's daughter. To my relief, Vicente laughs. "See, Bella. You've even turned Julian's head tonight."

Cat blushes.

I hand over a burgundy velvet jewelry box.

"Aww. Here we go." Vicente faces his daughter again and pops it open.

The crowd leans in and gasps.

Cataleyna's face lights up as she recognizes the glittering fourteen-million-dollar Heart of the Kingdom ruby necklace.

"You like it," her father declares, puffing out his chest.

"But how did you . . . ?"

"Come now. You know by now that there's nothing I can't do for my only daughter." Gently, he lifts the necklace out of the box, walks behind Cat, and drapes the jewel around her neck.

"Lift your hair," he orders.

She obeys, sweeping up her long tresses and then looks up at me—her secret lover.

I smile back—briefly. We don't want any calculating eyes discerning the truth. It isn't safe to show the slightest hint that there's something between us—not if I want to keep on living. I'm not going to lie. Cataleyna means the world to me. Not only is she beautiful, but also kind, sensitive and intelligent—

all the things that I wish for my future baby girl to be. At least I hope it's a girl. My eyes drop to her still flat tummy. Cat shared the good news yesterday. She's pregnant.

Cat awakened something in me from the first moment we met. She seduced me, I fought it. At least that's the lie I tell myself. The truth is probably more like I seduced her—despite the dangers—despite my being seven years her senior—despite fucking common damn sense.

We're like moths to a flame and it's a matter of time before we're burned—unless we play the game and plot our escape—break free from her father's long reach. We're not sure how far that is, but love demands that we find out.

"There we go," Vicente announces, grinning. "Turn around and let me take a good look at you."

Cat releases her hair and faces her father.

One look and his eyes mist again. "Isn't she perfect?"

The two-hundred-plus crowd unleashes thunderous applause and cheers. In the next second, she's ushered away by a gaggle of women, gushing about her beauty and how lucky she is to have a father who adores her so much.

I watch intently as the women pull her away.

Our eyes periodically lock across the room while she does her thing and mills around. After an hour of this, a sudden hush falls over the crowd.

I tear my attention away and spot Carlos and Tomas Vazquez entering the mansion with a small entourage. "What the fuck?" I reach for my Glock.

The other men in the detail go for their weapons as well.

Vicente restrains my hand and then gives everyone else a stand down signal. "It's all right. I invited them."

There's no fucking way that I heard that shit right. Rosales and the Vazquez brothers have been beefing for supremacy for the past decade. Only the Sinaloa and Zeta cartels have stacked more bodies in Mexico's never-ending drug wars. The Vazquez brother's reign of terror colors outside the line of drugs and their reach goes deep into the heart of the Mexican police and military.

I'm still staring at Vicente in disbelief when he turns around and greets his former enemies with open arms and a big smile.

"Welcome," Vicente greets before kissing Carlos on both cheeks and embracing him. "I'm glad that you could join us for the festivities."

"We wouldn't have missed it for the world," Carlos says, smiling.

The Vazquez brothers are rich, powerful, and even handsome men. Their power radiates throughout the room and an undeniable tension thickens the air. I don't know what Vicente is up to, but this move signals weakness.

"So where is the birthday girl?" Carlos asks, lifting his head to search among the crowd. "I brought her a gift."

"Did you, now?" Vicente asks.

"Well, one doesn't show up to a birthday party without a gift," Carlos laughs. "My mother did teach me *some* manners."

"Of course." Vicente turns towards me. My hand is still on my weapon. He gives a disapproving shake of his head and I remove my hand from the butt of my gun. "Bring Bella here. I'd like for her to meet some of her distinguished guests."

"Cataleyna," I correct.

"Hmm? Oh. Yes. Yes. That's what I meant. Just bring her to my study." Vicente faces the Vazquezes. "Care to join me for a brandy while we discuss business?"

"Absolutely," Carlos answers.

The men migrate behind the solid oak doors of Vicente's study.

I make a beeline to Cataleyna and announce, "Your father would like to see you."

Cat drains her champagne glass, deposits it on a waiter's passing tray, and then makes her excuses. "Duty calls, ladies. I'll be back."

I flash her a smile and then offer her my arm.

"I can't wait for this whole charade to be over and we can leave this place," she grumbles.

"Shhh." My eyes dart around, making sure her words aren't overheard.

"I'm serious, Julian. Once we're gone I don't ever want to look back."

I keep walking.

"You haven't changed your mind, have you?"

"Not now, Cat."

She stops on a dime. "Answer my question."

I round on her. "What are you doing? Are you trying to make a scene?"

"I'm trying to get to the truth. Have you changed your mind?"

"Calm down." I swipe another passing champagne flute. "Drink this," I order while smiling to inquiring minds.

"I don't want another damn drink," she spits, but accepts the glass anyway. "Answer my question."

I like her spitfire attitude, but not right now. Our gazes lock. "Of course I haven't changed my mind. I've been planning this night for months. I can't believe that you're even asking."

Relief floods Cataleyna's eyes to the point that she looks ready to weep.

My fear triples. If she can't keep her emotions under control, we can't survive this game.

"Cataleyna, you've got to pull it together."

"You're right. Sorry." She downs her champagne. "I'm fine now. Promise."

I give her more assurances. "Everything is arranged. By this time tomorrow we'll be on our own private island as Mr. and Mrs. Arias."

She beams at me. "You have no idea how happy that makes me."

"About half as happy as it makes me." I wink and then offer my arm again. "Now let's go. Your father is waiting."

Cat's smile melts as she links her arm back through mine. "Any idea what he wants?"

"He wants you to meet his new business partner."

"Business partner? Carlos Vazquez? What the hell is that all about and why didn't you talk him out of it?"

"No clue. I was left in the dark about this one." That bothers me, but I can't tell her that.

We arrive at the door to the study and Cataleyna sucks in a deep breath.

"Ready?" I ask.

She releases my arm. "As ready as I'll ever be."

I open the door.

"Aww. Here she is now," Vicente declares, spinning on his heel with his customary bourbon and cigar in hand.

"Hi, Daddy. You wanted to see me?" she asks innocently.

"Yes." He walks over to her and then escorts her to his guest. "I'd like for you to meet my new business partners. Carlos and Tomas Vazquez, my daughter and birthday girl, Cataleyna Rosales. Cataleyna, Carlos and Tomas Vazquez."

"Pleased to meet you," she says, offering her hand.

Carlos steps forward, accepts her delicate hand and brings it to his lips. "I assure you that the pleasure is all mine." His gaze devours her with open lust.

My blood morphs into volcanic lava as my hand inches toward my weapon. I glance at Vicente. Why is he tolerating this open disrespect and grinning like a fucking idiot?

Cataleyna holds onto her smile like a seasoned actress and it restores my trust in her to continue our deception.

When I think that I'm going to have to surgically remove the man's lips from Cat's hand, Carlos lifts his head.

"I brought you a gift."

"A gift?"

"For your birthday." He snaps his fingers and his brother, Tomas, steps forward with another velvet box.

Cat looks to her father but he remains mute. *Something is up.*

"It's a little trinket on your special day." Carlos opens the box and reveals a jaw-dropping diamond bracelet that NASA can see from outer space.

Cataleyna gasps.

"You like it," Carlos says, pleased. "I'm glad."

She shakes her head. "It's lovely but . . ."

"Ah. Ah. Ah. No buts. A beautiful woman should always be draped in diamonds."

She hesitates.

"Please don't insult me by saying that you won't accept my gift of friendship."

"I, uh—" She looks at her father again and then over at me.

Carlos follows her gaze and then locks onto me, reading me like an open book.

"I wouldn't dare dream of insulting you," Cat says, pulling his attention away from me. "Thank you. I'll treasure it always."

"Nothing would please me more." He flashes her a tight smile before slicing me with an evil look.

An awkward silence settles in the room.

"I should get back to my guests. I don't want anyone thinking that I'm a rude hostess." Gently, Cataleyna removes her hand from his and backs away.

"I'll catch up with you later, Bella," he father says, pressing a kiss against her cheek and then closes the door behind her.

"Lovely girl you have there," Carlos says, toking on his cigar. "She has a certain glow about her."

"Thank you." Vicente downs the rest of his brandy and then strolls back to the bar. "Now about our deal . . ."

"How old did you say she was again—twenty-one? It's got to be a full time job beating the men back." Carlos's gaze cuts to me again. "I know that I'd have a hard time concentrating with a beautiful temptation like that walking around."

My temper snaps and I charge forward. Fuck the gun. I want to bone crush this *puta* old-school style.

"Hey! Hey! Hey!" Vicente shouts.

Tomas intercedes, shoving me back, but I'm on ten and I take a fucking swing. He ducks and delivers an uppercut with a fist made out of steel.

"Ooof!" Doubled over, I struggle to draw in air, but the effort sets my lungs on fire.

"Enough!" Vicente thunders.

Carlos cackles triumphantly behind his brother.

The shit gets under my skin so bad that it renews my anger and I come back up with an uppercut of my own that connects solidly underneath Tomas's chin and lifts his ass off his feet. I waste no time charging Carlos but this slick muthafucka whips out his piece and stops me dead in my tracks.

Luckily Vicente has my back and he whips his shit out too. "*Ah. Ah. Ah.* It's not that kind of fucking party."

Rosales's cavalry bursts through the door, guns raised.

Carlos glances at Vicente and then back at me while his brother peels himself off the floor. "I thought that we were invited here to talk business?"

"You were. But all talk about my fucking daughter is off the table. You got it?"

The tension could choke a horse.

"Got it?" Vicente asks again.

Carlos lowers his gun, but he gives me a look that tells me that this shit isn't over. Not by a long shot. "Yeah. I got it. My apologies. I didn't mean to offend."

Vicente takes an extra few seconds to weigh whether to accept the drug lord's thin, unfelt apology before holstering his shit. "One day you'll be cursed with a daughter and you'll understand." He turns to our crew. "Everything is under control now."

Even they hesitate. We all trust the Vazquez's about as far as we can throw them. Once they see that Vicente is serious, one by one they lower their weapons.

However, Tomas's gaze is still burning a hole into the side

of my head. I return my attention to him to let him know that we can finish this shit right here right now.

"Julian, take a walk," Vicente orders.

"What?"

"You heard me. Take a walk. Go cool off."

All eyes are on me as I take a step back.

Vicente crosses over to me. "It's all right. I can handle these guys—but I appreciate you defending my daughter's honor."

He slaps me on the back and then nods me toward the door. I choke on my pride and own damn sense of honor as I turn and head out the door with my tail tucked between my fucking legs. I return to the party just in time as Cataleyna's seven-tier red velvet birthday cake is being rolled into the center of the party while her favorite singer croons *Tu Amor Me Hace Bien* from a stage.

At the end of the song, the guests erupt into thunderous applause and the birthday girl blows out her candles. Despite the festivities, the hours crawl by. Late in the night Vicente emerges from his meeting with the Vazquezes, smug and smiling, to present Cataleyna with a brand-new candy-apple-red Maybach convertible.

I'm left to wonder about what kind of deal with the devil my boss made. *It's not your problem. You and Cataleyna are out of here after tonight.* Still, it doesn't mean that I don't care about the old man. My emotions are a tangled web.

Near midnight, fireworks light up the sky.

I choose that moment to slink to Cataleyna's bedroom balcony where she stands watching the display. When the time is right, I grab her hand and pull her behind the velvet drapes.

"Julian," she gasps. "You scared me. Is it time?"

"Shhh. Not yet. I just wanted to see you." I draw her body flush against mine and then drink from her red lips. "It won't be long now," I whisper, coming up for air. "The boat will be at the dock at four. Be prepared and ready to leave."

"I will. I promise."

Our lips meet each other again and we drown in our forbidden sin.

Stop. This isn't the time or the place. But I can't stop kissing her and touching her. I'm addicted to everything about her. Before I know it, I'm lifting her heavy, beaded dress and rubbing my fingers against her dewy wet panties. "You're so fucking wet."

"It's because I need you right now." Cataleyna nibbles on my bottom lip and mewls sexily.

"We can't. Someone could—"

"You can't leave me like this, baby." She reaches down and grabs my cock.

It's rock-hard and ready to override my common sense.

"We can make it quick," she pants. "I promise." Her soft nibbling moves from my lips to my right earlobe. She knows that's one of my spots. "Please, baby. It's my birthday." With ease, she unzips me and frees the beast.

There's no fucking way I'm stopping now. I snatch her panties to the side and hike one of her long legs over my hip and then dive in. Her sweet pussy is so warm and tight that I nearly pop off right then and there. I take a second to compose myself, but my impatient nymph starts grinding on my shit and sending my ass to the moon.

"You feel *sooo* fucking good, baby," Cat moans, dragging her nails down my back. "Sling it to me harder."

My hips drill like a jackhammer, each stroke deeper and sweeter than the last. I've never had a woman who felt this good and made me feel like King Kong. Watching her orgasmic expressions bathed in exploding lights, I can't imagine life without her.

"Oh. Oh. I'm coming, baby," she pants while her pussy tightens.

"We'll come together," I say, knowing that I have less than a dozen strokes in me.

She's moaning and I'm groaning and at any minute we could be cold-busted, but all that matters is our coming together.

"Look at me, Cat," I command her.

She does as she's told and we stare into each other's eyes as our orgasms rip through us at the same time.

"*Aaaaaaagh!*" I bury my head into her jasmine-scented hair while my body trembles with aftershocks. We cling to each other, hot and sweaty. "I fucking love you so much," I confess.

"You better," she laughs. "I'm going to have your baby."

Thump!

"What was that?" I ask.

We spring apart.

My eyes dart around the room, but I'm unable to make out anything. The fireworks explode outside while the band plays.

"You think that somebody saw us?" Cataleyna asks.

"I don't—"

Thump!

Someone is in the closet. I slip my dick back into my pants and then reach for my gun.

"Be careful," Cat warns.

I press a finger to my lips and she nods in understanding.

Creak!

I reach for the doorknob.

Rat-a-tat-tat-tat

Rat-a-tat-tat-tat

Screams erupt outside and throughout the house.

"What the fuck?" I turn from the door and race to the balcony. A sea of party guests race across the lawn in their glittering gowns and penguin suits only to be gunned down by an army dressed in black. "We're under attack!"

"What?" Cat steals a look for herself. "Where's Papa?" Alarmed, she wrenches herself from me to bolt toward the door.

Rat-a-tat-tat-tat

Rat-a-tat-tat-tat

"Cataleyna, wait!"

Before I can stop her, her closet and bedroom door burst open with a *BANG!*

I'm rocked back, but then take aim at the intruders. Something hits my arm as I tap the trigger.

Cat screams and then collapses to the floor. "Cataleyna!" I make one move toward her and I'm whacked on the back of the head and the world disappears.

CHAPTER 2

THE BOSS

Rat-a-tat-tat-tat
Rat-a-tat-tat-tat
My heart sinks at the sound of each bullet fired. "What the fuck?" I can't wrap my head around it. One minute I'm throwing the party of the year and then the next thing I know my entire estate is under siege. Bullets and bodies are flying everywhere. My men counterattack and hustle me to the estate's panic room. *What's going on?* Whose fucking balls sag this low to try to pull this shit off tonight—of all nights?

The Vazquez brothers.

Shit. The very thought of them being the masterminds sets my blood on fire. Why did I go against my better judgment and bring those two snakes into my inner circle? I know fucking better—but the Sinaloa and the Zetas cartels have all but boxed me in; strong-arming connects, destroying my distribution and turning my own men against me. Bottom line: they have my dick in a vise and I had to start thinking outside of the box if I want to survive.

The drug game has changed over the years. There is no longer honor among thieves and killers. There is no respect for families and tradition with this new generation of degenerates. The wars are now fought with heavily armed militias that practice scorched-earth tactics and strike fear in the heart of everyone from clients to law enforcement and even politicians.

I'm not a fool. I know what's up. I can feel the walls closing in on me. One by one, my connects have dried up. However, I keep the illusion going and had devised a plan to combine forces with another cartel. Even that is difficult. The old guard is being slaughtered, jailed, or running scared.

Hell. I've even thought about cutting my losses and getting out.

Then they killed my Bella—the love of my life. I was a nobody and I had nothing before I met her. It was because of her I was able to build this empire. In the back of my mind I always knew that there would be a hell of a price to pay for the lives I've taken or ruined. And yet, I was still caught off guard when the devil took his due and mowed down my wife right in front of my daughter and me.

I've relived the moment where she lay in my arms, bloodied and struggling to breathe. I begged her not to leave me, but it did no good. A merciless God refused to answer my prayers.

But I still have a piece of her: Cataleyna. She is the sole reason I wake up every morning. The world that I fought to give Bella, I now aim to leave to my daughter. Impulsively, I reached out to the Vazquez cartel. The patriarch, Alejandro Vazquez, had been killed in a car bomb two years back, but his sons, Tomas and Carlos, have taken over and not only managed to hold their ground, but made some surprising gains in members and distribution against the Sinaloas. The history between us is a bit tricky. In the nineties there was a lot of bad blood spilled between the two families, which included Alejandro and I falling in love with the same woman.

I won and married Isabella Benitez. Bella. Alejandro never got over it.

But all of that was of a different time and I'd hoped that we could let that be water under the bridge and pursue a mutual interest.

I was wrong.

The gunfire continues.

"Where's my daughter? Somebody find her and bring her down here," I order, rushing into the safe confines of the panic room hidden behind the walls of my study.

"Yes, sir. We're on it."

I rush to the bank of security cameras to grasp the landscape, but the chaos on the screens makes it hard for me to decipher what the fuck is going on.

Rat-a-tat-tat-tat

Rat-a-tat-tat-tat

"Bella—Cataleyna, where are you?" I search for her red dress on the screen while my blood pressure spikes. *I can't find her. Maybe she's in her room.* It is the one place I don't have a camera. I turn to one screen where I can see my men race to my daughter's bedroom door.

I hold my breath.

One minute. Two minutes. A lifetime passes before my men rush back out, carrying a bleeding Julian.

"What the fuck?" Forgetting about my own safety, I bolt out of the panic room.

More gunfire.

I duck low and zigzag around dead bodies. "Where is she? Where is my daughter?" I grab Julian by the shirt and jerk him forward.

"I don't know. The bastards got the drop on me."

"Who?"

A distraught Julian shakes his head. "I don't know that either. They wore masks."

Bullets whiz by.

"They're headed toward the dock!" Salazar yells.

There's still time. "After them!" I release Julian and he takes off. I try to follow, but my entire body seizes up. *What the fuck?*

I drop to my knees, gasping. *I'm having a heart attack.*

CHAPTER 3

THE PRINCESS

"Move it! Move it! Move it!" Men shout all around me.

I wake with an explosive headache as I'm being jostled around. For a few seconds, the world doesn't make any sense until I realize that I'm hanging upside down—or rather over someone's shoulder.

"Get her into the boat. Hurry! Hurry!"

Who is that? I know that voice.

Panicked, I scream for help, but my mouth is stuffed and bound tight. I kick and punch, but that doesn't work either because my hands and feet are tied with rope that's digging into my skin.

Julian. What happened to him? Dear God. Is he hurt? Did they kill him? I can't even process the possibility. He's the love of my life. *Papa! What about him? Where is he?*

Blood drips down my head and blends with my angry tears. I know the kind of thugs my father deals with. There is no doubt in my mind this shit has something to do with him. It always does.

My heart races at the sound of gunfire whizzing by my head.

My kidnappers return fire as they hop into a speedboat and I'm tossed into a corner.

Carlos Vazquez snatches off his mask. "Be careful with her."

"We don't have time for your shit right now." Tomas snatched off his mask as well. "Get us the fuck out of here!"

Rat-a-tat-tat-tat

Rat-a-tat-tat-tat

I flatten myself against the floor of the boat while my heart gallops inside my chest.

The boat's engine roars to life. A second later, the horse-power kicks in and we rocket across the Caribbean Sea. I pray for a miracle.

Another boat roars onto the scene, sluicing through the turbulent waves as the inky-black sky cracks open with a luminous bolt of lightning. The sky rips open and unleashes a torrent of rain, drenching me on the spot. There's no end to this nightmare.

Rat-a-tat-tat-tat

Rat-a-tat-tat-tat

"Cataleyna!"

Julian! My heart leaps as I lift my head.

A bullet whizzes past my head and I dive back down. One of the kidnappers, inches from me, is hit. His body jerks around from a barrage of bullets while his finger remains on his AK-47, spraying even more lead around the deck.

It's a toss-up as to whether my rescue squad or the kidnappers will kill me first.

"Can't this muthafucka go any faster?" Tomas yells. "They're gaining on us!"

"Ooof!"

Men hurl themselves onto the Vazquez's' speedboat. I have no trouble making out the black knight riding to my rescue.

"You muthafuckas!" Julian delivers a hard punch across Tomas's jaw. *Crack!*

It sounds like he broke that shit.

Tomas doesn't even have time to recover before another punch rocks his head in the opposite direction. *Crack!*

Bullets dance around the two men as they engage in hand-to-hand combat and more of my father's men fling themselves onto the boat.

Carlos abandons the wheel and rushes to his brother's aid. When he gets close, he raises his gun but hesitates for a clean shot at Julian.

Without thinking, I swing my legs around like a two-by-four at Carlos's knees, surprising his ass and knocking him to the deck.

The shot goes wild and takes out another member of his crew.

Carlos turns his dark, evil gaze toward me. "You shouldn't have done that."

I scramble away, ignoring my rope burns.

Julian finishes whaling his bloodied fist on Tomas's face and then looks around and spots Carlos.

Neither man pays attention to the ongoing battle around them, but jump to their feet and charge each other like raging bulls. At the moment of impact, another thunderbolt booms. However, nothing distracts Carlos and Julian from their epic battle.

My desperate battle against my restraints intensifies. I cry, pray, and beg until I feel the rope give one centimeter at a time. At long last, I snatch one hand out and then rip the thick duct tape from my mouth.

"Julian! Help!"

I attack the ropes around my legs. Tomas is stirring from being knocked out and the gun is inches away from his finger-tips. Dread sinks into the pit of my gut. I know exactly what's about to go down and it doesn't seem like I can get my hands to go fast enough.

The rain falls faster, the punches land harder, and Tomas's hand is wrapped around the gun.

Hurry, Cat. Hurry. My fingers are numb and cold, but, at last the rope unravels around my ankles. I jump to my feet and race toward the two fighting men as Tomas raises the gun.

"*Noooooo!*" I leap in front of the bullet. Pain explodes in my chest and I'm propelled backwards against Carlos and Julian, knocking us all over the side of the speeding boat and slamming into the dark, infinite sea. "Help! Julian, Help!"

My nose and mouth fill with water as it feels like I've plunged a mile below the surface. I force myself to hold my breath and proceed to kick my way back up—but the pain in my chest and the burning in my lungs cause me to panic.

I'm not going to make it.

I can't see anything and I have no idea how much farther I have to go.

Julian, where are you? Why isn't he here to save me?

Kick. Kick. In the back of my mind I know that I'm not going to make it. I can't hold my breath or fight off the pain any longer.

Let go.

I can't. I argue with myself, but then the decision is taken from me as I draw in a watery breath and watch as the world fades to black.

Julian.

CHAPTER 4

THE NURSE

Playa del Carmen
Six months later . . .

"Malena, bitch, you still here?" Nichelle asks, switching her wide hips behind the nurses' station with her arms loaded with snacks from the vending machine.

"All right now. I got your bitch." I roll my eyes, but Nichelle ignores me with her rude ass.

"Then why is your ass still here?" she asks, opening a bag of Cheetos. In two seconds that orange-powdered shit is going to be all over every-damn-thing.

"Working a double."

"Again? Isn't this like the fifth time this week?"

"I don't know. Dawn's kid is still sick or some shit. It's cool, though. My ass got a shoe addiction that is maxing out my damn credit cards."

"Girl. I hear you. I'm a label ho, too. But purses are my thing. Louis Vuitton is pimping my ass like a bitch." She laughs and then plops down in her seat so hard it's a wonder that her ass doesn't splat onto the floor.

I conceal my disgust. "I thought you said that you were on a diet?"

Nichelle shrugs. "I fucked up and had *posole* for lunch—so

that blew through my calorie count for the day—but damn that shit was good." She chuckles before adding, "I'll start on Monday."

"What's wrong with tomorrow?"

"Hubby's birthday. There's no point in me acting like I'm not going to suck up half that chocolate cake I ordered him."

"Tsk. Why don't you just love your three hundred pound ass and call it a day?"

"Nuh-uh, girl. I'm going to get this weight off and rock a bikini next summer. Watch and see. You're not going to be the only size four up in this place." Nichelle crams a handful of Cheetos into her mouth and then wipes her orange-stained hands all over her nurse scrubs.

I shake my head. *She spits the same shit every week.*

"Have you checked on your boyfriend yet?" Nichelle asks.

"He's *not* my boyfriend," I snap.

Nichelle's head rocks back with a high-pitched laugh. "Girl, I don't know why you bother denying that you got a thing for our John Doe in room four-ten. Shit. All the nurses and half the resident female doctors do, too. Coma or no coma that man is fine as hell." She shoves off from her desk and rolls next to me. "You know those sponge baths are the highlight of your night. You ain't fooling nobody. We've all seen that anaconda he got beneath those sheets. Shit. I wouldn't mind surfboarding all over that good-good myself. HA!"

She laughs so close to my ear that I shove her away. "Get the hell on with that shit." I pop out of my seat. "I got work to do."

"Uh-huh." Nichelle reaches for a Snickers bar. "Take your time. Make sure that you get him good and clean. *Ha!*"

I flash a tight rubber-band smile, hoping that it will be enough to shut the bitch up.

It's not.

Nichelle's irritating laugh travels down the hall behind me and then leaps on my last nerve for another wild ride.

"I hope that you fuckin' choke on that damn chocolate

bar," I mumble. What gets under my skin more than anything is that she's right. I've had a few fantasies about our John Doe. But who hasn't? Now that his bruises and bones have healed, there's no denying that John Doe is fine as hell. He's a sexy chocolate combo with a Latin twist: chiseled features, square jaw, broad shoulders, and muscles that ripple from his chest to the V-cut of his hips. *Sweet Jesus.* I'm hot just thinking about him.

The story goes that a couple of beach joggers spotted him washed up on the beach. At first they thought that he was dead, but the emergency responders found a pulse—barely.

He had no identification on him. He was a mass of broken bones, scars and third-degree burns on the left side of his chest. No one knows where he came from, and in the six months that he's been at the hospital only one person has come around who was mildly interested in him—a reporter, but even that was months ago.

I breeze through my rounds, take blood, empty bedpans and up pain medications for my other patients before heading to room four-ten. I pretend that I'm not anxious to see him, but the moment I push open the door, my heart gallops inside my chest.

Get ahold of yourself. "Hello, handsome. How are you this evening?" I stretch out a genuine smile. "I hope that the other nurses have been treating you well today."

The heart monitor's steady *Beep! Beep! Beep!* is my usual answer.

"Well. It's that time again." I head toward the adjoining bathroom door and gather supplies for his sponge bath. It's routine, but every time I pull back the sheets and remove his hospital gown, I flush like a fucking teenager at his model-perfect profile: strong chin, sharp cheekbones, nice nose, and pillowy lips that tempt my ass nightly. Of course my gaze zeroes in on his thick, two-toned dick with its fat mushroom head. *Damn. How long has it been—a year—since I ended my last real relationship? Jesus, please say it hasn't been that long.*

I shake myself and get back down to business.

"First things first," I say. "I got to do your blood draw." I reach into my pocket and remove the four vials I need to fill from the butterfly needle secured on his right hand. While his blood drips into the small vials, I take note of how well he has healed over the past six months.

"You know that you can't hide here forever," I whisper. "You're going to have to wake up sooner or later."

Beep! Beep! Beep!

After dipping the sponge into the soapy water, I wash his feet and then proceeded to work my way up. I love touching him. I love how his erect dick stands straight up.

Ten and half inches. I've measured it a few times. I tsk under my breath and lick my lips. "Damn shame to let all of this to go to waste."

I slide the soapy sponge around the base of his cock and then down around his nut sack. Before long, I have a good rhythm, daddy-long-stroking his ass. Listening to the soapy sounds of his dick gliding between my fingers gets me wet. *Damn.* What I wouldn't give for this man to wake up, grab my ass and then fuck the shit out of me. Hell. If I'm not careful, I'll wind up with cobwebs on my pussy.

I abandon the sponge and used my soapy hands to slip and slide over the only dick I've held in months. It's wrong but this shit feels so good. "I should get up here and ride this fat muthafucka," I mumble and I work my hands up and down and around and around.

Just for a few minutes.

I glance over my shoulder to the door. *No one is going to come in.*

Up. Down. Up. Down.

My pussy is getting wet. *This shit is so wrong.*

"Mmmm," the patient moans.

"Aaahhh!" I jump back, bumping over the bowl of soapy

water. I slip and bust my ass, but I keep backing away from the bed. "Aaahhh!"

Nichelle thunders through the door, panting like a racehorse. "What the hell is going on in here?"

I point toward the bed. "He's awake!"

Nichelle looks up at a dazed and confused John Doe with his soapy dick still pointed straight in the air.

"Page the doctor on call!"

I scramble back onto my feet and bolt out of the room. At the nurses' station, I'm out of breath, but manage to punch in the doctor's pager number. While waiting for him to return the page, a slew of questions race through my head. How long had he been awake while I damn near molested his ass? And why didn't he say anything? *Shit. I'm going to lose my damn job over this.*

I peek down the long hallway and realize that he could be ratting me out to Nichelle right now. *Fuck.*

The phone rings. "Nurses' station."

"Yes. This is Dr. Woods. Someone paged me?"

"Yes, doctor. John Doe in four-ten is awake."

"I'll be right there," he says, disconnecting the call.

Unsure what to do next, I stay put—embarrassed and ashamed. Fuck my job. I could go to jail. *I feel sick.*

"Malena," Nichelle shouts.

Rolling my eyes, I head back down the hall. When I reach room four-ten, Nichelle has tied his gown back on and has tucked him back into bed.

"The doctor is on his way," I tell her.

John Doe's gaze follows the sound of my voice. His curious eyes land on me and I turn red.

"Call someone to clean that water up," Nichelle orders.

Nodding, I back out of the room and track down one of the janitors on duty. When I return to room four-ten, Dr. Woods has arrived and is taking the patient's vitals.

"Follow the light," he instructs, shifting a penlight back and forth.

But John Doe's eyes shifts to me again.

I hold my breath. *Is he going to snitch me out?*

The doctor clicks off the light.

"Let me introduce myself. I'm Dr. Woods. Currently, you're in the hospital—and I'm afraid that you've been here for some time. Can you tell us your name?"

Silence.

I lean in close.

Deep lines groove into John Doe's forehead as he shifts his attention back to the doctor. After a few long seconds, panic clouds his eyes. "I—" He erupts into a bad coughing fit.

I rush for the pitcher of water next to the bed and pour him a cup. "Here. Drink this." I place it up against his lips and tip it up. "Slowly. There you go."

He follows my directions and stares at me over the rim.

"Th—thanks," he croaks.

My knees knock at his rich baritone. It's far sexier than I've imagined.

"Now. About that name," the doctor asks. "Do you re-member it?"

Three sets of eyes lock on our patient while he struggles with the question.

"Do you remember anything? Anything at all?" Dr. Woods prods.

John Doe shakes his head, panic-stricken. "No," he croaks. "I—I don't. I don't know who I am."

CHAPTER 5

THE PATIENT

Blank.

I can't think of a damn thing. How the fuck is something like that possible? I keep trying, but all I get for my troubles is a massive migraine.

Beep! Beep! Beep! Beep! Beep!

"It's all right. Calm down," Dr. Woods says, placing a hand on my shoulder and flashing me a weak smile. "Don't get yourself worked up. I'm sure that everything will come back to you in due time."

Beep! Beep! Beep!

"That's better. What we're going to do is let you relax for a little while. Get you comfortable—and then first thing in the morning, I'll return with your primary doctor, Dr. Diaz, and one of our staff psychologists. They will update you on your time here and work through any issues that you might have. Okay?"

My gaze slices back over to the nurse at my side.

She flashes a smile that reassures me. "It's going to be all right."

I relax and nod. "All right."

"Then we'll let you get some rest. Ladies." The doctor directs everyone toward the door.

When the nurse next to me sets down the cup and turns to leave, I shoot out my hand and grab her by the wrist.

Startled, she jumps.

"Don't go," I say, and then add, "Please."

She relaxes and looks to the doctor for permission.

Dr. Woods nods. "Just for a few minutes."

The larger nurse speaks up. "If you rather that—"

"No. It's fine. I got this."

"Uh-huh." Some kind of static passes between the two nurses. But the other nurse and doctor clear out and the janitor enters the room.

"Uhm. Is there something that I can do for you, Mr . . . Doe?" the nurse asks me.

"Doe?" I frown. *Odd name.*

"I'm sorry—but that's what we've named you. Mr. John Doe."

I let that settle for a moment before I notice her looking down at my hand. "Sorry." I release her and then erupt into another painful coughing fit.

"Hold on, hold on." She pours me another cup of water. "Here we go."

I lean forward and guzzle most of it down. "Thank again Ms . . . ?"

"Castillo," she supplies. "Malena Castillo."

"Malena." I nod, easing on a soft smile. "Thank you."

Her brown cheeks flush. "It's not a problem. I'm just doing my job."

"Was that what you were doing earlier, too?"

She drops the cup, soaking the front of my hospital gown. "Shit. I'm so sorry." She turns and runs into the janitor, who is ear-hustling in on our conversation. "Damn. How long does it take to mop a fuckin' floor?" she snaps.

The janitor gives her a sharp look.

"Sorry. You just—please finish that up." She steps around him. When she returns from the bathroom, the janitor is rolling his yellow plastic bucket out of the door, but gives her another disapproving look.

Malena ignores him and returns to the bed and struggles to talk. "About what happened earlier—I apologize if you misunderstood what I was doing."

"Misunderstood? You were jerking me off," I say flatly.

"No. I—I was bathing you."

My brows lift to the center of my forehead. "In that case, thank you. My dick is as clean as a whistle."

Malena backs away. "I should get back to work."

"Why? Am I making you uncomfortable?"

"No. It's just that—"

"I don't mean to. I—I . . ." I struggle for the right words, but get frustrated when I keep smacking into the brick wall inside my head.

Beep! Beep! Beep! Beep! Beep!

"Okay. Okay. Calm down." Malena presses me to lie back against the bed. "Whatever it is, it can wait. Don't get yourself worked up." She smiles.

I nod and then stare at her. My gaze roams over her ink-black hair and something stirs in the shadows of my mind. "You're pretty."

The compliment catches her off guard. "Uh, thanks." She moves back, but I grab her hand again. "What's happened to me? Why can't I remember anything?"

"I don't know," she answers, to my disappointment. "All I know is that some joggers found you lying on the beach six months ago."

"Six months?"

Beep! Beep! Beep! Beep! Beep!

She panics. "Okay. Okay. I can't stay in here if you're going to keep getting worked up."

"But—but—I don't understand. How could I have been

here for that long? I—I—has no one come looking for me? I have family or something—don't I?"

Malena shrugs. "I don't know."

Frustrated, I close my eyes and draw in a deep breath. Doing so, I catch a whiff of her perfume. "What is that?"

"What?"

"That smell." I bring her hand up to my nose and inhale. A hazy memory stirs.

"Oh. You mean my perfume? It's Bulgari's Jasmine Noir. You like it?"

"It's . . ." I take another whiff. "Familiar."

Malena perks up. "Really?"

Serenity washes over me. "It smells wonderful."

"Thank you." Malena's smile widens as she relaxes. "Well, uhm." She clears her throat. "But this is a good sign."

"It is?"

"Yeah. You have some sensory memory."

Hope flutters in my chest.

"Get some rest. If you need anything, press this button for the nurses' station." Gently, she removes her hand from mine. "Everything will be fine. You'll see."

CHAPTER 6

THE PATIENT

Forty-eight hours later . . .

I can't sleep.

Every time I close my eyes I feel as if I'm suffocating—drowning. And if that's not enough, every forty-five minutes another nurse pokes her head into the room to check up on me. By the time dawn breaks and the nursing staff rotates, I'm so anxious to get out of the bed that I feel like crawling out of my skin.

I'm scheduled for another full day of CT-scans, MRIs and X-rays. Not to mention another day of people asking every five minutes if I remember anything yet. Some people look at me as though they think I'm faking this shit and this is all some elaborate scheme for me to get attention. After dinner, I receive my first visitor not on the medical staff: a reporter.

"*Hey*. How are you doing?" he asks with a fake grin that stretches across his entire face. "You still seem to be quite the mystery around here." He laughs to himself. "Oh. I'm Felix by the way. Felix Garcia for the *Playa Times*." He jets out a hand and starts pumping mine with exuberance. "I did a story on you when you were first found on the beach. I can't believe that you've been in a coma all this time."

"And you found out I woke up how?"

The reporter's neck reddens with embarrassment. "A good journalist never rats out his sources." He winks.

I'm instantly annoyed.

"Anyway. I came to get the story before the cops swoop in. Have they been here to see you yet?"

I shake my head.

"Good." Garcia slaps and rubs his hands like some evil genius. "Well, let's start from the beginning. What's your name? Where are you from?"

"I don't know."

"Wow. A real, honest-to-God amnesia case, huh?" He whips out a camera phone and snaps a picture.

"*Hey!*"

"Oh. I'm sorry. Do you mind?"

"Well—"

"You never know. Maybe someone out there will see my story and step forward."

He has a point. I squash my objection and endure an awkward interview during which I don't have much to say.

I'm a man without a name—without a past. Yet I can't help but feel like I'm in sort of danger. Then again, that could be the paranoia talking.

CHAPTER 7

THE CAPTOR

Cartagena, Colombia

"What the fuck is this?" I slap down a printed copy of the *Playa Times*. "Is this shit for real?" I eyeball the team leaders assembled before my desk. "Is there a chance that this is really him?"

Danny speaks up. "We don't know, boss. The shit came over the wire today and I thought that you might want to see it. It does kind of look like him, doesn't it?"

I lace my knuckles on the desk and lean forward to take another look. Despite the patient's beard and lean frame, I'm certain that I'm looking into the eyes of a ghost. I hesitate only because I've already been on numerous wild goose chases in the last six months and I'm not anxious to get involved in another one. But if there's a chance . . .

"All right. Have this shit checked out," I tell them. "If it's him, bring him to me."

"You got it, boss," Danny says, snatching up the paper.

I watch them as they file out of my office before I turn my attention to the bank of monitors that are my eyes and ears in every part of my family estate. The screen that holds most of my attention lately is the one that shows Rosales's prized princess,

Cataleyna, pacing back and forth. My heart quickens a beat as I watch her move gracefully in red silk and diamonds.

She looks like a queen. My queen.

It was a miracle we rescued her out of the ocean that night. All of our intricate plans went up in smoke—mainly because Cat's charging lover caught up to us and then put up such a fight. When our boat exploded on the ocean there were two more of our boats nearby.

Now I have Vicente's most prized possession and I have no intention of ever letting her go. All I plan to do now is sit back and watch his empire slowly crumble to the ground. The old fool actually thought that he could erase decades of animosity between us. Vicente had no clue that my brother and I had already cut a lucrative distribution deal with the Zetas. Now our product flows seamlessly through the southwest market without a single police dog sniffing around.

Our father would be proud. He always hated Vicente Rosales, and never forgave him for marrying the woman he'd wanted as his wife. I remember Isabella Rosales well, and her daughter Cataleyna is her spitting image. I see now how she's enchanted so many—including my brother. Her long ebony hair, flawless skin and . . . my gaze roams over her protruding belly. *His baby.* She's soiled. With a flash of anger, I crush out the cigar that I'd absently picked up. I toss it into the wastebasket and start pacing.

My mind zooms back to the newspaper article. *Is it him?* The question loops in my head until I feel the need to let off some steam. Exiting the office, I descend down into the ten-thousand-square-foot estate's dungeon. A crescendo of screams and wails greets my ears and carves a smile onto my face.

Nothing clears the mind like engaging in a little torture. And I have the right touch that can get the hardest gangsters to piss in their pants and sell their souls to make me stop. There's nothing quite like power. My brother taught me that.

As I walk down the center of the dungeon, I can hear the six prisoners I have chained down here scurry behind their iron bars. Today, I have my mind set on one prisoner. My current pet.

I stop before his cage, look up and meet his black stare. My pet looks up, at least as far as his spiked collar will allow him. When he thrusts up his chin with a false bravado, my dick hardens. "Why don't we play for a little while?" I reach for the medieval morning star flail and then unlock the cage.

My pet squirms on the floor, but he's unprepared when I club his chest and the iron spikes flail open his skin.

"AHHHHH!"

I laugh and hit him again. Twenty minutes later the stone walls are painted my favorite color: blood red.

CHAPTER 8

THE BOSS

Cozumel, Mexico

"It's him! The muthafucka is still alive!" I toss a copy of the *Playa Times* at Salazar. "Look at the fucking picture and tell me that isn't him."

Salazar picks up the newspaper and squints at the image. "I don't know, boss. I mean, I guess it sort of looks like him."

"It's him." I survived a stroke, and I'm now confined to this fucking wheelchair—the shit has slowed me down. After I saw the Vazquezes' boat explode on the water, my body turned on me. My empire has suffered, too. I lost most of my good men at my daughter's birthday massacre. Most of the rest were pilfered by the Sinaloa and Zetas cartels. Now I'm left with just a handful of loyal men. Then again, after Julian Arias's betrayal, maybe there's no such thing as loyalty.

"Have it checked out. If it's him—bring me back his head."

"You got it, boss." Salazar grabs the paper and races to carry out my orders.

Once alone, I exhale and then knock down that pinprick of hope growing within me. I can't afford to get my hopes up again. For months I refused to accept my daughter's death. How could I after reading her letter?

I power the wheelchair to my desk and then remove Cat's crumbled letter from my top drawer. The anger I felt when I first read it has long since ebbed away and has been replaced with anguish and sadness.

> *Dear Papa,*
> *By the time you read this letter, I should be long gone. If you love me, you'll let me go. Julian and I are in love. We want to get married and raise the child that's growing inside of me, far away from the madness of the cartel. I'm sorry, but it's not the life I want for my baby or myself. I can no longer live in the beautiful cage that you've built for me. I have to find and live my own life. I hope that you understand. And please, don't hate Julian. He didn't pursue me, I pursued him, because I fell in love with him the moment that I laid eyes on him. He didn't stand a chance. I know all of this will come as a shock and you'll be angry, but I hope in time you will find it in your heart to forgive me. And maybe one day you can even be happy for us.*
> *Love,*
> *Cataleyna*

Unlike the first dozen times I read the letter and crumpled it up, I carefully fold and return it to my top drawer. Though I still want Julian Arias dead, I prefer the thought of him and Bella off together with my first grandchild than at the bottom of the ocean with the Vazquez brothers. It's either one or the other—but right now, it's the not knowing that's driving me mad. "She's out there," I whisper under my breath. "Please, let her still be out there."

CHAPTER 9

THE PATIENT

"Help, Julian! Help!"

I wake up gasping and choking. It takes a few seconds for me to realize that I'm not sinking in some dark water, paddling for my life. But echoing in my head is that voice—that blood-curdling scream that leaves me anxious and powerless. *Who is she?*

I rack my brain for a full minute, trying to get a name to fall off the tip of my tongue. Instead, my migraine worsens.

The clock on the wall tells me I've managed to sleep for a full ten minutes. With that woman's screaming in my head I can't see my sleeping pattern changing any time soon.

I've got to get out of this place. I swing my legs over the side of the bed and decide to test their strength by standing up. Almost instantly, the room starts spinning. My arms flail out and I grab hold of the IV stand until the spinning stops. After that, I take my time hobbling toward the bathroom, convincing myself that I'm getting stronger as I go.

When I enter the bathroom, I come face-to-face with my reflection. I look like a woolly mammoth with purplish burnt-crêpe skin beneath my chin and stretching halfway across my chest. On top of that, my eyes are bloodshot and weighed down with thick bags. In short, I look like hell.

Quickly, I splash water onto my face. Even that causes more images to click pass my closed eyes. *Moon. Rain. Gunfire. Scream.*

I'm dizzy again and I pull away from the mirror. Not ready to climb back into bed, I decide to take my IV stand for a stroll. Exiting the room, I step into the bright light. There's a steady sound of beeps and trilling phone—but there's no one in sight. The hair on my neck stands up, but then I remind myself that the third shift probably operates with a skeleton crew. Pushing my unease to the back of my mind, I inch down the hallway. When I arrive at the nurses' station, I'm taken aback at seeing Nurse Nichelle face planted in a bag of Cheetos.

"Excuse me, ma'am?"

She doesn't move.

I lean forward to see whether I can hear her snoring.

Nothing.

In fact, I'm not sure that she's even breathing. "Ma'am?" I reach down to shake her shoulder. The second my hand touches her; I know that she's dead. "What the fuck?"

Creak!

I glance up to see one of the room doors opening.

"Hey. I need some help over here!"

A man dressed in black but with the words *Policia Federal* stitched across his chest looks up. Then I notice the gun.

"Holy shit." Abandoning my IV pole, I dive toward the other side of the nurses' station as muffled shots sound off.

Poof! Poof! Poof!

The needle is ripped out of my arm as I spring back to my feet and scramble around to the back of the station.

Poof! Poof! Poof!

One bullet grazes my right ear. I duck lower while still sprinting down the other side of the hallway.

Poof! Poof! Poof!

I corner onto the next hall, ramming my shoulder into the wall. "Shit." Stars dance before my eyes. The elevator doors up ahead are starting to close. Digging in deep, I race forward with all my might. I dive into the small box at the last second.

Poof! Poof! Ping! Ping!

A bullet ricochets around me and punctures the key panel. But at least my ass made it.

Bam!

Something lands on the roof. Startled, I look up and see a door open and a cop jumps down into the compartment. Instinct takes over, and I deliver a high kick to the man's gun arm, knocking his weapon to the ground. Next, I go in hard, delivering blows to his eyes, gut, and thorax. My attacker drops to the floor like a stone but I belatedly realize it brings him closer to the gun.

I go for the weapon as well, but he's able to get his hands around the butt and I have to wrestle him for it. I don't know where my strength is coming from but I'm fighting this dirty muthafucka with all I got.

A bell dings and the doors slide open.

"Aaaaah," a woman screams.

He squeezes the trigger. *Poof! Poof!*

The woman is silenced as she drops to the ground and the elevator doors close. The elevator descends as we wrestle and sweat like pigs. With my injuries, I'm the first to weaken. A second later, the gun arches in my direction.

Ding!

The doors open. I have to get out of here.

I jack my knee straight up and crush the man's balls.

"Oof!" He releases his grip enough for me to grab control of the gun and point it his way.

Poof! Poof!

The cop's body jumps and I look into his face to see his widening eyes. Slowly, a trickle of blood oozes from the corner of his mouth. He's dead.

Quickly, I shove the body off of me and then scramble out of the elevator and into the parking deck.

Panting and clutching the dead cop's gun, I have no idea which way to go or even where to go. Everything within me is telling me to run—that I'm not out of danger yet.

A police car turns onto the deck. I immediately hunch down and creep in between two cars. I move from car to car as the police car rolls closer to the elevator. Suddenly, it stops and I hear the car door open. "Fuck! Frank!" The cop races to elevator where his buddy is still lying in the doorway.

"Shit." I crouch even lower, hold my breath, and wait.

The police radio squawks.

I eyeball a ramp that leads toward an upper deck. I weigh whether to make a run for it. I'll risk exposure.

At the next squawk, I suck in a deep breath and then go for broke.

"Hey!" the cop barks.

I take off.

Gunfire follows in my wake. Chips of cement bite into my ankles but I keep going. On the upper level, I hear the revving of a car's engine shortly before a pair of red and white lights bolt toward me. Unable to stop, I hit the back of a silver Mercedes convertible.

"Yo! Wait! Help!" I pound on the trunk and then rush around to the passenger door.

It's locked.

"Open up! Open up!"

I make eye contact with the woman behind the steering wheel—and recognition sets in.

"Malena! Please! Open the door!"

Her confusion barely clears when her passenger-side window shatters. Without thinking, I punch out the rest of the glass and dive in. "Go! Go! Go!"

She ducks and screams as more gunfire explodes, but she does have the sense to shift into drive and punch the accelerator.

CHAPTER 10

THE NURSE

"What the fuck is going on?" I screech, cornering onto the next ramp. We speed past all the green arrows pointing us toward the exit.

"Why are the police after you? Why were they shooting?"

"I wish I fucking knew," he barks, looking around.

My eyes zoom in on the gun clutched in his hand and I feel the knot in my throat grow. "Where did you get that?"

"Off one of the cops that was trying to kill me."

"What?" My gut hits the floor.

"Look. I don't know how to explain it. There were crazy cops shooting up the hospital."

"But what do you want—with me?"

"At the moment? To get the fuck out of here."

"What happened to the cops?"

He glares at me.

Oh shit. There is a murderer in my car. Tears swell and burn the backs of my eyes. I've heard about kidnapping cases in the news. They usually find people out in the desert somewhere with their heads missing. *Oh God. Oh God.*

The tollbooth is up ahead. I breathe a sigh of relief, thinking this is my chance to send some kind of signal that I need help. As if reading my thoughts, he taps the gun barrel against my shoulder. "Don't stop."

I panic. "What?"

"You heard me. Punch it," he growls.

Scared, I close my eyes and floor it through the toll's wooden arm.

The attendant jumps out yelling and waving his arms.

"Don't stop! Don't stop!" my captor yells in my ear.

In my rearview mirror, the cop car bursts out of the parking deck. I'm scared he both will *and* won't be able to catch up with us.

The gun taps my shoulder. "Take the next right."

Tears rolling, I follow orders—but the cop remains hot on our trail.

"Look. It's not too late to surrender. I'm sure that they'll go easier on you if you turn yourself in."

He laughs. "The only thing those cops are interested in is putting a bullet in the center of my head, even though I didn't do anything but go for a late night stroll around the floor. Next thing I know there's a dead nurse at the station and psycho cops trying to take me out."

"What? That doesn't make sense."

"Tell me about it." He huffs out a long breath, while his eyes dart around for an escape route. He truly does look bewildered and I wonder if perhaps he's telling the truth. But why would the police be after him?

"I don't—I can't think," he admits frustrated.

I study him and then the distant flashing police lights. I got to make a decision—and I'm thinking about doing the wrong thing.

"Fuck it." I make a hard left, flooring the accelerator.

"What are you doing? Where are you going?"

"You want to get away or not?" I challenge him.

A spark of paranoia flashes in his eyes. He's weighing whether he can trust me now.

"Don't worry. I'll get you out of here." I corner onto a couple of more side streets and one back alley. Who ever thought that having a juvenile criminal history would come in handy? Ten minutes later, the flashing lights disappear from my rearview.

"You lost him," he says, physically relaxing.

"You're welcome," I say sarcastically.

Our eyes meet in the mirror.

"You believe me," he says matter-of-factly.

"Should I not?"

He shakes his head. "I swear to you, I don't know what's going on. I only know those cops were trying to kill me."

In Mexico, dirty cops are not that uncommon, but the question remains: why? A light goes off in my head and I answer my own question. "The article."

"What?"

"Maybe someone recognized you from the article that ran in the paper." My sleuth instincts kick into gear. "Are you getting any of your memory back?"

"No," he answers so quick that I'm not sure that I believe him.

"Look. If I'm going to put myself out on the line then you're going to have to come clean."

I'm telling you the truth," he shouts. "I don't remember shit!"

"All right. All right." Our gazes meet again in the mirror. His smoldering eyes have me raging a war between my head and my heart. My head is screaming for me to kick him out of the car while my bleeding heart chants that I need to help him. And like an idiot, I listen to my heart.

CHAPTER 11

THE BOSS

"What the fuck do you mean he got away?" I thunder at a twitching Salazar. "I thought he was bedridden?"

Salazar shrugs his big shoulders. "I'm not sure what happened. Angel's contractors were supposed to do the job, but he found one of them dead in an elevator. Angel caught sight of the target and he went in pursuit—however the guy commandeered a vehicle that was leaving the parking deck.

"Did he happen to catch the license plate?"

Pause.

"Fuck! I'm surrounded by incompetent idiots!"

"He got a partial plate. Don't worry. We'll find him. You have my word on that."

"Careful," I warn. "I'm going to hold you to that."

Salazar nods and then slowly backs out of the room.

I pour another brandy, toss it back and then pour another one. My baby is out there—somewhere. My one good working arm starts trembling.

My brandy spills all over the front of my shirt.

"Aargh!" I toss the glass across the room. It smashes against the wall—its crash doing nothing but elevate the rage boiling in my veins. "I'll find her," I swear. I just don't know if I believe myself anymore.

CHAPTER 12

THE NURSE

I've listened to John Doe's story three times. Each time he tells it, I find myself believing and trusting him more and more. But then again, I've always had a thing for bad boys.

"So what do we do now?" I ask.

"I appreciate that, but you've done enough. If I can stay here for the night, I'll be out of your hair first thing in the morning."

I cross my arms. "Uh huh."

"I'm serious. I don't want you to get any deeper in this than you already have."

"So—fuck off. Is that what you're telling me? What if those cops got my license plate? Have you thought of that? Face it. I'm in this shit with you."

"You can always say that you were coerced," he says.

"Are you kidding me? They kind of seem like the kind of cops who are only interested in shooting first and then asking questions."

"Then what? I—I don't know what you want me to say. I'm sorry that I've dragged you into this. I'd get you out of it if I could." He looks like he's about to explode.

"All right. Calm down. I believe you. But you're going to need help—like a private investigator."

"An investigator?"

"Well in order to find out what we're running from we first have to find out who you are—or at least who they think you are."

"All right." He thinks about it. "That makes sense. You know an investigator?"

"No—but there's always the phone book."

CHAPTER 13

THE P.I.

"Yes. The check is in the mail, I swear." I cram my hands into my jean shorts for my office key. It's hot as hell in here, which is why cut-off jeans, bikini top, and flip-flops have turned into my staple office uniform.

"C'mon. Cut me some slack," I huff into the phone as I stop in front the Vega's Private Investigations door. "I sent you one month's payment. I'm going to need a little more time on the other two months. Things are crazy here. It's not like I'm eating paper and shitting money. Give me another month. Business is going to pick up soon. I—" I catch a noise over my right shoulder. "Hold on, Sal." I lower the phone. "Can I help you?"

"Uh . . ." A woman covered up from head to toe and sporting black sunglasses rushes up to me and starts looking around like she's expecting gremlins to jump out of the hedges. I'll be damned if this job doesn't bring out all kinds. She steps forward and extends her hand. "Hello. I'm Malena Castillo. I'm looking for a . . ." she glances down at a business card again. ". . . an Emilio Vega? Is he around?"

Not another one. "I swear, I don't know how many of you

chicken heads Emilio had stashed around town, but the gig is up. Your sugar daddy has bit the dust. He's gone—so go find a real job."

The woman frowns and starts looking around so hard that she makes me itch.

The woman's shoulders droop. "I think there's some kind of misunderstanding. Is there any way we can go inside and talk?"

Hot damn. A client! "Yeah. Sure. C'mon in." Excited, I place the phone back against my ear. "Sal, are you there? Hello? Damn. He hung up." I push open the door just when the woman waves to someone inside a silver convertible.

A tall, broad-shouldered man with a matching pair of black sunglasses climbs out of the car and jogs over toward us.

This should be interesting. I open the office door and welcome them inside. Whatever the hell this is about, I hope these people can pay cash up front. "Please excuse the mess."

"It's okay," Malena says, looking around.

"I'm sorry but my husband Emilio passed away," I tell them.

"Oh." The couple shares a look. "We're sorry to hear that."

"It's all right. The bastard had it coming."

Shocked, they buck their eyes at me.

"I didn't knock him off—his best friend did the honors when he caught Emilio in bed with his wife. His *boy* permanently terminated their relationship. Saved me a bundle on divorcing his ass." *Shit. I'm talking too much.*

Awkward pause.

"Well . . . okay." The guy smiles and backs away. "It was nice meeting you."

"Wait." I call after him. "If you're looking for a private detective, you still came to the right place." I extend my hand. "I'm Amalia Vega. I'm a licensed private investigator, too. Please. Sit down." I gesture to two cluttered chairs and then rush to clear them off. "Sorry. The cleaning woman . . ."

"She died, too?" the man asks.

I laugh, probably too hard, and then remind myself to calm down and not look desperate.

"Look, Ms. Vega—"

"Amalia. Please call me Amalia." I drop into my chair. "How can I help you two?"

"Uh . . . Amalia," he starts. "I don't know if this is going to work out."

"Why not?"

He stammers for a second and then looks to Malena for help.

"This is a delicate matter," Malena says.

"I can be discreet," I assure them.

"No. I mean . . . see. This man is a former patient over at the hospital. He's currently suffering from . . . memory loss. He doesn't remember who he is or where he's from."

"For real? Like . . . amnesia?"

"I'm afraid so," he says.

"Oh. Wait. I think I read about you in the paper." I rack my brain. "They found you on a beach, right?"

"So I'm told."

"Ooooh. I'd *loooove* to work on a case like yours."

"There's more." He removes his sunglasses and reveals an intense pair of black eyes. "Some people are trying to kill me. I have no idea why."

"That's where we'd like you to come in," Malena jumps in and then looks me up and down. "Excuse me, but how long have you been an investigator?"

"Well. Let's see. Emilio passed away almost two weeks ago soo. . . . about two weeks—officially."

Their eyes buck again.

"*But* I worked alongside Emilio for ten years. I just always kept putting off getting my license until . . . well . . . it was too late." I laugh awkwardly.

"Well . . ." he stalls, still inching toward the door.

"I'm flexible—and I can do the job."

They exchange looks again.

"Look. You need a P.I. and I *reeeaally* need a job. Let's make a deal."

He hedges. "How much?"

"Usually, there's a five-thousand-dollar retainer. Fifty-five dollars an hour, plus expenses."

"That much?" Malena says.

"I can lower it to say . . . three thousand?"

"That's still too high," she haggles.

I lean back in my chair. "*Okay.* I'm cheap—not free. A girl still has to make a living."

"All right," she says. "I can pull it out of savings."

"I'll pay you back," he promises her.

I watch the exchange, wondering what the deal was between these two. Friends? Lovers? Sugar Momma? "Do we have a deal?" I ask.

He nods. "Deal."

We shake hands.

"Great." I pull out a notepad and pen from my top drawer. "Let's go over what you do know. First things first: What's your contact information?"

"Excuse me?"

"Where are you staying?"

"You can take my number," Malena interjects. "He's staying at *my* place."

My brows shoot up. "Oh?"

"It's temporary," he says.

My gaze shifts to Malena in time to catch her annoyed expression before it vanishes behind a plastic smile.

"*Sooo* you two are just friends?"

Malena's hands fall to her sides. "Of course."

"Uh huh." I return to my notepad. "And your contact info?"

Malena rattles off her phone numbers and her address.

"And . . . what do I call you?" I ask him.

"Call me?"

"A name. I have to call you *something*."

"Oh. They were calling me John Doe at the hospital," he says, shrugging. "So . . . John, I guess."

"Humph. They're not too creative over there, are they?" I cock my head and evaluate him. "You don't look like a John, though. You think he looks like a John?" I ask Malena.

"*Nooo*. Not really," she agrees.

"I don't?" he asks, frowning.

"No." I tap my chin with the pen, thinking.

"How about Nicholas," Malena suggests.

"Nicholas is nice, but he looks more like a Ramon, or a Tomas . . . or . . . Julian."

He jerks as if I'd punched him in the gut.

Malena frowns. "What it is?"

"I'm not sure," he says, "—but that name . . ."

"What? Julian?" I ask.

He nods. "Yeah. I think . . . it might be my *real* name."

CHAPTER 14

THE LOVER

Three months later . . .

"Fuck me, Julian! Fuck me," Malena begs while moonlight bathes her dark, satin skin.

I lift up her baby-oiled body and jam her up against the bedroom wall. She wraps her long legs around my hips and I slide effortlessly into her tight pussy.

"God, you feel so good," I growl into the crook of her neck.

It's the only truth I've told lately.

Shit got real complicated the second I moved into her place. Friends became friends with benefits within a matter of days. My sex-starved body now ravishes her nightly. Malena loves it, even though she complains that I'm insatiable. That is probably true, too—at least as long as she wears her jasmine-scented perfume. That shit drives me wild.

"Oh. *Oooh. Oooh.*" Malena rakes her nails down my back.

I hiss because they course the same tender path every night. Still, the shit doesn't stop my dick game. Hell, I can't stop. A blinding lust that I don't understand takes over my body—but it has nothing to do with Malena personally. Yes, the sex is good, but no matter how hard or long I fuck her she never fills the hole inside of me.

The longing.

"That's it, baby. Ah. I'm coming!" Malena's legs lock around my waist as her pussy squeezes my cock.

I close my eyes and allow a cloud of jasmine to take me away where a shadowy woman teases my mind and body. *Who is she?*

"Oh. *Fuuuck*," I roar, thrusting my hips harder, deeper, and faster.

"Julian," the other woman whispers in my head.

"*Awwww*." As I rock my head back my entire body quakes before I blast off inside of her.

Malena screams out my name as she explodes and coats my dick with her body's thick honey. Spent, we remain entwined up against the wall, panting and struggling to get our breath.

Hot and sweaty, we tumble into bed.

I'm the first to come back down to earth and when I stare into Malena's moon-glow face, I'm disturbed by how little I feel for the woman who's taken me into her home, who feeds, clothes and even fucks me on a nightly basis. What the hell is wrong with me? Why can't I feel something for her?

As usual, Malena curls into a spoon.

I hate this shit, but I force myself to endure it because I owe her. Everything I have I owe to this woman. This shit is frustrating. So far, my ace detective hasn't been able to find jack shit. Something has to happen. I don't know how much longer I can fake it.

"What are you thinking about?"

The question comes out of left field and jars me.

When I don't answer, she glances over her shoulder and peers up at me through the silvery moonlight. "Julian?"

"Nothing . . . everything."

"You've been so distant lately."

Huffing out a long breath, I roll out of our spooning position and let my mask slip. "Don't start this shit again."

"What?" Malena gasps and sits up straight. "I just want to talk to you."

I toss the silk sheets off and sit on the side of the bed. "Talk about what? We keep talking about the same shit over and over again." I try to reel in my anger but her needling has gotten under my skin. All she does is yap, yap, yap. I could fucking strangle her some fucking times. I've actually dreamed about it.

"Is it something that I've done?" she asks.

"I don't know why you can't understand that I'm frustrated about this whole situation. Not everything is about you."

"Ouch."

"You asked." I climb out of bed and pace.

"Sorry. I was—"

"You were *what*?" I snap. "Can't we ever just fuck and go to sleep? Do you really have to know what the hell I'm thinking about every damn second of the day?"

"You know what? Fuck you!" She hops out of bed and storms to the adjoining bathroom.

Slam!

I glare at the closed door. "I got to get the fuck out of here." *And go where?* Pissed, I pace like a caged animal. Finally, I stomp out of the bedroom to the kitchen where I down two beers in two minutes. It's also where Malena finds me.

Irritated, I'm not ready for another round of 'talks'. "I'm going to move out," I tell her.

"What? No. Why? Is it something I did? I can change. I can fix it."

"The last thing I want to do is to overstay my welcome. I don't want you to feel like I'm taking advantage of you."

"No. I've never said that."

"But it's time for me to face the real possibility that I may never get my memory back. I have to start building a life."

"Without me?"

I stop pacing. "I didn't say that."

"But you've been thinking about it."

Tell her the truth. "You deserve much better than . . . damaged goods."

"Don't say that. You're not damaged goods—even if you never get your memory back. You have so much to offer."

I shoot her a dubious look, which compels her to continue. "Look. You're good-looking, intelligent, strong. Even if you have to start over, you can do anything that you set your mind to. My brother Diego says you're doing great over at the club, right?"

"Diego. Humph." I roll my eyes. I hate that job, but there was no point in bringing that up. We can go around and around on that shit all night.

Malena reaches out and grabs my hands. "Come back to bed," she coos. "I'm not ready to go to sleep yet."

I let her lead me forward and she peppers kisses along my neck. I close my eyes as jasmine floods my senses and seduces me.

CHAPTER 15

THE LOVER

Club Fuego

It's another Saturday night at Playa del Carmen's hottest club. It's wall to wall with scantily-dressed women and testosterone-charged men. The hard-driving beats from the DJ's turntable have everyone turned up. Guarding the door, I'm amused at how the bougie transforms into the rachet within five seconds of walking through the door.

Multicolored strobe lights splash over the crowd while a thick, potent cloud of ganja, soured cologne, and funk pollutes the air. After three months of this shit, I'm bored with it all. However, it's a job that pays under the table and is tiding me over so that I don't feel like I'm taking advantage of my living situation.

"Yo, man. Are you all right?"

"What?"

Kaleef, another bouncer shakes his head and chuckles under his breath. "Damn, man. You're really zoned out, huh?"

"Nah. Nah. I'm cool. What's up?"

Kaleef jets his thumb over his beefy shoulder toward the closest bar. "You got some chick asking for you."

"Me? Are you sure?"

"Yep. She asked for Julian. You're the only one that works here."

My gaze sweeps to the bar where I spot Amalia, a bona fide knockout in a gold, shimmering number that showcases her chiseled abs.

"Hope you don't mind my saying that your new baby girl is thick as hell," Kaleef jokes, pounding me on the back. "Better not let wifey find out that you're dipping your dick in random chicks."

I frown. "Thanks, but she's not my girl—and Malena isn't wifey."

"Uh-huh." Kaleef says. "Well, boost a nigga up and send baby girl my way when you're through talking to her. You know how I do."

I smirk and share a fist bump with the brothah, but when I walk away I roll my eyes and toss Kaleef's request out of my mind. "Hey, you," I greet Amalia. "I thought that you only remembered me on paydays."

"Not likely." She meets my gaze. "You're kind of a hard man to forget."

My brows shoot up as I take my time to do a slow drag over her shapely figure. She doesn't stir my blood either—not like the woman who teases me in my dreams nightly. "Can I buy you a drink?"

"Tempting—but I'm on the clock. I need to keep a clear head."

"On the clock? Dressed like that? You must have another job that I don't know about."

Amalia laughs. "You'll be amazed how far a ho's uniform can get you in my line of work."

I laugh. "Okay. So what *business* brings you here this time of night?"

Amalia's smile fades. "Well, you're still quite a mystery. So far you're a man that appeared out of thin air."

"Great."

"So I brought this." She reaches down for her clutch bag and pulls out a few items.

"What's that?"

"A do-it-yourself fingerprinting kit."

"You carry a fingerprint case?"

"I do now." She smiles. "Look, I know that you don't want to deal with the police."

"Because they like to shoot at me," I fill in for her.

"Well. I have a contact that I can trust at the department. I can have him run your prints for me on the down low."

"No." I shake my head. "No cops. I told you that."

"Look. I trust this guy—and my going door to door flashing your picture has gotten me nothing but blisters."

Frustrated, I look down at the small kit and then notice the bartender clocking us. "Hey. Let's not do this right here. Let's go in the back."

Amalia glances around. "Good idea." She gathers her things and follows me to the club's storage room.

"All right. We should have some privacy for a few minutes," I say.

Amalia places the inkpad and the print card down on top of a box.

"So what happens if it uh . . ."

"Comes back dirty?"

I nod.

"I promise to call and give you a heads up before the cavalry bangs down your door. Deal?"

I hesitate. A voice in the back of my head is telling me not to this, but at this point I'm ready to do this and get the shit over with.

"Well?"

"All right. Let's do this before I change my mind."

Amalia flashes me a reassuring smile. "Relax. It won't take long." True to her word, the process takes less than a minute.

"Now what?"

"Now we wait," she says as she seals the print card and then crams the kit back into her clutch. "You should be used to waiting."

"For how long?"

"No more than forty-eight hours. If I get something sooner than that I'll call you. Promise. You're still at Ms. Castillo's place?"

"Yeah. But let me give you my cell phone number. It's a pre-paid but it does the job." We exchange numbers and then I proceed to take her back into the club. The throng of people has thickened near the dance floor where a tall brothah shoves into me, but instead of apologizing, the man turns toward me with an attitude.

"Yo, nigga! Watch where you're . . ."

My chest swells up as I step up to this Goliath, who has an ugly scar across his face. "Is there a muthafuckin' problem?" I challenge.

"Holy shit," the man mutters, stumbling backward and reaching for something tucked behind his back.

I waste no time going for my own piece and shoving Amalia off to the side—a second before the bullets start flying.

I return fire.

Screams go up and people dash everywhere.

I clip the man's shoulder. In retaliation, the scarred man grabs a petite woman and shoves her into my direct line of fire.

I take my finger off of the trigger and then shove the woman out of the way. However, that gives the man time to bolt toward the front door with the crowd.

I chase after him and have to dodge more bullets for my trouble. By the time I make it through the door, the shooter is long gone. "What the fuck?"

CHAPTER 16

THE BOSS

"He's alive," Salazar announces.

I power the wheelchair around from my office bar and face him. "Are you sure?"

"I saw him with my own eyes," Salazar says. "His hair is different. He's scarred and burned, but I'm *sure* that it was him."

I draw in a long, measured breath. More sightings. I'm almost too scared to believe.

"Where?"

"Club Fuego in Playa del Carmen. He was there with some woman."

I perk at this news. "Cataleyna?"

Salazar drops his gaze and scratches at his scar. "No, boss, but—"

"But what?"

"The woman did look a lot like her."

Against my will, hope needles its way into my heart. "Check it out. If it's him, you know what to do."

A mischievous grin slides across Salazar's mangled face. "Yes, sir." He turns and marches out of my office.

CHAPTER 17

THE PRINCESS

"Push! Push!" the large midwife, Maria, coaches from between my legs.

"I can't! I can't!" Sweat pours down my face while every muscle in my body seizes with pain. "Please, make it stop." The baby is ripping me in two.

"You can do this. You can do this. I know you can," Ruthie, a girl who's no more than fourteen, presses a cool compress against my forehead, but I'm in too much pain to notice. No doctor. No epidural. And no Julian by my side. The pain only intensifies my anguish.

"Wait. This is all wrong."

"Wrong? What's wrong?" I pant, peering down at the woman between my knees. I can't take it if there's something wrong with my baby. The baby is all I have left of Julian.

"I have to turn the baby."

"What?"

"Hold on," Maria pushes in her hand.

"Aaaarrgh!" My body turns into one large spasm.

"Don't push."

I hear the order, but my body has a mind of its own and it wants the baby out.

"Stop pushing!"

"I'm trying." I toss and turn while the midwife battles to keep me still.

The wild-eyed teenage mops the sweat from my hair and neck.

When is this torture going to end?

"I almost got it," the midwife says, still turning the baby.

I hope so. I don't know how much more of this I can take. I twist and squirm on the huge California-king sized bed. My gaze finds the two cameras in the corners of the room.

They are watching me. They are always watching me. *The fucking assholes.* Why do they get off doing this shit? How much longer will this nightmare last? Why isn't my father doing anything about it? Does he even know that I'm still alive?

"All right. Got it. Get ready to push."

Tears well up. I'm too weak to fight them back. That only makes me angrier. Once upon a time, I was a lot stronger than this. I wasn't afraid of anything. Now I'm this weak, pathetic, groveling creature imprisoned in yet another golden cage while a set of mad men pull the strings in my life.

"All right now. *Push!*"

Exhausted to the point of delirium, I lay in a pool of my own sweat. "I can't. I can't."

"Señorita, you must," Ruthie says. "It's almost over."

I want to believe her, but I can't. The pain is all-consuming, and it feels like it's going to go on forever.

Ruthie sets aside the compress and takes my hand. In the next second, I crush her fingers as the next spasm hits, but the teenager bears the pain without complaint.

"*Aaaaaaaah!*" I push down with all I have.

"It's coming. It's coming. I can see the head," the midwife cries.

I pant a few more breaths and push again.

"That's it. That's it. You can do it."

"*Aaaargh!*"

"One more," the midwife coaches. "We're almost there. Give me one more big push."

Panting, I don't know whether I have it in me to continue.

"One more," Ruthie whispers.

"Julian," I beg, needing to believe that he's with me now. "I don't know if I can."

"Yes, you can, Señorita," Ruthie encourages. "Push."

Digging deep, I find a strength that I didn't know I had. "*Aaaaargh!*"

The baby's shoulders clear and the rest of its body slide out.

"I got it. It's a girl," Maria announces, and then turns to clean the baby.

"Oh thank God," I moan, closing my eyes for a prayer of thanks. But something isn't right. "What's wrong? Why isn't she crying?"

Ignoring me, Maria continues to clean the baby.

"Answer me. What's wrong with my baby?"

Suddenly, the door bursts open and *he* strolls into the room, his dark gaze raking over me with contempt.

Fear creeps into my heart. "W—what do you want? What are you doing here?"

Maria finishes cleaning my baby and then wraps her in a thin blanket.

"Give her to me." I hold out my arms, expecting Maria to hand me the baby, but instead she makes a beeline toward Vasquez. "What are you doing? No! No! Give her to me!"

Maria lays the baby in his arms.

At long last, the baby wails at the world. "*Whaaa! Whaaa!*"

"Give her to me!" I block out my pain and scramble to get up from the damp and bloody sheets. "Give me back my baby!"

His lips curl sinisterly. "What baby? You don't have a baby."

"What? No!"

He turns back toward the door.

"You can't do this." I stand up onto my wobbly legs and stumble after him. "You fucking monster. Give me my baby!"

Ruthie makes a feeble attempt to pull me back, but I shove her so hard that she careens into the wall.

The midwife gets into the act and the two struggle with me.

He laughs, never breaking his stride toward the door. "You'll be doing yourself a favor if you could forget all about this."

"*No!*" I wrestle free. "You can't do this! You can't do this!" I reach the door just as it slams in my face.

Locked.

I pound on the door, desperate. "Give me my baby back!"

Laughter rumbles through the door.

Bam! Bam! Bam!

"Give me my baby!"

The laughter fades as I slide to the floor, a broken woman. "Please, give me my baby."

CHAPTER 18

THE LOVER

"*Help! Julian! Help!*"

I bolt straight up, sweaty and confused. I realize that it's the middle of the night and I'm crashed on Malena's couch. *It was that damn dream again.* Dropping my head in between my hands, I exhale a long, frustrated breath. How much longer is this shit going to go on? Night after night, it's the same gunfire, the same woman's screams, and the same dark water. What the fuck happened that night? If I can figure that shit out then I'll know why muthafuckas are trying to kill me.

A sound catches my ear and my hand snakes out for the .45 tucked beneath one of the couch cushions. Malena clicks on the living room's lights and finds herself staring down the barrel of a gun.

"What the hell?" She jumps, eyes wide.

"Oh. It's you."

"Who else would it be?" she snaps.

I lower my weapon. "Sorry."

She keeps her gaze locked on my weapon. "Diego said that there was a shooting at the club last night. Why didn't you tell me?"

"Yeah. I don't know what the hell that shit was about. Dude took one look at me and started blasting."

"This isn't good. We now have my brother mixed up in this shit."

"What did he tell the cops?" I ask.

"Nothing. He said it was a couple of party goers—but the cops confiscated his security tapes. It's just a matter of time before that tape jams Diego up."

"He's going to rat me out?"

"I don't know what he's going to do—but I doubt that he's going to risk losing his baby to protect you. He gave you the job as a favor to me."

"I get it. I get it."

Malena's eyes tear up. "I'm sorry but I think whatever's going on it's a little too much."

"What are you saying?"

"I'm saying that . . . I'm scared. I think I'm in over my head. Maybe in your past life you . . . you . . ."

"I—what?"

"Maybe you weren't such a nice guy," she says and then looks contrite for having spoken her mind. "Look, Diego said—"

"Diego. Diego."

"My brother has done nothing but try to help you out," she defends. "And he's pretty adamant that the man that tried to take you out is a known drug lord with the Rosales cartel. A cartel! So that means if they know you then . . ."

My blood boils at her insinuation. "Then what? I'm one of them? That's what you think of me—that I'm some low-life drug dealer? C'mon. Give me a fuckin' break."

"And what about the police?" she asks.

"What about them? They're some dirty fuckin' cops. What do you want me to say?"

"I don't know. I just know that you're in danger or danger-ous—and the longer you stick around here, I'm in danger, too."

I want to understand, but the more she talks the more she's pissing me off. "Just fucking say it already. You want me out of here."

There's a long pause before she finally says, "I'm sorry."

"Whatever." I stomp past her toward the spare bedroom and toss what little clothes and stashed money I have into a duffle bag.

Malena rushes into the room. "Wait, Julian. You don't have to do it right now."

"Now is as good a time as any." The idea of bouncing suddenly feels liberating. I don't know what's waiting for me out in the streets but it's got to be better to meet my fate head-on than to suffocate in this damn house, fucking this needy bitch to keep a roof over my head.

"Julian, please wait. Please." She is frantically wrestling my arms and trying to block me from grabbing more clothes.

"I didn't mean it. I didn't mean it," she raves. "I'm just under a lot stress. Don't go. I don't want you to go." She gives up holding my arms and instead tries to cradle my face and force me to look at her.

I easily pry her hands away from my face, but she springs up onto the tips of her toes to pepper my face with kisses. The shit annoys me at first—but then my dick gets hard and the next thing I know I'm ripping her clothes off.

CHAPTER 19

THE P.I.

I curse Emilio's ass for the millionth time, leaving me with all these damn bills. I should've listened to my mother and married for money instead of love. Emilio Vega was a sexy, smooth-talking devil that never met a set of tits that he didn't like. When he wasn't off fucking everything he could nail down, he was gambling us into a debt that'll take two generations of Vegas to pay off. If I didn't love being a nosey bitch, I would pack up my shit and start all over again somewhere else. Somewhere like Argentina or Brazil. The same places that Emilio had always promised to take me.

There's a knock on the door.

"Who in the fuck is that?" I glance at my watch and wonder who could be here at this time of night. Standing from my desk, I retrieve my Glock and then creep to the front of the office. I immediately recognize Angel peeking at me through the glass.

I relax, click on the safety and then rush to answer the door. "What are you doing here?"

He comes through the door, looking around. "I got your results back and since I was coming through the neighborhood, I'd figured I'd drop them off."

I frown. "You could've called."

He continues to look around. "You got a minute?"

"Sure. C'mon in." I lock the door behind him and then lead him back toward my office.

"*Sooo.*" I sit my gun on the desk, drop back into my seat and kick up my feet. "Please tell you got good news."

Angel draws and levels his gun on me.

"What the fuck?" I drop my feet.

"*Ah. Ah. Ah.* No sudden moves," he warns.

"What the hell is this about?"

"Where is he?"

"Where is who?"

"Don't play stupid. Where is your *client?*"

"Who?"

He laughs. "Don't play stupid. You only have one client."

"Why? Who is he?"

"Let's just say that he's someone with a mighty big price on his head that I'm going to cash in. So I'm going to ask you again. Where is he?"

"How much of a price on his head? You know a sister is looking for a come up, too."

He hesitates and studies me hard. I can't believe that up until a minute ago I thought Angel was one of the good ones—a rare commodity in the crooked police department.

"The address," he presses.

I can't make a move for the weapon on my desk—but chances are he doesn't know about the .22 taped underneath it.

"What's the reward?" I ask, equally serious.

Silence.

"C'mon. How much?" My hand inches toward the .22.

"Twenty-five *million,*" he answers.

I release a long whistle. "That some serious fucking cash. Who posted the reward?"

Angel hesitates. "Vicente Rosales. Dead or alive."

I whistle again. What the hell does a drug king like Rosales want with my client? "If I give you the address how much will you cut me in for?"

He waivers.

"Fifty-fifty?"

"Hell, no."

"Sixty-forty. I'm not greedy."

"Eighty-twenty," Angel counters. "That's five million. Take it or leave it."

I smile as my hand closes around the .22. "Oh. I'll take it," I tell him.

He lowers the gun and I blow his fucking balls off.

CHAPTER 20

THE LOVER

Malena pulls me down onto the bed, lifting her silky legs and hooking them over my shoulders to allow a deeper penetration. I lose myself in her jasmine scented body, but it's another woman I see. She appears more clear to me now than ever before. The heart-shaped face, sleek nose, rosy cheeks. She's dressed all in red and glittering with diamonds.

"*Oh! Oh! I'm coming!*" Malena pants.

My hips pound deeper while an image of a pair of ruby-colored lips spread wide over a pearly white smile comes into focus.

More. More. I need to see more.

Wrapped up in the fantasy woman in my head I don't hear Malena telling me to stop, or even feel her fist hammer against my chest.

Finally, Malena slams a hard right across my jaw.

Enraged, I lock my hands around this bitch's throat, cutting off her air supply. "What the fuck is your goddamn problem?"

Startled and scared, Malena claws at my hands. "Julian! Please. Julian!"

But I'm too pissed about the disrespect that I can't think straight. *Who does this bitch think she is?*

Slowly, my red rage ebbs away and reality sinks in. *What the fuck am I doing?* I jerk my hands off of her neck and spring off of the bed. "Oh my God," I pant, looking down at my hands.

Coughing and crying, Malena backs away and takes a tumble off the edge of the bed.

I rush to help her.

"Don't touch me," she screeches.

I jump back. "Malena, I'm sorry. I—I don't know what came over me."

"You tried to kill me," she screams, pressing into a corner.

"No. No. I—I . . ." *What?* I don't know what to say or what the hell had come over me. "I'm sorry," I repeat. It's the only thing that I can say.

Malena breaks down sobbing, making me feel like a bigger shit.

"Don't cry." I kneel and crawl over to her. "Baby, please don't cry. Please." I gather her into my arms and let her tears wash my chest. I whisper my apologies over and over again.

Thump!

Malena and I freeze.

Creak!

Malena gasps. "Someone is in the house."

"Stay put." I stand, pressing my finger against my lips. Quickly, I snatch up my black boxers from the floor, slip them on and then creep toward the closed bedroom door. It's not until then that I realize that I left the gun in the living room. Holding my breath, I twist the knob and then ease out into the dark hallway. I remain calm as my senses heighten. All I hear is the soft whir of the air conditioner blowing through the house vents. However, every hair on my body stands at attention.

As I enter the living room, the darkness persists because of the closed blinds and curtains on the windows. *The gun is gone.* Inching by the fireplace, I pick up one of the iron pokers and continue surveying the house.

Nothing.

But everything within me says there's someone else here.
Breathing.
Watching.

Yet, as the seconds tick by, doubt creeps around the back of my mind. Had I imagined the whole thing?

"Julian, is everything all right?" Malena calls out.

I relax, feeling foolish. "Yeah. Everything is fine." I head back toward the hallway.

"What was it?" she asks breathlessly from the bedroom door.

"Nothing."

Malena reaches out and flips on the hall light. *"Julian, behind you!"*

I duck and turn as the gigantic intruder fires off a shot.

Malena screams.

I swing the iron poker like a nine-iron and clock the large, masked intruder under the chin. *Thunk!*

The man is lifted a few inches into the air and then crashes onto the floor.

Another shot goes wild but I waste no time leaping on the muscled intruder with my fists flying. Each power blow cracks bones.

Despite being dazed and confused, the black giant regroups enough to counterattack. His first punch misses, but the second one slams into my jaw with the force of a wrecking ball.

I crash into the wall.

"Where is Cataleyna?" the man growls.

Who? Shaking off the punch, I launch my full weight into my attacker. We tumble backward into the living room. A set of curtains rips off the windows while an end table splinters in half. When I look up, a big lamp is coming straight toward my head. I spring to my left and it crashes against the floor. Shards of glass spray me, a few slicing across my face and chest.

"I'm going to ask you again," the man hisses through his bloody teeth. "What did you do with Cataleyna? Tell me and I *might* let you live."

"I don't know what the fuck you're talking about. And I have no intention of letting *your* ass walk out of here alive."

Judging by the widening smile, my words are right down his ally. "Bring it on, tough guy." He waves me forward.

Too happy to oblige, I again hurl my body toward my opponent. Dude tries to sidestep the attack, but my arms lock around his waist and we flip over the arm of the couch and crash-land on the glass coffee table.

I don't even feel the pain. A black rage takes over my body and we go at it like gladiators.

Pound for pound, we're evenly matched.

At least that's my assessment until the ugly gorilla grabs me up and hurls me out of the living room and over the breakfast bar. When I hit the porcelain floor, the air is knocked out of me.

My attacker hits the kitchen light and snatches a large knife from the butcher block. "You know, I'm going to enjoy carving you up!"

I scramble back onto my feet, but I slip backward against the sink and knock over all the dishes.

The gorilla takes the blade between his fingers.

My hand edges toward the cutting board still on the counter.

Laughing, the man throws the knife at my head.

With lightning reflexes, I bring the board up in front of my face. The blade *thunks* into the center of the board.

He goes for another knife on the butcher block while I snatch out the one in the cutting board and then launch it right back at the muthafucka, who's about to throw the next weapon.

But it's too late.

Thunk!! My knife slices into the middle of his throat like warm butter.

Eyes wide, the gorilla drops his weapon and tries to pull the knife out of his neck. The blade moves only an inch before he sinks to his knees. Blood spews like water from a fire hydrant across the kitchen floor.

Our gazes lock. I watch the life drain from him before he keels over with a final *thud!*

I stand and walk over to him. "Now who in the fuck are you?" I roll him over and frantically search the body for some type of identification. There's a wallet in the back left pocket. "Duane Salazar," I read the name from the driver's license. I repeat it in my head, hoping it will rattle a memory loose or something. When it doesn't, I continue my search: credit cards, receipts and a couple hundred dollars. Tossing that aside, I dive into the man's front pockets and find an open pack of gum and a photograph. I take one look at the picture and my heart stops.

It's her. The same woman who's been haunting my dreams. That hair. Those eyes. That smile. *She's real—but who is she?* I flip the picture over, but there isn't anything written on the back.

"What the fuck?" I don't understand.

I hold onto the picture, stand and then step over the body. It isn't until I'm in the hallway that I even remember Malena. "Oh fuck!" I race to her even though she looks like a broken mannequin on the floor. I check for a pulse though I know that I won't find one.

"Shit." Lowering my head I wait for grief to come, but oddly I feel nothing. After a minute, my pre-paid smartphone chirps from the bedroom.

Amalia Vegas, reads the name on the screen.

In the distance, sirens fill the air.

"Hello."

"Julian! Thank God you're there," Amalia says.

"Yeah. Listen there's . . ."

"You got to get out of there."

"What?"

"I don't have much time to explain—or argue—but you got to leave the house. *Now!*"

CHAPTER 21

THE LOVER

I disconnect. Turning, I look back at Malena's twisted body. I don't want to leave her like this. It doesn't seem right. I walk over to her and gently rearrange her so that she looks like she's sleeping. Guilt twists in my gut, but the sirens draw closer.

I got to get out of here.

The sirens grow louder. My survival instinct kicks in and I scramble to get the rest of my belongings into the duffel bag. Seconds later, I snatch Malena's car keys off a hook in the foyer and then take off out of the front door. The moment I rev up the engine, a line of house lights turns on across the street. *The neighbors.*

I jet out of the driveway and peel off. Briefly, blue and white lights flash in my rearview mirror as a police car corners onto the street. Without missing a beat, I slam my foot onto the accelerator and speed out of the housing complex like a bat out of hell.

Unfortunately, I don't get too far before I blow past another cop car hiding in the median. I groan at the sound of the siren and the flashing lights.

I make a sharp right. My back tires drift, forcing me to

course-correct. Seconds later, the police follow suit, swinging wide and swiping other vehicles. However, they stay in pursuit.

"Shit." I floor the accelerator and weave between slower motorists. I fly through two lights. Horns and tires squeal as cars swerve to avoid T-boning me. I make it through.

The chasing cop cars aren't so lucky.

Crash! Boom! Crash!!

I glance up into the rearview mirror and see a growing car pile.

My cell phone rings.

"Where are you?" Amalia demands.

I search for street signs but can't find one. "I don't know."

"How far are you from the Aerosaab?"

I frown. "I have no idea. What is that?"

"It's a private landing strip three miles east of the hospital. Do you think that you can get there?"

"Uh, yeah. I think I can find it."

"All right. I'll meet you there. We got to get you out of town."

"And go where?" The problem with running from trouble with amnesia is that I have no idea where is a safe place to hide.

"I have a friend who can fly us across the way to Cozumel."

"Cozumel? Why there?"

"You got a better idea?"

I wish I did. I don't like the idea of putting my fate in someone else's hands—but what choice do I have?

"Well? I'm waiting," Amalia says. "I'm trying to help. I can hang up and wash my hands of this, if you want."

"No. No. It's not that," I huff over the line. "I'm thinking."

"Well, think a little faster. I have a guy flying out in the next twenty minutes. He's not going to wait."

"Fuck it. All right. I'll meet you at the airport." I disconnect the call and toss the phone back into my bag. I scan the rearview for signs of police. They're nowhere in sight.

I remain jumpy throughout my race to the airport. True to her word, Amalia, dressed head to toe in black, is pacing near a blue Toyota Camry.

"There's our ride," Amalia says, pointing to a small plane on the landing strip.

"*That* thing?"

"What? You don't have a fear of flying, do you?"

"No." I think it over. "At least I don't think so."

She pats me on the back. "Don't worry. You'll be all right."

"Always cutting it close," the pilot says, greeting Amalia with a friendly hug.

"But I always come through," she boasts.

"That you do." He turns his attention to me. "Welcome aboard."

"Thanks." I accept the man's hand, but I'm put off when he doesn't release my grip.

"I'm sorry," the pilot says. "Do I know you?"

I tense. "I don't know. Do you?"

Amalia jumps in. "Marcus, we better get going. That is if you're going to stick to your precious schedule."

The pilot nods, but is still slow to release my hand. "I'm usually pretty good with faces."

"I wish I could say the same thing," I counter with a touch of humor.

Amalia laughs. She then takes me me by the hand and leads me up the plane's boarding stairs.

I buckle myself in even though my long legs make me feel like a giant crammed into a matchbox. When the pilot climbed on board, our eyes met again. The way he's eyeballing me, I'm not sure if I want him to be able to place my face. Within minutes, we are in the air. God only knows what's waiting for me in Cozumel.

CHAPTER 22

THE P.I.

"Welcome to Cozumel," Marcus announces.

Given the late hour, we can barely make out much of anything, but I have a rental car arranged to pick us up when we land.

"Where to now?" Julian asks, climbing into the passenger seat.

"Right now we need to find somewhere to crash so that you can figure out what you're going to do."

"How do I do that when I still don't know who I am? Did your contact at the department call you yet?"

"Uhm—no. Not yet."

He frowns. "Then how did you know that I needed to get out of town?"

Fuck. "Look. I have eyes and ears everywhere. You're paying me to be on top of things, right?"

He doesn't answer. He stares at me like he knows I'm lying through my teeth.

"Anyway. We can talk about everything tomorrow. Right now we need a good night's rest and then we can put our heads together in the morning. Deal?"

He doesn't answer. Instead, his black gaze burns into me.

This twenty-five-million dollar man is dangerous and I'm playing with fire.

"Are you going to say anything?" I ask.

"There's not really too much to say now, is there?" He turns and looks out the window.

Relieved, I exhale. There is a small chance that this whole amnesia thing is a crock and I should be more scared of him than of Rosales.

"This place looks familiar," he says suddenly.

"What?"

He twists around in his seat and then scans the street. "There's a shopping plaza up at the corner," he announces.

Sure enough, Cinco Soles shopping plaza comes into view.

Then he starts naming Tequila bars and clothing stores before we reach them.

"I've been here before," he says excitedly.

"Apparently."

Then Casita de Maya comes into view and his color drains. "There. Pull into that hotel."

I glance up. "Where? There? Casita de Maya?"

"Yeah, there. I think I've been here before, too."

You got to be kidding me. Do you know how much a place like this costs?"

"Pull over," he insists. "Now, goddamn it."

"All right. All right. I'm pulling over."

I pull into the lot, bypasses the valet and park in the parking deck.

"There's something I got to tell you," Julian says. "It's about Malena."

I sigh. "Can it wait? I really need a hot shower and some shut-eye before I deal with anything else tonight. How about we talk at breakfast?"

"She's dead."

I stare at him, not sure that I heard him right. "What do you mean—*dead?*"

"We had a break-in tonight. That muthafucka from Club Fuego came to finish the job. Malena took a bullet to the chest."

"And the guy?"

"A knife through the neck."

I stare at him. I don't know what to say.

"You still want to help me?"

I don't know what to do now. "Yeah."

His eyes narrow. "Why?"

I blink. "W—why? What do you mean?"

"Do you normally make a habit out of helping murderers?"

"Murderer?"

"I've now killed my second person in three months."

"So what are you saying? You don't want my help?"

His stare unnerves me. "Why don't we get some rest," I say, feeling sweat beading on the back of my neck. "Sleep on it and we'll talk in the morning."

Finally, he nods. "All right." He climbs out of the car.

Swallowing the knot in my throat, I climb out of the car, too. Together we walked into the hotel in silence. Because of the late hour there is only a handful of people milling about the hotel lobby.

"I've definitely been here before," he continues, whispering under his breath. He makes a three-hundred-sixty degree turn, taking in his surroundings.

"Really?" I walk back to him, studying him. "What else do you remember?"

He shakes his head as if willing his brain to give him something—anything. "*She* was here."

I frown. "Who is *she*?"

He looks at me, hesitates. "Nobody. Forget it." He takes a step and I stop him. "Is your memory coming back?"

"No. Not exactly."

I cross my arms. "Look. I've put myself out on a limb for you. There's got to be some level of trust."

"Humph. Trust." He impales me with another black stare. "I suspect that trust and truth go hand in hand. I don't think you're being too truthful with me tonight."

Oh shit. "I don't know what you're talking about."

He nods and heads toward the receptionist. "We need two rooms," he tells her.

The young woman grins at him. "Yes, sir. Let me see what we have."

As she searches her computer, I steal glances at him, weighing his mood. But he's a hard read.

The receptionist asks a series of questions before checking us in as Mr. and Mrs. Tony Montana.

"What are you, a Scarface fan?" I ask.

He looks genuinely confused.

"It's a famous gangster movie," I tell him.

"Oh. No. The name . . . came to me."

I nod, not sure whether I believe him.

He hands over cash for the rooms.

The receptionist smiles. "Okay. Here are your keys. Rooms eight-twelve and eight-thirteen." She hands us the room keys. "Enjoy your stay."

"Thank you." We ride up to our floor in silence.

"See you in the morning," he says, sliding his card key into the lock.

"Night." I enter my room and quickly close the door.

I wait a full minute and then head straight for the phone. So far, so good. I dig through my jeans pocket and retrieve the reward leaflet that I lifted from Angel. "Twenty-five million dollars," I whisper. With this kind of money, I can settle all of Emilio's debts and live the rest of my life without worrying about money.

I glance at the number printed at the bottom and weigh my options. After another minute, I pick up the phone and dial.

CHAPTER 23

THE LOVER

I shut off the shower and step out into a stream-filled bathroom. Though I'm more relaxed, my body still aches from the number of body blows that Salazar dude dealt me.

"Where is Cataleyna?" Salazar's repeated question loops in my head.

Who?

Help! Julian! Help!

The woman in red flashes in my head again.

I grab the hotel robe from the back of the bathroom door and march out into the room. From my duffel bag, I pull out the woman's picture I lifted off Salazar. The woman isn't dolled up like the image in my head. She's still gorgeous with minimal makeup and her hair billowing in the wind. She looks like the kind of girl that a man could take home to meet the parents. The kind of woman a man would love to make beautiful babies with. I smile, liking that idea. Before long I'm running my finger along the side of her face in the photograph. This woman meant something to me. She's important. A wife? A girlfriend? A lover?

Guilt crushes me. How can I not remember her? I lay down, staring at the photo. At least now it makes sense why

I've never been able to feel anything for Malena. My heart be-longs to someone else.

"Where are you?" I whisper, but as soon as I ask the ques-tion, I sense that something horrible has happened to her.

I need a drink. Badly.

I abandon sleep and get dressed. With any luck the hotel bar is still open. In the hallway, I stop in front of Amalia's room. Maybe I should invite her down. After a few knocks and no answer, I assume that she's crashed for the night.

It's 3:00 a.m. and the bar is still open. I count six patrons spread out in the place as I walk up to the main bar. A grinning bartender with a brass nametag that reads Jimmy approaches as soon as my ass lands on the stool. "Ahh. Welcome back! I won-dered what happened to you!" He frowns. "What happened to you? Did you get into a fight with a burning Mack truck?"

I blink. "I know you?"

The bartender laughs. "Who can forget Tony Montana?"

My smile withers. "Montana?"

"Hey. I don't ask too many questions. I just try to remem-ber all the good tippers."

"I need a drink."

"Your usual?"

I have a usual? "Sure. Why not?"

"One Manhattan coming up."

"Thanks," I say, once the drink is delivered. One sip and a warm familiarity washes over me.

"Good?" Jimmy asks, puffing out his chest.

"Perfect." I sit the glass down. "Mind if I ask you a few questions?"

"Sure. Shoot."

"How often would you say that I used to come in here?"

"Well . . . it's been a while . . ." He seems to start counting in his head. "I'd say it's been what—nine, ten months?"

I have no idea. "Something like that. And how often would you say I'd come here?"

The bartender slaps his drying towel over his shoulder. "It's hard to say—I only worked part-time back then, but if I had to put money on it, I'd say you came around here maybe twice a week. Why?"

I sigh. The last thing I want to do is rehash my memory problem. "It's a long story."

"Aren't they all?" He laughs.

I drain my drink. "Hit me again."

"You got it."

When Jimmy disappears again, I wonder how I can get more information from the guy without seeming like some wacko.

My second drink is delivered.

"Bottoms up," Jimmy grins.

"Thanks."

"Mind if I ask you a question?" Jimmy asks.

Oh, great. "All right."

"How did it go with you and the girl?" he asks, grinning.

My heart stops. "The girl?"

"The last time you were here you were . . . juiced, if you don't mind me saying so, and were going on and on about some woman that you couldn't get out of your system. Said that you were ready to make your move. I figured that you were finally about to pop the question."

I was going to ask her to marry me. I smile.

"Ahh. It went *that* well, huh?" The bartender knocks on the counter. "Tell you what, the next drink is on the house."

"Thanks." At least I have another piece of the puzzle. I remove the picture from my front pocket and stare at it.

Fiancée? For some reason that feels right.

"Is that the lucky woman?" Jimmy asks, peering down. "May I?"

Proud of the beauty's identity, I hand over the picture. The bartender shocks me again.

"Wait. I know her." Jimmy looks up at me. "Cataleyna Rosales is *your* fiancée?"

CHAPTER 24

THE PRINCESS

I'm losing my mind. I want my baby. What kind of monsters would snatch an innocent baby from its mother? I've done everything that they've asked. Why won't they let me and my baby go?

It's never going to happen. They are never going to let me leave.

After days of crying my eyes out, I've reached my limit.

There's no point in my carrying on. I don't want to live. I've stopped eating, but death is too slow. A year ago, I thought my father had isolated and sheltered me. Now I truly know what it's like to be a prisoner.

Tears swell and roll down my face. Disgusted, I swipe them away. I'm fucking tired of crying. I'm supposed to be tougher than this. I'm Cataleyna Rosales—a cartel princess. I'm supposed to be fearless. My father would be ashamed if he saw how easily our enemies had broken me.

And I *am* broken.

I finish mopping my eyes and realize that I have to win back my power. After all, I'm the master of my fate. I'm in control of what happens next.

I peer up at the full moon. It's a peaceful night. The stillness calls and seduces me. In death, there'll be no more pain.

There will be no more tears. More importantly, I'll reunite with Julian. He's waiting for me. I'm convinced of it.

Minutes later, I dry my tears, walk from the chair by the locked window and into the adjoining bathroom where I fill the tub with hot water. On the ledge is a jar of jasmine bath beads that had been a gift from my abductors. I've been given a lot of gifts for reasons I fail to understand. They are probably from Carlos, even though he has yet to show his face. Tomas does all of the dirty work.

When the tub is filled, I shut off the water. Standing, I walk over to the bathroom counter and pick up the hand mirror from the vanity tray. I take one look at my reflection and don't recognize the gaunt, melancholy woman staring back. Turning, I head back to the tub with the mirror in hand, strip, and climb inside. As I ease into it, I block out the sting of the hot water. I take the mirror and smash it against the ledge. The glass shatters onto the marbled floor.

I pick up a large shard and then slash my wrists. The pain is instant, but I don't cry out. Blood streams into the water. Calm, I ease back against the tub and wait for death.

A minute later, there's a crash from the bedroom and then the slap of feet running toward the bathroom.

"What did you do?" Tomas thunders.

Death, hurry. Please.

A pair of strong arms dives into the tub.

"No! No! *No!"* I pound my bloody arms against his chest. He struggles to get a firm hold. "Stop it. *Stop it!"*

"Leave me alone," I wail. "I want to die!" I fight until he loses his grip and drops me.

I bang my head on the tub's ledge and slip underwater.

Tomas snatches me back up and hauls my limp body out of the bathroom.

Weak, I renew my fight. "Please," I beg. "Let me die."

"It's not going to happen," he growls.

But it is happening. I'm slipping away.

CHAPTER 25

THE LOVER

"You know her?"

"She's kind of hard to forget," Jimmy laughs. "Cataleyna Rosales. She used to come around here all the time—like you." He cocks his head as if snapping the pieces of the puzzle together. "*Ahhh*. I get it now. You two had a little weekly rendezvous thing here at the hotel. I gotcha. I gotcha. So you found her then?"

What did you do with Cataleyna? Salazar had asked.

"Found her?"

"Yeah." Jimmy pauses to think back. "Months ago her father sent an army to comb the whole damn town. I don't know if she ran away or was kidnapped. Hell, I didn't even know that she was a cartel princess when she was hanging out here. Goes to show that you never really know about people. You know what I mean?"

I nod.

"Anyway, I know it was a big deal around here for a while. There was some huge massacre out at that big compound north of here. A lot of people in town say the Zetas were behind that shit, others say that it was the Vazquez brothers of Columbia. And some say she just ran off. So which was it?"

Vazquez. The name sounds familiar.

"Sir?"

"Hmm?"

"Which was it? I mean they *did* find her, right?"

I don't know what to tell him.

Jimmy pales as if he realized he's been talking too much. "Oh wait, man. If that's your girl, I'm sorry. I—I didn't mean anything by it. I—I was—"

"It's all right." I drain my drink. "Hit me again." I don't want him to stop talking.

"Yes—yes, sir." Jimmy refreshes my drink.

"The cartel. Tell me what you know about them."

"Which one?" Jimmy chuckles.

"All of them."

Hours later, I hike up to my room with my head buzzing. I know what I must do now: Find Cataleyna Rosales. She must be still missing. Why else was that Salazar guy still looking for her? Her disappearance lines up with my washing up on the Playa del Carmen shore. I was there that night she went missing. I'm sure of it.

I hop off the elevator and rush to Amalia's room, excited to share everything I've learned tonight. Again, she doesn't answer the door. After knocking for a full minute, I give up and resign to wait for a more appropriate hour.

Stumbling into my room, I collapse onto the bed, hoping to get at least an hour of sleep. As soon as I close my eyes, Cataleyna appears in her smoldering red beaded gown. There's a group of women who giggle and laugh around her. I want to walk over and touch her, kiss her, but I can't. I watch her move as if she's floating on air and when she laughs, it's pure music.

That vision stays with me until I open my eyes an hour later and spot my door creeping open. *What in the hell?* A silencer-capped gun takes aim.

I bolt to my left, rolling off the bed as the intruder taps the trigger.

Poof! Poof!

One of the bed pillows spit up feathers.

I scramble across the floor to the bag for my gun. The door bursts open and I return fire, forcing my attackers to take cover.

When they shoot back, I tuck and roll to the room's desk before four bullets punch into the floor and desk.

Moving on instinct, I advance to the other side of the desk and fire with deadly precision.

Two bodies drop dead.

Stunned, I stand and creep toward the hit men who now have identical bullet holes in the center of their foreheads.

"Holy shit." I don't know whether to be proud or repulsed by what I've done, but I do know that I have to get the hell out of here.

I grab the duffel bag and Cataleyna's picture from the bed. At the door, I tense at hearing voices in the hallway. I look around to see if there's another way out.

No such luck.

"Fuck it." I rush into the hallway with my gun in hand. People gasp and scramble into the rooms. I stop and bang on Amalia's door.

No answer.

"Amalia, open up!" I pound on the door again.

Where the fuck is she? Heads peek out of the rooms again. I can't wait around here any longer. I race off. Taking the stairs, I fly down eight flights. When I rush into the lobby, I damn near run straight into the police. Dropping my head, I tuck my weapon beneath my shirt and make a beeline for the front door.

Out on the sidewalk, I hang a left and keep it moving.

Police sirens and flashing lights barrel down the street. I tuck and hide my face until the cop cars pass. After that, I take off running—not knowing where in the hell I'm going.

CHAPTER 26

THE BOSS

"Damn!" I slam down the phone and suck in an angry breath. Once I get hold of myself, I lift my gaze to a nameless foot soldier standing by the door. "Bring me the girl."

"Yes, boss." The soldier speeds out of the room.

I power over to the bar and pour a drink.

"Let go of me! *Let go!*"

I down the drink and then quickly pour another one.

"You're making a big mistake, Rosales. You can't keep me here."

"Calm down, Señora Vega." I wheel around to face her. "No one is going to hurt you. You're a guest."

"Where I come from people don't lock up guests overnight. That's called kidnapping."

"You say tomato and I say *tomahto*. You came to me, re- member?"

"For the reward."

"I'm not in the habit of handing out twenty-five million dollars to every stranger with a wild story. I had to check you out."

Ms. Vega straightens her shoulders. "And?"

"So far your story checks out, *but* I'm going to need for you to bring him in. Seems my men missed him this morning."

"What do you mean?"

Instead of answering the question, I roll across the room to a wall of bookshelves. I move one book and then the whole thing slides to the right to reveal my safe.

"Like I was saying," I continue, grabbing stacks of cash. "If you want the reward money, you bring him to me."

She hesitates. "How do I know that you'll fulfill your end of the bargain?"

"You don't."

"And *that's* a problem." She folds her arms. "I don't trust you."

"That makes you a smart woman," I say. "But this is a one-time offer. You'll get nothing if I have to get him myself."

We engage in a long staring contest. Despite my half-paralyzed face and slight slur, I still get my point across. "You already tried to bring him in," she says.

"That's where you are wrong. I didn't try to bring in. I tried to kill him. There's a difference."

She fidgets nervously, but eyeballs the stacks of cash.

"Don't worry. It's not your affair. You're here for the reward money, right?"

She pauses again. "Right."

"Tell you what . . . I'll give you half upfront: twelve and a half million dollars. The rest when you deliver him. Deal?"

Pause. "Deal."

CHAPTER 27

THE PRINCESS

I float in a space and time unfamiliar to me. I want to languish here forever away from the pain and misery that has become my life. I'm safe. Protected. Is this death—a dark, numb and soundless paradise?

Disappointment pricks my heart. I'd hoped to see Julian's loving face again—maybe even my mom's or dad's. How many times have I wondered if he was dead since he hasn't rescued me? Don't think about that. It doesn't matter. Nothing matters anymore. Not since those monsters stole my baby.

My sweet baby. I didn't even have a chance to see her face or give her a name.

Bit by bit the shards of my broken heart tear me apart. In a snap, my dark safe haven transforms into another private hell. The pain comes rushing back and so do the voices around me.

"Stupid, stupid, stupid, girl," a man growls over me. "What the hell did you think you were doing? You can't die. I'm not going to let you. Not after the hell I went through to get you here. Not after what it's cost me."

Groggy, I peel open my eyes. Everything is still hazy. I blink, but my vision refuses to focus.

"You can forget it." He paces beside the bed. "You're never

going to get out of this compound. You'll never see that kid again." He stops and bends over me until our faces are inches apart. "You'll die when I say that you can die and not a *second* sooner. Do you hear me?"

I groan, weakly twisting away. He grabs hold of my chin and forces our gazes to meet.

"Good. We understand each other." He reaches up and gently streams his fingers through my hair. "You're still a very beautiful woman. Maybe if you soften your heart a little . . . ?"

In horror, I choke on a sob.

He stands. "Fine. Have it your way." He strolls toward the door. "But you'll come around—eventually." He looks up. "Maria, watch her. Make sure that she doesn't do anything *else* foolish."

"Yes, Señor."

He storms out of the room.

I look down at my bandaged wrists and more tears flood my eyes.

"Señorita, why do you insist on angering him?" Maria asks.

Tears swell. I turn my face into my pillow and sob.

Maria pats me on the head. "There. There. Everything is going to be all right."

No it isn't. Nothing will ever be all right ever again.

CHAPTER 28

THE P.I.

Casita de Maya is crawling with cops. I don't dare risk going back in there. Right now I have to figure out how to find my client. I keep calling his cell but the calls go straight to voicemail. I can't give up on my twenty-five million dollar man. I come through Main Street and even take a few trips to the shadier side of town.

No luck.

"C'mon. C'mon. Where are you?" Then like a mirage, he appears in front of me, crossing the crosswalk toward a jewelry shop. "Julian!" I power down the window and shout again. "Julian!"

Cagily, he glances over his shoulder. When he spots me, he rushes over and climbs into the car. "Where in the hell have you been?"

"Looking for you!"

"I went to your room several times and you never answered the door. Two dudes broke into my room and tried to kill me."

"I'm starting to lose count how many people have it out for you."

He shakes his head but he doesn't press me any further. "We have to go to Cartagena," he says suddenly.

"Cartagena? Columbia? Why?"

"I think that's where Cataleyna is being held."

"Where? Who? What?"

"Cataleyna Rosales." He reaches into his back pocket and removes a photo. "This is Cataleyna and she's my fiancée. She's also a cartel princess that has been kidnapped by her father's rivals, the Vazquez brothers. They own and control a lot of territory, but they're originally from Cartagena. I'm willing to bet that's where they've taken her."

"Do you have your memory back?"

"No."

"Then how do you know all of this?"

"Jimmy the bartender. I talked to him for hours. He remembered me. Said I was a regular at the hotel and usually went by the name Tony Montana."

"You sound crazy right now."

"I'm not crazy!"

I stare at him. "How about this, we go and see a friend of mine?"

"No. We don't have time for that. You need to call your pilot friend and see if he can take us to Cartagena."

I laugh—but he doesn't. "You *have* to be joking."

"You don't understand. I've been dreaming about this woman since I woke up in the hospital. I believe I was there the night she was taken. I *have* to find her. And if you won't help me then you can drop me off up at the corner and we can go our separate ways."

Fuck. Fuck. Fuck.

"Are you in?" he asks.

"Of course. Sure," I tell him. My gaze cuts to the rearview mirror and I spot a Benz that I'm almost certain that has been following me since I left Vicente Rosales. What a tangled web I've weaved.

"Call him now," he urges. He's not going to take no for an answer.

I grab my cell phone and call Marcus. At first he laughs, then we haggle and then we strike a deal. Now I have to get word to Vicente Rosales before I end up on his hit list.

CHAPTER 29

THE LOVER

Hours later, Amalia and I are on a private plane for Cartagena, Columbia.

During the long flight, I keep studying Cataleyna's picture. In the back of my mind, I know that there's a chance that she's dead, but I don't want to believe it. Hell, I could be on a wild goose chase to Cartagena. Maybe the Zetas took her or another cartel. Why am I pinning everything on what some chatty bartender says?

Because it's the only thing I have to go on.

After landing, we check into a rundown motel and get one room. This is a time when maybe less flash will do us some good. I don't want Amalia disappearing on me again. I eyeball her, noticing that she's real fidgety lately.

"So what's your plan?" Amalia asks.

"The best I can come up with is we start asking the locals about Carlos and Tomas. Maybe suggest that we got some weight to move."

"You're joking," she says.

I shrug. "What? You got a better idea?"

"Yeah. How about we don't go asking about dangerous

cartels in their backyard? It sounds like the fastest way to end up in the morgue."

"Well, it's all I got. And until your genius ideas kick in why don't we go with mine?" I toss my bag onto the bed while she makes a beeline to the bathroom—with her phone.

"I'll be out in a minute," she says, exasperated.

I nod and watch her close the door. For the first time since we've met, I don't trust Amalia Vega.

CHAPTER 30

THE PRINCESS

I no longer keep track of the days. I don't even give into the pretense of being interested in the things and events around me. I'm also no longer trusted to be alone. Maria and Ruthie watch me in shifts. They wash, clothe and even feed me as if I'm a child.

Most days I sit in front of my locked window, staring at how the waves crash against the jagged rocks. The scene is both violent and beautiful at the same time.

"How much longer do you think that you can keep this up?" Maria asks, running a brush through my thick hair. "Things will go much better if you would be nicer to Señor Vazquez. Clearly, he has feelings for you. Look at the nice dress that he sent to you today." She gestures over to the bed where a shimmering blue Prada gown lies. "Won't you come down and have dinner with him—just this once?"

I refuse to even answer that ridiculous question. The only way that I'd share a meal with that man is if he physically tied me down to a chair, which he'll probably do any day now.

Maria sighs, but at least she finally shuts up.

Hours later, the sun disappears and Maria gathers her things as her shift ends. Out of the corner of my eye, I see Maria drop her door key onto an area rug near the bed. I hold my breath while Maria exchanges a few words with Ruthie by the door.

Slowly, I stand up and wander over to the bed to feign interest in the Prada gown. Picking it up, I stealthily place my foot over the key. After so many months, hope returns.

"Are you thinking about changing your mind, Señorita?" Maria asks.

I scoff and toss the dress back down onto the bed. *"Never!"*

Maria sighs.

There's a rap at the door. The kitchen has sent up my dinner tray. Ruthie opens the door with her key and Maria says her goodbyes and leaves the room.

Hope spreads like a virus through me and a plan formulates. *I'm going to escape*

CHAPTER 31

THE LOVER

I'm a man on a mission.

For days we keep our noses to the grindstone, but everyone we talk to feigns ignorance of the Vazquez cartel or refuses to talk. I must be intimidating most of them because they clam up when I ask them questions.

During this time, I get the distinct impression that we're being followed. Whoever it is, they're good at blending into the background. Whenever I ask Amalia about it, she tries to convince me that after three attempts on my life I'm being paranoid.

She's hiding something.

As a result, I'm alert around her and while casing the streets. Our paths cross a drunken woman at a hole-in-the-wall bar. She rambles on about a baby. At first, I don't pay the woman any attention until the name *Vazquez* crosses her lips. A few patrons hush her, but the liquor has taken hold. I send the woman a few more drinks and keep my ears open.

"They're monsters," she slurs. "That baby never did nothing to nobody. And now the mother is always looking for ways to kill herself. I don't blame her. A cage is a cage is a cage, you know?"

"Maria, lower your voice," her female companion hisses. "You shouldn't talk about such things here."

Maria shoulders the friend away. "Don't shush me. If I want to talk, I'll talk. What are they going to do—throw me into their little dungeon?" She laughs, while looking like she wants to cry at the same time. "What he's doing to that girl is awful." She tosses back her drink.

I signal the bartender to pour another.

Grateful, the large woman twists around on the stool and from our dark corner, I give her a small nod.

"N—now there's a gentleman who knows how to treat a woman," she slurs before continuing to drown her sorrows in the bottom of her glass. Minutes later, she grows loud and belligerent and the bartender throws her and her friend out.

"Showtime," I tell Amalia. We pay our tab and tail the women.

Out on the dark streets, the women struggle to walk a straight line.

"Excuse me, ladies. Can we talk to you for a minute?" I ask.

Maria turns, but spins around too fast and slips out of her kitten heels.

She tumbles to the street and I snatch off my shades and rush to help her up. "Careful, now. You don't want to hurt yourself."

"She's okay," her friend insists. "I can get her home." She tries to push me away.

Maria takes one look into my scarred and burned face and screams her head off. "Oh, Dios mío. Es el Diablo!" Maria scrambles, losing her shoe trying to get away from me.

"What? Wait!"

"Ahhhh!" Not waiting to hear a damn thing, Maria and her friend take off.

Crowds spill out into the street and rubberneck to see what the hell all the commotion is about.

Amalia tugs on my shirt. "We better get out of here."

I look around and don't like the growing crowd. "You're right. Let's go."

We backtrack to our rental car.

"What do you want to do now?" Amalia asks.

"Let's see if we can catch up with them. They're walking so maybe they live around here."

Instead of starting the car, Amalia huffs out a long breath.

"Problem?"

"Do you think that is a good idea? The woman was terrified of you."

"I need her to talk to me—to tell me where the Vazquez compound is located."

Amalia shakes her head.

"Two minutes," I tell her. "That's all."

Sighing, she starts the car. "Okay."

We cruise off into the direction the two drunken women ran off. Less than a mile down the road, we spot them stumbling through a row of shanty houses. A man steps out of one of the houses and shouts at Maria and her condition. The two go at it even as she pushes her way into the house. Their screaming voices carry throughout the neighborhood. None of the neighbors react, which tells me this is a normal thing with them. An hour later, the fighting ends and the unmistakable sounds of fucking emanate from the house.

"We got a screamer," Amalia jokes.

My gut knots in frustration.

"So *now* what?" she asks.

"What else? We wait."

CHAPTER 32

THE PRINCESS

I didn't mean to hurt Ruthie, but my anxiety and fear made me strike her head harder than I intended. It was a rare chance when I got her out of view of the room's cameras and I attacked. I don't check for a pulse and I push my guilt to the back of my mind. I jet for the door with Maria's key.

Fear nearly paralyzes me but somehow I find the courage to push through. I ease out of the door and creep through the long hallway. It takes forever to reach the end of the damn thing and, even then, I expect to run into a pack of guards or even Carlos and Tomas themselves. But there's nobody here.

The voice in the back of my head parrots that I'm walking into a trap, but I keep placing one foot in front of the other. One hall leads to another and then another. Am I trapped in a maze?

Maybe I should try one of the doors? I don't like that idea. There's no telling what I might find in this place. Maybe I went the wrong way. Maybe I should've taken a left from the room instead of a right.

I turn around, but doubt that I can remember all the turns I've made.

Suddenly, there are voices. Men talking. Panicking, I reach

for the nearest door and then offer up a quick prayer of thanks when I discover it isn't locked. However, the door doesn't lead to a room, but to a staircase.

Tears of relief swell and roll down my face as I tackle the stairs two at a time. It didn't matter that I don't have a plan. I only know that I have to get out of this stone prison. Down and down the stairwell until I'm certain that I've reached the pit of hell. A new wave of panic washes over me. At the bottom of the staircase, I stand still as my eyes adjust to the darkness. It's freezing. I wrap my arms around myself for protection and to ward off the cold.

Clang! Clang! Clang!

I jump back and then trip over the bottom stair. When I hit the ground, the wind rushes out of me.

"W—Who's out there?" a gruff voice rumbles through the dark, dank air.

I scramble to get back up, but before I take off up the stairs, the voice asks another question. "What day is it?"

I stop.

"Please. Talk to me," he begs. "It's been days since someone has been down here."

The man's desperation pulls at my heart. Despite my best judgment, I turn around and inch further into the darkness. The deeper I go the colder it gets. Every hair on my body stands at attention while goose bumps pimple my skin.

This is a bad idea.

Still, I keep moving. At the end of the corridor, I round a corner and finally see a pool of moonlight flood through a stone window with iron bars. I can also see that I'm in an underground prison. Metal drags against the stone floor and then a pair of dark hands wraps around two bars.

"Are you still there?" the voice rasps.

I stop, certain that I've reached the end of my rope of courage.

"Please," he begs. "Some water."

"I don't have any—"

"Over there." He gestures toward what looks like an iron bucket propped up on a wooden table.

I don't move.

"Please." He drops to his knees and bows his thick, shaggy head. "Please."

I close my eyes and tell myself that I shouldn't care what happens to this man. I have my own damn problems and I don't know how much time I have before my captors—our captors—discover I'm gone. I open my eyes, but don't turn to leave.

You can take two minutes to give him some water.

Sucking in a deep breath, I move forward again.

"Thank you," he says, before I help him. "Thank you."

I reach the bucket. There's water but nothing for me to pour it into. "I, uh . . ."

The man coughs and hacks so hard that I can hear his ribs rattling in his chest. It sounds horrible and painful.

I pick up the whole bucket, carry it over and set it down at the bars.

Immediately, he dives his hands into the small pool of liquid and scoops as much as he can into his mouth. He gets more on him than in him.

I flinch, watching him go at it like an animal.

"Thank you. Thank you." He turns his beaten, black-and-blue face up.

Recognition bolts through me and I jump to my feet and scream.

Unfortunately, I hadn't heard the man who'd walked up behind me, but I bump right into him. I scream again and whip around.

"Ah, here you are." Tomas grins. "You've been a bad girl again."

CHAPTER 33

THE CAPTOR

My princess has claws. I like that. I smile the whole way back to her room. On the floor is a still very unconscious Ruthie. I should've known better than to have a child watch Cataleyna. After all, she is a Rosales. Being evil and conniving surely runs through her veins.

As I tuck her back into bed, I can't help but notice how angelic she looks with moonlight spilling onto her face. Entranced, I caress her smooth, heart-shaped face. I never understood my brother's fascination—until recently. Carlos fell for Cataleyna the first moment he laid eyes on her. Then he watched her when she would sneak away from under her father's watchful eye to meet her lover: Vicente's right hand man, Julian Arias. Both men were like dogs in heat, following her wherever she went. Carlos would even bug the hotel rooms the lovers frequented so that he could watch the couple make love.

It was an obsession.

I was convinced that Carlos had lost it, but he managed to talk me into this kidnapping scheme. I went along because I wanted to strike back at a man whom our father went to the grave battling. Carlos did it because he simply wanted something that he couldn't have.

Now I'm wondering if I've fallen under her spell, too.

I stand from the bed, order one of my men to take Maria's niece out of the room, and then head back to my office. As soon as I enter, the phone rings.

"Patrón, we have another sighting."

I exhale a frustrated breath. "Are you sure that it's him this time?"

"I'm not, patrón, but we're fielding an awful lot of calls all around town."

"In Cartagena?"

"Yes, sir. What do you want us to do?"

"Have *you* personally seen him?"

After a long pause, my man responds, "No."

I sigh. I'm not about to send out a whole cavalry for another false alarm.

"Patrón?"

"You and Stefan check it out and report back to me. If it's him, you know what to do."

"You got it."

CHAPTER 34

THE LOVER

We sit on Maria for two days. The stakeout is pure hell between Amalia and me. It gets so bad that we start snapping at each other. I can't figure her out and I can't get her to tell me who she's constantly calling.

"Look. If you need to get back to your life in Playa del Carmen, I understand. I'm out of money and you got to know that it's going to take me a while to pay this tab I'm running up."

"No. It's all right. I want to see this through. If you think you can rescue this fiancée then I want to help."

"Really?" I ask, dubiously.

"Really," she says, avoiding my eyes.

Maria emerges from the house looking like a completely different woman. All cleaned up, she looks like a nurse or a caregiver.

I'm convinced that we're finally going get some answers. "Don't lose her."

"I'm on it." Amalia starts the car.

As we make it to the town's main road, a black Mercedes pulls up next to us. I glance their way in time to see the barrel of a gun. "Amalia, drive!" I go for my piece, but it's too late.

A barrage of bullets flies our way.

My window explodes as Amalia jams her foot onto the accelerator.

I'm waving and blinking away shards of glass as another blast goes off.

Despite all hell breaking loose, Amalia guns the car through the streets of Cartagena like a pro. "Shit. Hold on," she orders, making a sharp right on two wheels.

I finally get hold of my weapon and fire back—only the bullets bounce off our attacker's vehicle.

"See? This is what you get when you start asking around about drug cartels," Amalia shouts, making another sharp turn. Then I hear her cry, "FUCK!" She slams on the brakes. Tires screech. Rubber burns.

I fly into the dashboard and hear a rib crack.

Crash!

The car flips. Once. Twice. Three times.

Without our seatbelts buckled, we're tossed around like rags until the car slams violently into its roof.

In shock, I can't feel my body. Blood drips into my eyes. *Where's Amalia?* I turn my head, but I can't find her. *Was she thrown from the car?* I try to call out, but can't. I hear feet running toward me, but then tires screech and another eruption of gunfire explodes around the car.

What in the hell is going on?

While the war rages on outside, pain seeps into my nervous system.

A head pokes in through the broken window.

"Is he alive?" someone asks.

The man reaches in and touches me.

I groan.

"He's alive!"

"Grab him and let's get the fuck out of there before more of those muthafuckas show up."

When the man grabs me by the shoulders and drags me out over broken glass I nearly black out.

"Hurry! *Hurry!*"

Once I'm out of the car, the big muscle-head tosses me over a meaty shoulder.

"Let's go. *Let's go!*"

My head ringing, I try to hang on for as long as I can, but the pull of oblivion is too strong. I close my eyes and immediately see Cataleyna's face. Shame and guilt overwhelm me. I'm never going to find her.

I've failed.

CHAPTER 35

THE BOSS

Cartagena Colombia . . .

"What the fuck do you mean lost him?" I thunder. "How in the hell did you lose him?"

My men stutter and stammer. "W—we tried to detain him after the accident, but some goons showed up and took out two of our men. By the time backup arrived, they—disappeared."

"Of course. We're on their fucking turf. They were bound to find them, especially with them roaming around asking questions like that. Maybe that damn P.I. wasn't lying about his amnesia."

"Well—she's dead," one of the men, says. "She was thrown from the car."

"And my money?" I ask.

"We're looking for it," he says. "I'm sure that she stashed it somewhere close."

Pulling in an angry breath, I try to think of my next move. Vega said that her client believed that Cataleyna was brought here. I don't know how much of this amnesia story was true or if they were leading me on yet another wild goose chase. Now with both of them gone, I'm back to square one. Do I pack up and head back home or see if I can get anywhere near the Vazquez compound?

Suddenly, a stabbing pain seizes my right side. I struggle to breathe. "No, God, please, not yet."

The pain intensifies and I slump out of my wheelchair and hit the floor.

"Boss, are you all right?" My men scramble around me.

"No. No. No," I beg. "Not until I see my daughter again." My vision blurs, and my breathing thins.

"Hold on. We're going to get you some help!"

I roll onto my back as my life story speeds before my eyes. It's all there: The pain, the mistakes and then, lastly, the two greatest joys of my life. Isabella and Cataleyna. "Please God, don't take me yet. Please. Not until I see my daughter again. *Please.*"

CHAPTER 36

THE LOVER

*W*here the fuck am I?

Ears ringing, head spinning, I glance around. I'm in a huge room with grand furniture that looks familiar. I sit up, but everything gets worse, especially the pain. I push through it until I'm on my feet. My chest is bound and my clothes have been changed.

By who?

I creep around the room, looking for anything that I can use as a weapon. There's nothing. I head toward the door, halfway expecting it to be locked.

It's not.

"Hello?"

Nothing.

I step out of the room and peer down the hallway. "Hello?"

Silence.

I ease out further as the ringing and spinning intensifies. Images, one after another, flicker inside of my head. A full life flashes. A woman. A man. *My parents?*

Laughter. Sunshine. Children. Love. Heartache. Obsession. Pain.

I'm overwhelmed and nausated.

Moon. Rain. Gunfire. Scream.

Dropping to my knees, I struggle to catch my breath.

Someone comes up behind me. "Good to see you're finally awake."

I turn and my gazes crash into a dark figure. A name tumbles to my lips. "Carlos," I growl. "Where is she?"

The man stares at me. "Are you all right?"

"I know that you have her. Tell me where she is!"

"Is this some kind of joke? If it is, it's not funny." He smiles. "I don't know how you pulled it off," he says. "I thought you were dead."

"Sorry to disappoint you. Now where is she, Carlos?" The ringing in my head grows louder. The images fly at warp speed. "Where's Cataleyna?"

"Carlos? What are you talking about? I'm not Carlos."

"Don't play me for a fool. I know you have Cataleyna."

"Of course I do."

"Then where is she?" I surge to my feet and yank him to me. "I'll fucking kill you if you've harmed one hair on her head. Where is she, Carlos?"

He jerks out of my grip. "What the fuck is wrong with you? And what's this Carlos shit? I'm not Carlos—*you* are!"

CHAPTER 37

THE VILLAIN

The ringing in my ears is deafening. "What?"

"I'm Tomas. Why in the hell do you think that I'm you?" He cocks his head and frowns.

I shake my head and take a retreating step. "You're trying to confuse me. I know who you are. Don't change the subject. Where is she?"

"Cataleyna?"

"Of course Cataleyna! She's here, isn't she?"

Tomas weighs his answer. "Yes. I brought and kept her like we originally planned. Don't you remember?"

Moon. Rain. Gunfire. Scream.

"I—I . . ."

Moon. Rain. Gunfire. Scream.

"I have to see her. Take me to her," I demand.

Tomas shakes his head.

"I said take me to her!"

"Not until you tell me what the hell is going on with you. Why don't you remember who I am—who you are?"

"I told you I *know* . . ." The room spins faster. ". . . who you . . . are." More images assault me. Me as a kid, holidays, a father bouncing me on his knee. Me playing with another kid—a kid that looks like the man before me.

But that doesn't make sense. "I'm . . . Julian."

"Julian Arias?" Tomas throws his head back and laughs. "Who in the hell told you that?"

"I—I . . ." I struggle to think straight with the ringing and the memories. "I remember . . ."

Tomas turns and walks into the next room.

"Hey! Where are you going?"

Tomas ignores the question and picks up a silver picture frame and holds it up. "Look familiar?"

I glance down and recognized myself smiling in a cap and gown with this man by my side. "I . . . don't . . . understand."

"We're brothers. You're Carlos Demetrius Vazquez and I'm your younger brother Tomas."

I can't pull my eyes from the photograph.

"You want to meet Julian Arias? All right. I'll introduce you to him." Tomas marches out of the room, certain that I'll follow his lead.

I do—all the way down to the house cellar. I remember this place. My father, Alejandro, built it. The dungeon is where he— *we* make people disappear. Tomas leads me to an iron cage. Inside, a man who is just a pile of skin, bones, and matted hair is curled in a corner.

"Julian, you have another visitor," Tomas barks.

The man doesn't move.

Tomas turns and grabs a metal rod and bangs on the bars. "Wake up. *Wake up!*" He produces a set of keys and opens the cage.

I walk inside.

The man lifts his head. "Cat?" he asks.

I stare at the man's beaten and deformed face.

Tomas chuckles. "I hope that you don't mind, but I had a little fun with him while you were gone." He turns and looks at me with open emotion. "I blamed him for what happened to you that night on the boat. I thought that you were dead. When you went over the side . . ."

I remember. A gun battle on the boat. I wrestled with this man. Tomas shot at him but Cataleyna stepped in front of him, knocking us all overboard. "I'm Carlos."

Tomas nods with a wide smile. "Is it coming back to you now?"

I ignore him and kneel in front of the *real* Julian. Without even thinking, I wrap my hands around his neck and squeeze with everything I have.

Julian doesn't resist. It's as if he welcomes death. He chokes and turns a deep purple.

Disgusted, I fling him away.

Tomas laughs and pats me on the back. "Welcome back, *brother.*"

Now I remember everything: the months I watched Julian with his paws all over the woman I'd fallen in love with at first sight, an enemy's daughter, who I was determined to have at any cost.

"I don't understand how you're here . . . or where you've been," Tomas says. "I'm having a hard time wrapping my brain around all of this."

"I woke up in a hospital three months ago in Playa del Carmen. I couldn't remember who I was." I look at Julian again. "I thought I was him."

"However it happened. I'm glad you're back." Tomas laughs and then embraces me. "Welcome home."

I pull out of my shock and return my brother's embrace. However, I still have one question. "Cataleyna?"

There's a beat of hesitation. "I'll take you to her."

CHAPTER 38

THE PRINCESS

I wake with my entire face throbbing in pain. When I look around, I'm crushed to see that I'm still in my golden cage. "Julian." I press a hand over my mouth, remembering the beaten and broken man down in the basement. Though he was black and blue with eyes swollen shut, I know it was him. Has he been down there all this time?

A key rattles in the door.

I freeze, clutching the bedding in my tight fist.

The door creaks open and the Vazquez brothers walk into the room. My mind goes wild. "What the fuck do you want?" I shout, inching away from them across the bed.

Tomas hits on the light switch and floods the room with light. "Like I told you. Safe and sound."

A scarred and burned Carlos enters into the room. I glare at him in horror and disgust.

"You're here. I knew that I'd find you," Carlos gushes with visible relief.

I frown and keep moving backward until I fall over the side of the bed.

"Careful!" He races over to help.

"Don't touch me!"

"I want to make sure that you're all—"

"I said don't touch me!" I spin my hands like a propeller, hitting him in the face, chest, and head.

"*Stop it!*"

"You're both monsters! I hate you! I hate you! I hate you!" One punch catches Carlos in the lip. He explodes with anger and backhands me so hard that I crash back against the wall, sobbing.

Blinking, he immediately does a one-eighty and kneels down. "Cat, baby. I'm *so* sorry. I didn't mean to do that. I don't know what came over me."

I shrink away. "Go away! Leave me alone."

"I—"

"*Go away!*"

Gritting his teeth, he checks his anger. "All right. I'll—let you get some rest." Reluctantly, he stands and backs away. "I'll be back tomorrow. We can talk then—get to know each other."

"What?" I stare, shaking my head. "When are you two going to get it through your heads. I don't want to have anything to do with you. *Ever!*" I turn and throw everything I can get my hands on: a brush, a mirror, and a lamp. "Get out! Get out! *Get out!*" I wail at him until I've backed him and his sadistic brother to the door.

Defeated, Carlos turns and walks out behind his brother.

After its slams, I slump against the door.

"She'll calm down," I hear Tomas promise. "You have all the time you need, you'll bring her around."

My tears fall faster.

Carlos's voice rumbles through the door where I huddle shaking. "Yeah. She'll come around. After all, we have plenty of time."

I bow my head and cry.

CHAPTER 39

THE VILLAIN

Tomas's smile widens. "I can't fucking believe that you're really here." He stares at the scars on my face. "You look like shit, but I'm glad you're back home."

"Good to be back." We embrace with genuine affection. Memories of our close upbringing flood my head. Tomas is more than my brother, he's my best friend.

"This is a cause for celebration."

We head downstairs for a few drinks. The moment we step into the office, I notice the bank of monitors—all dedicated to Cataleyna's room. My hackles rise and I cut a look to my brother as he heads straight to the bar.

"Your usual?" he asks.

"Yeah. Sure." I eyeball him and then the bank of monitors again. "Did she give you much trouble?"

"Who?" Tomas glances to the monitor again. "Oh. You mean *her?* No. Though I did have to do a little dirty work and get rid of her love child."

"What?"

Tomas pours our drinks. "Don't worry. I had Maria and her niece Ruthie take care of the problem. Seems as though our little angel was soiled goods."

"*Our?*" My eyes narrow as suspicion creeps up my spine.

"Slip of the tongue." Tomas walks over and hands me my drink. "Cheers." He taps my glass in a lackluster toast—all the while avoiding my gaze.

"Where's the kid?"

"Dead." Tomas smiles. "The last thing the world needs is another bastard, right?"

I twirl the liquor inside of my glass while studying Tomas. "And what about you and Cataleyna?"

Tomas slips on a blank mask. "What do you mean?"

I'm not fooled and I'm sure that it shows on my face. "I've been gone a long time. You thought I was dead. You said so yourself."

"Yeah. So?"

Suspicion turns to anger. "So—she's a beautiful woman and you're a man. Anything happen between the two of you while I was . . . missing?"

"No." Tomas laughs, but it sounds fake as hell.

"No?" My blood boils. "Are you sure that's what you want to go with?"

Tomas's awkward laugh downgrades to awkward, puttering chuckles. His mask cracks. "C'mon," he says, going for the con. "You know that I wouldn't lie to you."

The room falls silent.

At the moment I can't think of a single time when my brother has lied to me or stabbed me in the back, but there's a first time for everything. "So what was the plan?"

"Plan?" Tomas shrugs and shakes his head. "No plan. For a long time I was holding out hope that you'd be found and . . . here you are!" Another awkward laugh.

I take the first sip of my drink, my temper rising.

Tomas returns to the bar for another drink.

I steal another look at the monitors and see Cataleyna pressed up against the door. By the way her shoulders are trembling, I know that she's crying. My heart goes out to her.

I wish she would allow me to comfort her and soothe her fears. I'm not such a bad guy. I can make her happy—make her love me.

When my attention returns to Tomas, I'm stunned to see the gun in his hand pointed at me. Now I have my answer. He has fallen in love with her, too.

"Why did you come back?" Tomas asks, shaking his head.

"So I take it that you're no longer happy to see me."

"I am—*was,* but . . ." He cuts a look to the monitors and then back. "I can't give her up—not even for you. I'm sorry, but I'm in love with her."

Enraged, I lunge for the gun.

Tomas is caught off guard and we tumble to the floor. The gun fires a wild shot as it's knocked out of my brother's hand.

Physically matched, we wrestle and exchange punches until we're bloody and slick with sweat.

Finally, Tomas gets the upper hand and dives for the gun. A hot pain pierces my shoulder. I push that shit aside and seize the hand with the gun.

He fires another shot, but it goes wild.

"You should have never come back," Tomas growls.

"And you should have remained loyal," I say, crushing his wrist and cutting the gun in his direction.

A fourth shot rings out.

Tomas' body jumps and his eyes go wide before settling on me.

Regret crashes into me as I watch the light fade in his eyes. At long last he collapses, dead. I shove him off and climb to my feet. At the door there's a crowd of our soldiers standing and watching wide-eyed—no doubt they didn't know which brother to jump in and try to help.

I look at them with my brother's blood all over my shirt. But before I can utter a word, the sound of gunfire fills the air.

Rat-a-tat-tat-tat

Rat-a-tat-tat-tat

What the fuck? An alarm goes off. We're under attack.

CHAPTER 40

THE PRINCESS

Gunfire rips through the night.

What in the hell is that? I jump to my feet and race to my locked window.

Rat-ta-tat-tat-tat

Rat-ta-tat-tat-tat

The compound is under attack. Hope returns and surges through my veins, but then I quickly tamp it back. It could be anyone laying siege. I could easily exchange this cage for another one—or they'll kill me along with everyone else in this place. But death no longer scares me.

I listen as the battle rages for almost an hour. I pace back and forth, anxious to know what's going on. Finally, a boot kicks in my door.

I burrow myself into a corner until a miracle wheels through the door. *"Papa!"* I leap up and race into his arms. "You found me! You finally found me!"

"Cataleyna," he chokes with emotion. "Is it you? Is it really you?"

"Yes, Papa! Yes. It's really me." I squeeze his neck even tighter. When I lean back, I note the change in his face. "What happened to you? Why are you in a wheelchair?"

"We can talk about that later. Let's get you out of here. *Nicco!*"

"But—" then I remember. *"Julian!"* I jump out of papa's lap. "We have to save Julian!"

"What? Wait. I don't—"

"Please, papa. He's in the dungeon. They've been torturing him this whole time." I temple my hands and beg. "I love him, papa."

He wars with his emotions. He clearly wants to tell me no.

"Nicco," my father shouts.

"Yes, boss?"

"Help me down to this dungeon."

A few minutes later, I lead my father and team of his men to the dungeon. But when we find Julian, my heart stops. *"Julian!"* I race to him, afraid for the worst, but then I find a faint pulse. "*He's alive!* We have to get him out of here! Papa, *please!*"

My father stares at Julian, who has been reduced to a sack of bones "All right, Cataleyna. Anything for you."

My father's men quickly take hold of Julian and rush us through the compound's battlefield to the waiting black vans.

"Did you find them?" My father shouts to another soldier.

"One of them, sir. We found Tomas dead in an office. We're still searching for Carlos."

Tomas is dead? I can hardly believe it. But if Carlos gets away I will never be safe.

The van door is slammed closed and I huddle next to Julian, whispering encouraging words the whole time. "We're getting you out of here. You're going to make it. *We're* going to make it. You'll see."

Slowly, Julian lolls his head toward me, but his eyes are so swollen, I don't know if he can even see me.

"Cat?" he whispers. "Is it really you?"

I gather his head into my lap. "I'm here, Julian. I'm always here for you."

His busted and bloody lips curl into a faint smile. "I love you."

"I love you, too." I bow my head and then pray the whole way toward the hospital.

EPILOGUE

THE VILLAIN

Three years later . . .

There's not a day, hour, or minute that I don't think about Cataleyna Rosales-Arias. All the hell I went through to kidnap her, only to lose her and my memory, and then the very day I get her back, I lose her all over again.

She's with *him* now: The *real* Julian. Somehow that sack of shit survived. It's my fault for not snapping his damn neck when I had the chance.

"Daddy! Daddy! *Look!*"

I glance up at my little Cataleyna twirling in her new princess costume. "*Ahhh.* You look beautiful, baby girl." I smile and stretch out my arms. "Come give Daddy a kiss."

My little girl beams a smile up and races into my arms.

I smother her with kisses and she breaks out in giggles. She looks exactly like her mother: black hair, soulful brown eyes, and her angelic heart-shaped face.

"Guess who is the most beautiful girl in the whole wide world?"

Little Cat giggles. "*I* am."

"That's right. And Daddy loves you very much." I place another kiss against her forehead and tell her, "Now go and play with your friends. They are here for your birthday."

"Okay." She pokes out her bottom lip, but then quickly joins the other children at the party.

Turns out, Maria and Ruthie didn't kill Cataleyna's baby like Tomas had ordered. Instead, they hid her in town. When I found out, I had them bring her to me. This way, I have a little of Cataleyna for myself. I'll raise her alone—for now. One day, we will both be reunited with her mother.

Cataleyna thinks she's safe in her new marriage to Julian Arias. Recently, they had their second child, but I'm watching. I'll always be watching.

DON'T MISS

Boss Divas by De'nesha Diamond

The most lethal ride-or-die women in Memphis now run their gangs and the streets. But the aftermath of an all-out war means merciless new enemies, time-bomb secrets . . . and one chance to take it all . . .

Available now wherever books and ebooks are sold.

CHAPTER 1

TA'SHARA

"STOP THE FUCKING CAR!"

Profit slams on the brakes while I bolt out of the passenger car door and race into the night toward my foster parents' burning house.

"TRACEE! REGGIE!" *They're not in there. Please, God. Don't let them be in there.* "TRACEE! REGGIE!"

"Ta'Shara, wait up," Profit yells. His long strides eat up the distance between us even as I shove my way through the city's emergency responders. I've never seen flames stretch so high or felt such intense heat. Still, none of that shit stops me. In my delusional mind, there is still time to get them out of there.

"Hey, lady. You can't go in there," someone shouts and makes a grab for me.

As I draw closer to the front porch, Profit is able to wrap one of his powerful arms around my waist and lift me off my feet. "Baby, stop. You can't go in there."

"Let me go!" My legs pedal in the air as I stretch uselessly for the door. "TRACEE! REGGIE!" My screams rake my throat raw.

Profit drags me away from the growing flames.

Men in uniform rush over to us. I don't know who they are and I don't care. I just need to know one thing. "Where are my parents? Did they make it out?"

"Ma'am, calm down. Please tell me your name."

"WHERE ARE THEY?"

"Ma'am—"

"ANSWER ME, DAMMIT!"

"C'mon, man," Profit says. "Give my girl something."

The fireman draws a deep breath and then drops a bomb that changes my life forever.

"The neighbors reported the fire. Right now, I'm not aware of anyone making it out of the house. I'm sorry."

"NOOOOOOO!" I collapse in Profit's arms. He hauls me up against his six-three frame and I lay my head on his broad chest. Before, I found comfort in his strong embrace, but not tonight. I sob uncontrollably as pain overwhelms me, but then I make out a familiar car down the street.

"Oh. My. God."

Profit tenses. "What?"

My eyes aren't deceiving me. Sitting behind the wheel of her burgundy Crown Victoria is LeShelle with a slow smile creeping across her face. She forms a gun with her hand and pretends to fire at us.

We're next.

LeShelle tosses back her head and, despite the siren's wail, the roaring fire, and the chaos around me, that bitch's maniacal laugh rings in my ears.

How much more of this shit am I going to take? When will this fuckin' bullshit end?

BOOM!

The crowd gasps when windows explode from the top floor of the house, but my gaze never waivers from LeShelle. My tears dry up as anger grips me.

She did this shit. I don't need a jury to tell me that the bitch is guilty as hell. How long has she been threatening the

Douglases' lives? Why in the hell didn't I believe that she would follow through?

LeShelle has proven her ruthlessness time after time. This fucking "Gangster Disciples versus the Vice Lords" shit ain't a game to her. It's a way of life. And she doesn't give a fuck who she hurts.

My blood boils and all at once everything burst out of me. I wrench away from Profit's protective arms and take off toward LeShelle in a rage.

"I'M GOING TO FUCKING KILL YOU!"

"Ta'Shara, no!" Profit shouts.

I ignore him as I race toward LeShelle's car. My hot tears burn tracks down my face.

LeShelle laughs in my face and then pulls off from the curb, but not before I'm able to pound my fist against the trunk.

Profit's arms wrap back around my waist, but I kick out and connect with LeShelle's taillight and shatter that mutherfucka. The small wave of satisfaction I get is quickly erased when her piece-of-shit car burps out a black cloud of exhaust in my face.

"NO! Don't let her get away. No!"

"Ta'Shara, please. Not now. Let it go!"

Let it go? I round on Profit. "How the fuck can you say that shit?"

BOOM!

More windows explode, drawing my attention back to the only place that I've ever called home. My heart claws its way out of my chest as orange flames and black smoke lick the sky.

My legs give out and my knees kiss the concrete, and all the while Profit's arms remain locked around me. I can't hear what he's saying because my sobs drown him out.

"This is all my fault," tumbles over my tongue. I conjure up an image of Tracee and Reggie—the last time I saw them. It's a horrible memory. Everyone was angry and everyone said things that . . . can never be taken back.

Grief consumes me. I squeeze my eyes tight and cling to the ghosts inside of my head. "I'm sorry. I'm so sorry."

Profit's arms tighten. I melt in his arms even though I want to lash out. *Isn't it his fault my foster parents roasted in that house, too?* When the question crosses my mind, I crumble from the weight of my shame.

I'm to blame. No one else.

A heap in the center of the street, I lay my head against Profit's chest again and take in the horrific sight through a steady sheen of tears. The Douglases were good people. All they wanted was the best for me and for me to believe in myself. They would've done the same for LeShelle if she gave them the chance.

LeShelle fell in love with the streets and the make-believe power of being the head bitch of the Queen Gs. I didn't want anything to do with any of that bullshit, but it didn't matter. I'm viewed as GD property by blood, and the shit hit the fan when I fell in love with Profit—a Vice Lord by blood. Back then Profit wasn't a soldier yet. But our being together was taken as a sign of disrespect. LeShelle couldn't let it slide.

However, the harder I fight the streets' politics, the deeper I'm dragged into her bullshit world of gangs and violence.

"I should have killed her when I had the chance." If I had, Tracee and Reggie would still be alive. "She won't get away with this," I vow. "I'm going to kill her if it's the last thing I do."

DON'T MISS

Wife Extraordinaire Returns by Kiki Swinson

Trice Davis and her husband, Troy, only had prize money on their minds when they signed up for the reality show *Trading Wives*—a knock-off of *Wife Swap*. The fact that they were swapping with a couple they knew, Leon and Charlene, made it seem harmless. But that couldn't have been farther from the truth . . .

Available now wherever books and ebooks are sold.

CHAPTER 1

TRICE

"Leon! No! Please stop!" I screamed, feeling blood rushing to my face.

"Motherfucker! You thought I was gonna let you fuck my wife and take yours back and live happily ever after?!" Leon yelled as he waved the gun at Troy.

Troy looked like a man possessed. His eyes were bloodshot, and his fists were curled tightly.

"Fuck you, nigga! I didn't fuck that skank Charlene! But you wasted no time fucking my wife!" Troy growled as he lunged at Leon. I ran to come between them. I didn't want them to fight over me. Just as I came toward Troy, I stopped in my tracks.

BAM! BAM! I heard the shots so loudly I didn't even feel any pain.

I could feel myself screaming, but amazingly, I couldn't hear myself. Next, I felt a hot burning sensation envelope my body.

BAM! BAM! Two more shots and everything in my world went black.

I jumped out of my sleep covered in sweat. I swallowed hard and looked over at Troy. He was sleeping soundly as usual. I guess it was easy for him, since he wasn't the one who'd almost died. I had been severely shot and almost died. The hospital staff saved my life when Troy thought the lifeless body covered with a white sheet belonged to me. He didn't know it, but I had been taken out of that operating room long before the other person had been brought in. God rest her soul.

Luckily for me, two shots went straight through—one in my shoulder, the other in my arm. It was the third shot that had done me damage. As a result, I had my spleen removed. But what hurt most were the infidelities that transpired between all of us. I don't remember much about that night, except that Troy had come over to the hotel I was hiding out in. Unfortunately, Leon came as well. Things escalated when Troy realized that during the spouse trade, Leon and I had had sex. As it turned out, it wasn't my fault things with Leon and I had gone to that level.

Leon's wife, Charlene, had convinced me that she had had sex with my husband first. She had said some very cruel things to me over the phone, and I was crushed to my core. When she told me Troy had just finished eating her out and that he was *indisposed*, as she put it, I was devastated beyond belief.

Out of revenge and hurt, I slept with Leon. I had no idea the feelings would grow into what we did. So, when he got sentenced to all that time, I was hurt.

It had been seven months since my husband, Troy, and I had participated in the hit reality show *Trading Spouses*. It had also been seven months since that fucking show ruined our lives and the lives of Troy's best friend, Leon, and his wife, Charlene.

The guys had been childhood buddies and best friends almost all of their lives. They had done everything together growing up, but all of that changed. When we'd agreed to trade spouses for one week for ten thousand dollars, none of us knew it wouldn't be worth it in the end. Because Charlene disconnected the cameras in our house, we were sanctioned and no was paid one red cent. The TV execs did pay for my medical bills, but aside from that, we didn't get shit.

Troy and I tried to repair our marriage in the aftermath of it all. But in my eyes, it was over. When I found out I was pregnant, I decided it would probably be best for me to hold on to someone for the baby's sake . . . rather than becoming a statistic.

Troy was the closest thing.

I looked around my bedroom, and a cold feeling came over me just thinking about the shit that had happened. I touched my very pregnant belly and felt my baby move inside of me. I closed my eyes and sighed. *Baby* was the operative word . . . because the father was an issue. Although Troy believed it was his baby, I thought for sure I knew differently.

"Trice? You okay, baby?" Troy asked, rousing from his sleep. I kept my back to him and closed my eyes.

"I'm fine. Just another nightmare," I said without looking at him.

Troy reached out and rubbed his hands over my back. His touch made me feel dirty and partly guilty. I had been thinking about Leon in that moment.

"How's my little bun in the oven doing?" Troy asked, still rubbing my back.

"Fine. The baby is fine," I replied, a little annoyed. I stood up swiftly and grabbed my robe from the end of our bed. I rolled my eyes as I left the room. I shuddered at Troy being all mushy and loving. He had been nothing but good to me since the entire incident with Leon. But I couldn't get my feelings to change toward him for anything. Somewhere in the back of my mind, I blamed Troy for everything that had happened.

I was still convinced he'd slept with Charlene. The producers of the show couldn't help me disprove it. And since that dumb bitch Charlene had disconnected the camera wires, that didn't do shit for my suspicions. Why else would she have disconnected the cameras if they weren't fucking?

I knew all about how grimy Charlene was from Leon. He told me how she was a lazy hood rat that barely took care of their son, and she never did any of the cleaning around the house. She was uneducated, and all she did was hustle the welfare system to make extra money. In other words, Charlene was a bum bitch.

Leon had assured me repeatedly that I had way more class than Charlene. He had also aired Troy's dirty laundry by telling me that Troy had thought about cheating on me once. Troy had gotten so close that he and the girl were naked before he backed out of it. Leon also told me that Troy complained that I didn't fuck him enough or suck his dick at all. Wasn't that some bullshit?

It was just like Troy to tell half the fucking story. I knew Leon wasn't making shit up because it was true. I refused to suck Troy's dick, and I also rationed out the pussy. I loved Troy for how good he was as a provider and person, but his dick game was whack. His dick was so skinny and short that most times I couldn't even feel it. It was like getting fucked by a baby.

When Troy and I dated, I tried to ignore the horrible sex by keeping my eye on the prize. The prize was having a house, nice car, nice things, and of course, security. I thought I could just look past the fact that his sex was horrendous and fall in love with everything else, like Troy's personality. He had the ability to provide the fairy-tale life we had.

Well, after we got married, I just couldn't do it. I tried and tried. Troy would beg for sex, and sometimes I would just give in for argument's sake. Most times, I would lie there praying for it to be over . . . all five minutes of it. I mean, he even had the nerve to be a fucking two-minute brother with a small dick.

I tried buying sex toys and that worked for a while, but sometimes I longed for some good ol' righteous hard dick. I wanted and needed some real skin-to-skin contact, not that plastic feeling from my toys. I wanted a man to use his God-given gift to dig my back out. Unfortunately for Troy, during the spouse trade, that's exactly what happened. Leon's dick was huge and oh so good. And during our lovemaking, I had an orgasm for the first time in ten years. Leon had fucked me in several different positions that I never dared to try with Troy. It was frustrating as hell to always have Troy's little dick fall out of my pussy. I couldn't imagine how frustrated I would get trying anything other than our traditional missionary position. Hell, even when we did the doggie position, his little dick would constantly slip out.

But Leon was different. He had me hooked. Although I was fighting the reality of what he had done to me. I tried to put Leon and his sex out of my mind, but between feeling vulnerable after finding out that Troy had the nerve to cheat on me with Charlene and having Leon comfort me with that beautiful piece of meat, I was all in. I was head over heels for Leon so fast that I had amazed even myself. I was ready to walk away from my marriage and even live a more modest life. Leon wasn't as successful and didn't have as much as Troy, but the sex had me ready to throw it all away—the house, the cars, the fat bank account, and everything Troy did for me.

But I knew Troy . . . and he wouldn't let go that easily.

I shook off the thoughts of Leon and his wonderful dick as I walked out of the bedroom and headed downstairs. It was still dark outside. I shuffled my swollen feet into the kitchen and poured a glass of milk. I quietly lifted a metal canister off the top of the refrigerator and retrieved the secret cell phone I had purchased. I slid it into my robe pocket and sat down with my glass of milk. I didn't hear any footsteps coming from up-stairs, which probably meant Troy had scratched his balls and went right back to sleep.

I looked around, ensuring I was careful. I took out the phone and powered it up. My heart raced feverishly as the missed calls began appearing on the phone.

"Damn," I cursed under my breath. They were all missed calls from the prison facility where Leon was housed. I had gotten the phone just to have secret communications with him. It was foul, I know, but I couldn't help it.

I was reading through all of the missed calls, trying to put together the last time Leon called me. I was so engrossed scrolling through the numbers and lost in thought that I didn't hear Troy enter the kitchen.

"Whatcha got there?" Troy asked, smiling from the doorway.

"Oh shit!" I exclaimed, dropping the phone into my lap. "You scared the shit out of me, Troy! What're you trying to do, make me go into labor early? And why in the hell are you sneaking up on me?!" I gasped, placing my hand over my chest.

He had caught me red-handed, but I had recovered fast.

"Damn, Trice, calm down. I just wanted to make sure you were okay. You got out of bed so abruptly," Troy replied, looking at me strangely as he walked toward the table where I was sitting.

"Well, make some noise next time. I mean, it's like you are always lurking in the shadows somewhere," I said, making sure the phone went into the pocket of my robe.

"Were you reading something?" Troy probed, standing over me.

"No, I wasn't. I happened to be saying my daily prayer," I lied. I got up from the table so hard the kitchen chair went slamming to the floor. "I didn't know you worked for the FBI now!" I snapped, stomping out of the kitchen. I had to get away from his ass fast.

"Damn, I can't wait for your moody ass to have that baby. You treat me like shit on a daily!" I heard Troy yelling at my back.

"Oh, shut the fuck up," I mumbled in response.

I needed to get the fuck out of the house so I could accept the twelve o'clock call from Leon. Speaking to him was the only thing that would make me feel better right now.

the CRitteR club

Marion Takes Charge

by Callie Barkley ♥ illustrated by Marsha Riti

LITTLE SIMON

New York London Toronto Sydney New Delhi

LITTLE SIMON

An imprint of Simon & Schuster Children's Publishing Division • 1230 Avenue of the Americas, New York, New York 10020 • First Little Simon paperback edition September 2015 • Copyright © 2015 by Simon & Schuster, Inc. All rights reserved, including the right of reproduction in whole or in part in any form. LITTLE SIMON is a registered trademark of Simon & Schuster, Inc., and associated colophon is a trademark of Simon & Schuster, Inc. For information about special discounts for bulk purchases, please contact Simon & Schuster Special Sales at 1-866-506-1949 or business@simonandschuster.com. The Simon & Schuster Speakers Bureau can bring authors to your live event. For more information or to book an event contact the Simon & Schuster Speakers Bureau at 1-866-248-3049 or visit our website at www.simonspeakers.com. Designed by Laura Roode. The text of this book was set in ITC Stone Informal Std.
Manufactured in the United States of America 0216 MTN   10 9 8 7 6 5 4 3 2
Library of Congress Cataloging-in-Publication Data
Barkley, Callie. Marion takes charge / by Callie Barkley ; illustrated by Marsha Riti. — First Little Simon paperback edition. pages cm. — (Critter Club ; #12)
Summary: When Marion finally gets the chance to babysit her little sister, she finds that the task is harder than she expected, especially when she gets called to the Critter Club to help with a stray cat and must bring Gabby along. [1. Babysitters—Fiction. 2. Sisters—Fiction. 3. Clubs—Fiction. 4. Animal shelters—Fiction.] I. Riti, Marsha, illustrator. II. Title. PZ7.B250585Maw 2015 [Fic]—dc23 2014049484
ISBN 978-1-4814-2409-7 (hc)
ISBN 978-1-4814-2408-0 (pbk)
ISBN 978-1-4814-2410-3 (eBook)

Table of Content

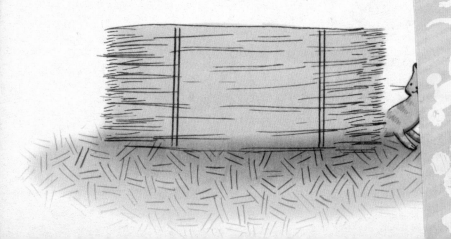

Marion, the Big Sister

"Here, Gabby," Marion Ballard said to her little sister. "I'll do that for you."

"No, I can do it!" Gabby replied. She was at the front door, tying her shoes. Marion thought she was doing it way too slowly.

Mrs. Ballard was waiting in the car. Marion checked her watch. It

was 8:35. School started at 8:45, and the drive was eight minutes long. If they didn't get going, they'd be late!

Finally, Gabby was ready. They rushed outside.

Phew! thought Marion as her mom backed out of the driveway.

Marion made sure she had everything. She had her lunch box.

She had her sneakers for gym. She
peeked inside her homework folder.
Yep, she had her homework.

"Do you have your lunch,
Gabby?" Marion asked her sister.

Gabby nodded. "Your home-
work?" Marion said.

Gabby nodded again. She was
in kindergarten. She usually had
a short math work sheet and some
reading homework.

"Your reading folder?" Marion asked.

Gabby's eyes went wide in alarm. "I forgot to read the new book in my reading folder!"

Marion looked out the car window. They still had a few minutes before they got to school. "Want to read it together now?" Marion asked.

Gabby smiled and nodded. She pulled out the book. It was called *My Bike.*

Marion held the book and turned the pages as Gabby read. She helped Gabby with words she didn't know.

It was a short book, and they finished just as Mrs. Ballard pulled up to the school.

"Thanks, Marion!" said Gabby, tucking her book into her backpack.

Marion smiled. She was glad she helped Gabby start her day off right.

Mrs. Ballard helped Marion and Gabby out of the car.

She gave Gabby a kiss on her

head. "Have a great day!" she said as Gabby walked off toward the school entrance. Then she looked at Marion.

"That was great, the way you helped your sister just now," said

Mrs. Ballard proudly. "In fact, I have a question for you. You know how you've always wanted to baby-sit Gabby?"

Marion nodded. It was true. She *was* always begging her parents to babysit.

9

"Well," said her mom with a smile, "Dad and I are having a party for some friends on Saturday. We'll be home the whole time. But I'm wondering . . . will you be in charge of watching Gabby during the party?"

Marion gasped. "Yes!" she cried. She jumped up and down with excitement. Her parents had always told her she was too young to baby-sit. But now they thought she was ready for the responsibility!

"Thank you, Mom!" Marion cried, hugging her mother. "Thank you, thank you, thank you!"

Then Marion hurried into school. She couldn't wait to tell her best friends the big news!

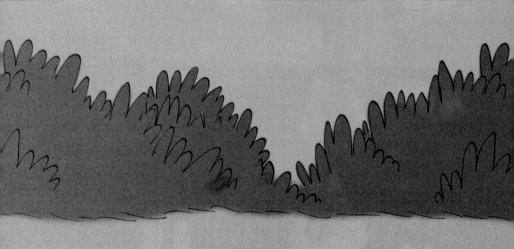

The Club's New Critter

Marion had gym later that morning. It was her first chance to talk to Amy, Liz, and Ellie.

"They're going to let me babysit!" Marion exclaimed. She'd told them about her parents' party. "I'm going to watch Gabby upstairs while they have their party downstairs."

The girls were standing in a

circle. They were playing Hot Potato with a ball. When the gym teacher turned off the music, who-ever was holding the ball was out.

Marion tossed the ball to Liz.

"Stewart babysat me one time," Liz said. Stewart was Liz's big brother. "But I think *I* should have been in charge. He was going to make a pizza bagel in the slice toaster. I stopped him.

That would have been a mess!"

Liz threw the ball to Ellie.

Ellie shook her head. "I would never want to babysit Toby," she said. Toby was Ellie's little brother. "He wears me out even when I'm not in charge!"

Ellie tossed the ball to Amy.

"I think I'm better at babysitting animals than kids," Amy said. Amy's mom, Dr. Purvis, was a veterinarian. She also helped the girls run their animal rescue shelter, The Critter Club.

Just then the music stopped. Marion, Ellie, and Liz looked at Amy.

"I know, I know," Amy said. "I'm out."

Amy stepped to one side. The music came back on. The girls continued playing. Ellie threw the ball to Liz.

"Oh, guess what?" Amy said from the sidelines. "My mom found a stray cat yesterday!" Liz threw the ball to Marion as Amy went on. "She said she seemed really weak at first," Amy said. "But my mom gave her some food and a couple

of shots. She's doing a lot better. She might be ready to come to The Critter Club by Friday!"

"Then we can figure out if she has a home . . . or if she needs one!" Marion said happily.

The music stopped. Marion still

had the ball. Her smile faded—
but only for a second. She was too
excited about the cat.

Marion *loved* cats.
Her own kitten, Ollie,
had been a guest at The
Critter Club once. He had been in
a litter born to a stray mama cat.
The girls had found homes for all
the other kittens. But Marion hadn't
wanted to say good-bye to Ollie. So
her family had adopted him!

Marion couldn't wait to meet the
latest Critter Club cat on Friday. And
then she'd get to babysit Gabby on
Saturday!

*This is going to be the best week-
end ever!* she thought.

Chapter 3

How to Calm a Cat

On Friday after school, Marion's dad gave her a ride to Ms. Sullivan's house. She hurried into the barn, The Critter Club headquarters. Liz, Ellie, Amy, and Dr. Purvis were there.

They'd had two animal guests for the last week. One was an iguana they were pet-sitting for a family on

vacation. The other was a mouse. His last owner was allergic to him. The girls were trying to find him a new home.

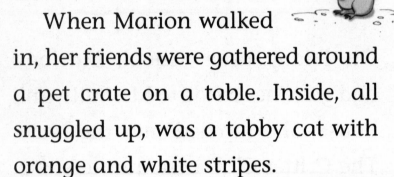

When Marion walked in, her friends were gathered around a pet crate on a table. Inside, all snuggled up, was a tabby cat with orange and white stripes.

"Girls, meet our new friend," Dr. Purvis said. She opened the door of the crate and stepped back. "She might be shy at first. Let her come out when she's ready."

While they waited, they talked about the cat's name. "She didn't have a collar," Dr. Purvis pointed out. "But it's possible she has an owner and a name already."

"How about we just call her 'Tabby' for now?" Liz suggested. All the girls agreed.

Finally, Tabby crept toward the crate's open door. She stuck her head out cautiously. Then, slowly, she stepped out.

Ellie cooed in her sweetest voice: "Hello there, kitty." She reached out to pick her up. But Tabby drew back and hissed!

"Whoa!" Ellie cried.

Dr. Purvis put a hand on Ellie's shoulder. "Don't take it personally," she said. "She's nervous. Let's not pick her up just yet."

Amy spoke up. "Maybe she wants to smell us first?" Amy rested her hand on the table a few feet from Tabby. But the cat turned away. "I

guess not!" Amy said with a shrug.

Dr. Purvis frowned. "Hmm. She probably just needs to get used to it here. Let's let her explore. Meanwhile, we can get her room ready."

Tabby's "room" was the empty horse stall at the back of the barn. It had four walls, a door, and plenty of space inside.

"This is perfect," said Liz. "When we're here, we can let her roam around. And when we're not, we can close the door. That way, she won't try to get into the other pets' cages."

Together, the girls worked to make the stall cozy. They piled old blankets in one corner.

"That's a nice sleeping spot," said Ellie.

33

Amy pulled a few cat toys out of her backpack. "I brought these from the clinic."

Marion set up a litter box in a little alcove. "She'll be needing this for sure," she said.

Just then Marion noticed her shoe was untied. She sat down on the floor to tie it. As she was making the double knot, she heard a soft *mew* at her side. Marion turned her head. Tabby was at her elbow, looking up at her. Marion didn't move. She wanted to give Tabby some time to decide what *she* wanted.

Slowly, Tabby came around in front of Marion. She stepped into Marion's lap. Then she lay down and put her chin on Marion's leg.

Marion looked up. Amy, Ellie, Liz, and Dr. Purvis were staring at Tabby in shock.

Then Dr. Purvis smiled. "Well," she said, "it looks like someone has made a friend."

Sister Sitter

Marion jumped out of bed early on Saturday morning. *Today I'm not just Gabby's sister. I'm Gabby's baby-sitter!* she thought.

She stood in front of her closet. Which of her outfits would make her look the most responsible? Marion picked out a long-sleeved shirt, a sweater, a corduroy skirt, and leggings. She was comfy, warm, and ready for anything.

Then Marion went to brush her teeth in the bathroom. She even flossed after. *Responsible people definitely floss,* she thought.

Down in the kitchen, Marion's parents had made breakfast. Gabby was at the table, eating her pancakes.

"Hungry?" Mrs. Ballard asked Marion.

Marion nodded and sat down.

Eating a good breakfast is very responsible, she thought. *It's the most important meal of the day!*

Mrs. Ballard gave Marion a plate of pancakes and berries. She poured her a glass of juice. Then

she sat down with the girls.

"So, the party isn't until this afternoon," Mrs. Ballard said. "But Dad and I have lots to do to get the house ready. Can you watch Gabby while we're setting things up?"

Marion nodded. "No problem!" she exclaimed. "Don't worry about us. I've got everything under control!"

Marion ran up to her room. She came back with her notebook. "I made a list last night," she explained. "It's a whole bunch of activities for us to do today!"

Mrs. Ballard smiled at both Marion and Gabby. "Okay, then!"

she said. "We will be in the living room. We'll be busy, but we're here if you need us."

Then she walked out of the room, leaving Marion and Gabby alone at the table. Gabby sat there quietly, staring at Marion.

Marion eyed Gabby's glass. "Do you need more juice?" Marion asked.

Gabby shook her head no. "No, thanks," she replied.

Marion peeked over at Gabby's plate. There was almost a whole pancake left.

"Aren't you going to finish?" Marion asked.

Gabby shrugged. "I'm full."

"You should finish," Marion said in her most adult voice. "You need food to keep your energy up!"

Gabby crossed her arms in front of her. She seemed to have her mind made up.

Marion ate her breakfast quickly.

Then she asked Gabby if she wanted to see the activities list.

"Okay!" Gabby replied excitedly.

Marion pointed at number one on the list. "Clean Gabby's room!"

Gabby's smile disappeared. "Clean my room?" she repeated. "That's no fun!"

1. clean Gabby's room
2. play a board game
3. drawing
4. play outside
5. take a bath

Marion shrugged. "But your room really needs it," she said, standing up from the table. "Come on. I'll help you."

Gabby groaned.

Marion led the way up the stairs. "I know this isn't the best thing on the list," she called over her shoulder, "but soon we'll be done. Then

we can get to the next activity: playing a board game!"

Marion got to the top step. She turned around, adding, "That sounds fun, right?"

Gabby wasn't there. She hadn't followed Marion. Marion could see her downstairs, still at the kitchen table.

Marion took a deep breath. *Maybe this is going to be harder than I thought.*

Chapter 5

A Call for Help

It took longer than Marion expected to clean Gabby's room. Maybe it was because only Marion was really cleaning up. Every time she looked over, Gabby was *playing* with a toy instead of putting it away.

Finally, Marion looked around and sighed. "Good enough." She and Gabby went down to the

Chess

Dress-up Clothes

Hats

playroom. They stood in front of the game closet. "What should we play?" Marion asked.

Gabby answered right away. "Candy Land!"

Ugh, thought Marion. She had played Candy Land a zillion times! "How about Scrabble Junior?" Marion tried. It would help her get ready for the spelling test next week.

Gabby pouted and said, "I really, really, *really* want to play Candy Land."

Marion sighed. "Okay. Candy Land it is." She was trying hard to be a good babysitter.

Gabby grabbed the green game piece. It was Marion's favorite from when she was little. But Marion let Gabby take it. Marion took red instead.

In the middle of the game, Gabby drew a card that made her go back lots of spaces. She wanted to pick again. Marion let her.

Marion was on a lucky streak. She was out in front. Then she picked the ice-cream card and got to skip even farther ahead. She was so close to the candy castle!

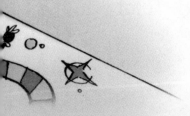

"I don't want to play anymore,"
Gabby said suddenly.

"What?" Marion cried. "I let you

pick the game. I let you have the green piece. I let you have a do-over. Now you're quitting?"

Gabby turned her back to Marion.

Marion was frustrated. She tried to calm down as she walked to the hall closet. She got out the big marker box for their next activity—drawing. So far, babysitting Gabby was *not much fun!*

Marion was in the hall when the phone rang. She heard her dad pick up in the living room. "Oh, hi, Ellie!" he said.

Marion perked up at the sound of Ellie's name. She poked her head in the living room. Her dad handed her the phone.

"Hey!" said Ellie on the other end. "I'm at Ms. Sullivan's house. Amy, Liz, and I got here an hour ago. Tabby wasn't in her room, and we still can't find her. We've looked everywhere!"

"Oh, no!" said Marion.

"I know!" said Ellie. "So we were

thinking. . . . Tabby really seemed to like you yesterday. Maybe she'd come if *you* called. Is there any way you could come over?"

Marion opened her mouth to say, "Yes!" After all, her friends needed her help. But she couldn't. She'd been wanting to babysit Gabby for *forever,* and she'd promised her parents she would. She needed to prove she could handle it.

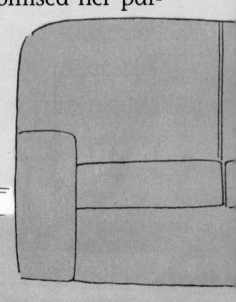

63

Chapter 6

Marion to the Rescue

Marion told Ellie she would come as soon as the party was over. "I'm sorry I can't come sooner," she said sadly.

Ellie said she understood. Marion wished she could be in two places at once.

Her dad heard her hang up the phone. "What's up?" he asked.

Marion explained that Tabby was missing and her friends needed her help. "But I know you need me here to watch Gabby."

As the words came out, Marion gasped. "Or maybe you don't need me *here*!" she cried.

Her dad looked confused.

"Dad," said Marion, "could I take Gabby with me to The Critter Club? She's always wanted to come!"

Mr. Ballard thought it over. "I don't see why not," he replied.

He called Ms. Sullivan to make sure she would be there with the girls. When he hung up, he gave Marion a thumbs-up. "I'll drive you both over," he said. "And I'll pick you up at three, when the party is over. Sound good?"

"Great!" Marion exclaimed.

She ran to the playroom to tell Gabby, who was even more excited than Marion was.

"You can help us find Tabby!" Marion told her. Gabby stood up proudly—all ready for her mission.

Marion tried to get Gabby to put

on a sweater. "Sometimes it's chilly in the barn," Marion warned. But Gabby didn't want to wear it.

Marion sighed. They hurried into Mr. Ballard's car and rode over to The Critter Club.

Ellie, Amy, and Liz ran out to

meet them when they got there. "We're so glad you're here!" Ellie cried.

"Hi, Gabby," Amy said kindly. "Are you going to help us too?"

"Yep!" Gabby exclaimed.

They all went into the barn. Liz showed Gabby where Tabby's room was. "This is where we expected her to be this morning," she said.

Amy pointed toward the litter box. Behind it, in a dark corner of

the room, there was a small hole in the wall. "We think maybe she squeezed out through there," Amy said.

"We're hoping she's still in the barn somewhere," Ellie added. "If she got outside, she could be *anywhere!*"

Marion tried calling. "Here, Tabby, Tabby. Here, kitty!"

She moved around the barn. Gabby followed her. Meanwhile, the others fanned out in all directions. They peeked in corners, under tables, and in the supply closet.

"Here, Tabby!" Marion called a little louder. "Where are you? Come out, Tabby!"

They kept at it for nearly fifteen minutes. Marion called and called until her voice sounded tired.

But there was no sign of Tabby anywhere in the barn.

Marion sat down on a hay bale in the corner. Gabby sat next to her. Marion's shoulders slumped. She looked at her friends. "I guess I haven't been any help at all!" she said.

Just then, from behind the hay bale, Tabby crept out silently. The girls all saw her, but no one spoke or moved. They just watched as Tabby padded slowly toward Marion. The cat climbed up into her lap. She sat down. And then she started to purr.

Chapter 7

Gabby Meets Tabby

Marion looked over at Ellie, Amy, and Liz. They were all smiling.

"It worked!" Amy whispered.

Liz and Ellie cheered silently. No one wanted to startle Tabby.

But Gabby didn't realize this. She was too excited to meet Tabby for the first time. "TAB-by! I'm GAB-by!" she shrieked, and leaned over eagerly to pet the cat.

Tabby's head jerked up. Her back arched. But Gabby didn't notice. She kept petting her fur from tail to head—the *wrong* way. Suddenly, Tabby screeched. *Rawrrrr!* She shot out of Marion's lap and was gone

behind the hay again.

"Gabby!" Marion snapped. "Look what you did!"

Gabby froze, startled by Marion's tone. Her brow wrinkled and her chin trembled. Marion had seen that look many times. It usually happened right before Gabby started to cry.

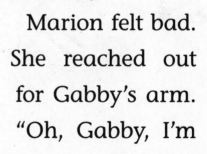

Marion felt bad. She reached out for Gabby's arm. "Oh, Gabby, I'm

sorry," Marion said. She tried to speak extra gently. "It's okay. It's just . . . Tabby is very jumpy. And most cats prefer to be pet the *other* way—from their heads toward their tails."

"But you didn't know that," said Ellie kindly. She and Liz and Amy came over. Ellie patted Gabby on the back.

"Yeah, don't worry," said Liz. "Now we know where Tabby is. We'll get her to come out again."

"Hey! I have an idea," Amy said to Gabby. "Do you want to meet the other animals staying here?"

A tiny smile lit up Gabby's face. She nodded. Amy and Ellie led her over to the iguana's terrarium and the mouse's cage. Meanwhile, Marion and Liz tried to get Tabby to come out of hiding again.

Soon, the barn was peaceful. Tabby was lapping milk from a bowl. The iguana and the mouse had also been fed. They'd cleaned out Tabby's litter box. The girls had written an ad to put in next week's newspaper. The headline read:

Cute Gray Mouse Needs a Home

Contact The Critter Club

CUTE GRAY
MOUSE NEEDS
A HOME. Then they had made some
flyers to put up around town. They
planned to put them up next week.

"What should we do now?"
Marion asked. "My dad isn't coming

to get us until three o'clock." They had all afternoon to spend at The Critter Club.

The girls thought it over. "Want to play Three, Two, One, Draw?" Ellie suggested.

"Yeah!" the others replied at once.

The girls kept the game in the barn's supply closet. They loved it—it was like a drawing version of charades. One person drew, and her

teammates tried to guess what she was drawing. Sometimes they just played a short speed round. Other times, they played the full-length game.

Liz started to set up the game. "Wait," she

said. "There are five of us. We won't have even teams."

The girls all thought it over.

"I have an idea," said Marion suddenly. "Why don't Gabby and I be on one team. You three can be on the other."

Marion winked at Gabby. She

wanted Gabby to know she wasn't
mad at her.

Gabby gave a huge smile. "Let's
play!" she said.

Chapter 8

Animals Everywhere!

Just as they started the game, Ms. Sullivan stuck her head into the barn.

"Hello in here!" she said cheerfully. "I have a favor to ask. I made a big batch of cookie dough. I need to roll it out and cut the cookies. It sure would go faster if I had a few helpers!" She flashed a sweet smile.

"And I'm willing to pay in fresh-baked cookies!"

All of the girls eagerly volunteered. But then Marion looked down at Tabby.

"Gabby," she said, "maybe you and I should stay here to

keep an eye on Tabby."

Amy agreed. "That's probably a good idea," she said. "But don't worry. We'll bring you each a cookie!"

Amy, Liz, and Ellie went off with Ms. Sullivan. Marion and Gabby were left alone in the barn with the animals.

Tabby had finished her milk. She curled up next to Marion. She licked her paws and rubbed her face to clean herself. She looked as calm as could be. Marion reached out and pet Tabby very lightly.

Tabby didn't hiss. She didn't flinch. She put her head down and closed her eyes.

"Look!" Marion whispered to Gabby. "I think she's really settling in, finally."

Gabby didn't answer. She was standing by the mouse cage with her back to Marion.

"Gabby?" Marion said. "What are you—?"

Marion didn't finish her question. Suddenly, Tabby was on her feet, bolting toward the mouse cage. At the same moment, Gabby let out a shriek as a small streak of gray fur scurried across the table.

The mouse was loose! And Tabby was chasing it!

Gabby shrieked again as Tabby ran between her legs. Startled and off balance, Gabby stumbled backward. She bumped into the table behind her. On the tabletop, the iguana terrarium teetered and fell over. The mesh lid came off.

"Oh, no!" cried Marion. She ran toward the terrarium. She had to

get the lid back on—quickly!

But it was too late.

The iguana scrambled out just as Marion got there. It scurried across the table, down a table leg, and across the floor.

Marion didn't know which way to go first! Everything was completely out of control!

"Tabby! I mean, *Gabby*!" she shouted frantically. "Follow that iguana! I'll try to save the mouse!

Come back here, Gabby! I mean *Tabby*!"

But Gabby just stood frozen to her spot, shrieking louder and louder. Ms. Sullivan and the girls must have heard her from the house. Suddenly they rushed into the barn.

Working together, Amy and Liz cornered

the iguana. They got him back into the terrarium and put the lid on.

Marion managed to catch up to Tabby. She held on to the cat. Meanwhile, Ms. Sullivan and Ellie slowly coaxed the mouse out from the supply closet.

Before long, all the animals were back where they were supposed to be. Everyone breathed a sigh of relief.

Everyone, that is, except for Marion. She was completely worn out. She turned and marched over to Gabby.

"What were you *thinking?*"

Marion yelled. "You *weren't* thinking, were you?"

Instantly, Gabby burst into tears. She turned and ran out of the barn.

Chapter 9

Sisterly Love

Marion sighed. No one needed to tell her. She knew she had sounded really harsh. *Gabby must have felt terrible about letting the animals out. And I just made her feel even worse,* Marion thought.

Marion went outside. Gabby was sitting under the big tree in Ms. Sullivan's backyard. Her head was buried in her hands.

Marion sat down next to her. She put her arm around her little sister.

"I'm so sorry, Gabby," Marion said. "I shouldn't have yelled at you."

Gabby looked up at Marion. "I wasn't trying to let the mouse out," Gabby sobbed. "I just wanted to pet him the way you were petting Tabby. It just . . . it just happened so fast!"

"I know," said Marion. "Animals don't always do what we expect. It's hard work taking care of them."

She paused, thinking about her day with Gabby so far. "It's hard work taking care of people, too."

They sat under the tree for a little while. Marion told Gabby about the times *she* had messed up at The Critter Club. "Like when Ollie and his brothers and sisters were here,"

Marion told her. "I was trying to feed one of them from a bottle. Instead, I spilled milk all over the kitten!"

Gabby smiled. She giggled, imagining Marion making a mess.

Mew.

Marion and Gabby looked up. There was Tabby, standing a few feet away in the grass. Marion crisscrossed her legs to make a lap for Tabby to climb into.

But instead, Tabby stepped

lightly into Gabby's lap. She sat down and put her head on Gabby's leg. Gabby gasped in surprise.

"She likes you, too!" Marion cried. Gabby beamed.

The sisters sat for a few more

minutes and then returned to the barn. Soon, all the girls were deep into their game of Three, Two, One, Draw. Marion and Gabby were winning. They made a fantastic team.

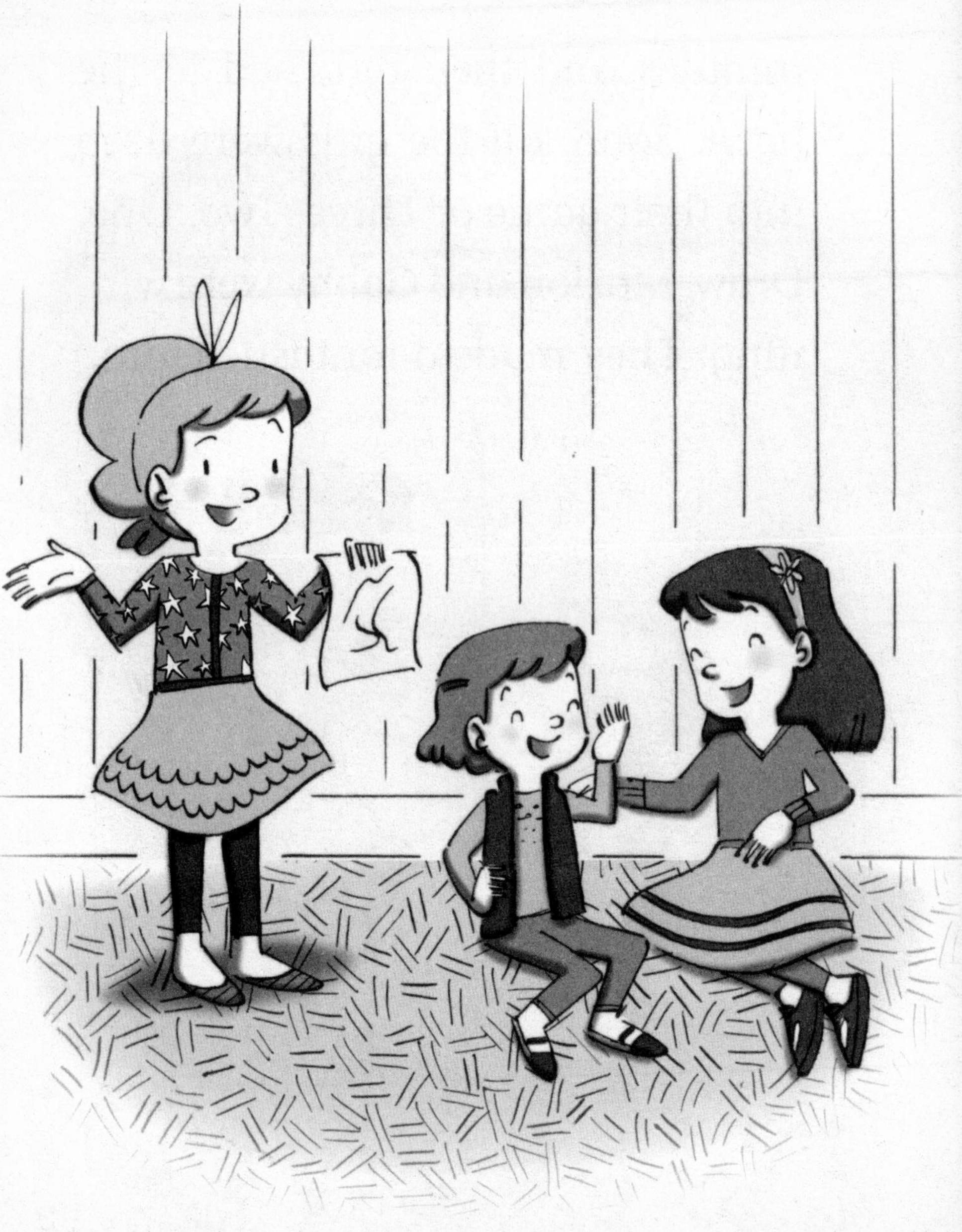

"It's no fair!" Ellie said. "Gabby makes two little squiggles on the paper. And just like that, you know it's a horse?"

Liz held up one of the drawings Marion had made. "And Gabby! How did you get 'helicopter' from *this*?"

Gabby shrugged and looked at Marion. The two of them burst out laughing.

"What can we say?" Marion said between giggles. "We know each other very well!" She put her arm around Gabby. Just then Gabby shivered. "Are you cold?" Marion asked her.

Gabby shrugged. "A little," she admitted.

I knew it! Marion thought. *I told her she should have brought a sweater.*

But Marion didn't say that to Gabby. Instead, she took off her sweater. She wrapped it around Gabby's shoulders. "Here. You can wear mine for a little while."

"Thanks," Gabby said.

Marion smiled. Then a thought popped into her mind. As much

as she had wanted the chance to babysit, she didn't really *need* to be Gabby's sitter. Because being Gabby's *sister* was a lot more fun.

Read on for a sneak peek at
the next Critter Club book:

#13

Amy Is a
Little Bit Chicken

Cluck, cluck, baaawk! A hen came wandering into the barn. Two more followed right behind her.

The chickens had arrived the day before. They had been wandering around downtown Santa Vista. They even walked into the road, stopping traffic! No one knew where they'd come from. And no one knew what to do!

Then Ms. Sullivan happened to pass by. She knew a place the chickens could stay while their owner was found: The Critter Club!

Already the girls had learned a lot about keeping chickens. For starters, they needed a coop, or henhouse. Luckily Ms. Sullivan's neighbors offered to help. Mr. Mack was a farmer and Mrs. Mack was a carpenter. Together, they made the perfect coop-building team.

The girls went outside to see how it was coming along. Behind the barn, Mrs. Mack was hammering a shingle onto the coop roof.

"Wow, it's almost done!" Ellie exclaimed.

"We have a few more things to add inside," said Mrs. Mack. "Let's try to get them inside of it."

Amy tried luring them with chicken feed. But when she tossed some toward them, the hens ran away from it.

"It seems like they're afraid of *everything*," Amy said to Mr. Mack.

He smiled. "Chickens sometimes are kind of . . . chicken."

the CRitteR club

Join the club!